BlueWood Publishing

THE GRAFFITI SCULPTOR

Latham Shinder earned an MBA at California State University and studied law at the University of Zimbabwe. While there, he traveled widely throughout southern Africa, where he began writing fiction. He lives and works near Dallas, Texas. *The Graffiti Sculptor* is his first novel.

THE GRAFFITI SCULPTOR

LATHAM SHINDER

BlueWood Publishing

BlueWood Publishing
1400 N. Highway 91, Suite 1127
Denison, Texas 75020

ISBN: 978-0-9799219-0-2

Printed in the United States of America
First BlueWood Publishing Edition 2007

For Sheila

THE GRAFFITI SCULPTOR

First of all, Billie Hannah's a professional critic, which ranks her up there with serial killers and dead baby eaters. And what's with the two first names? The woman is a cow with bad teeth and body odor, and if there's a god, she's suffering from an itchy yeast infection as I sit here on the bus reading her column. She uses words like maladroit, clumsy, off the mark, and tells her readers my work is as cuddly as the latest round of anti-abortion propaganda. She can offer only two words for the gallery-goer. "Don't go."

If I had it in me, I'd kill her.

The bus is filled with a handful of losers from my part of town heading north on Oak Lawn, zigzagging our way up to Hannah's hamlet in Highland Park. I've no idea what I'll do when I get there. I'd briefly thought of stuffing her critique, pages C2 and the continuation on C18, down her throat; but she's a goddamn elephant, as I said, and I might get trampled in the process.

I've got on your standard breaking-and-entering getup: black leotard body suit with matching black leather jacket that comes to my belly button. Black bra. Likewise the panties. I carry a black shoulder pack that never leaves my side. My watch says one a.m. If I get caught, I can always say I'm heading to a late-night aerobics class.

It turns out the house is easy to find if you're a jungle commuter or a mountain climber, but for a city girl like me it's not so easy. From Preston, where the bus drops me and a shaggy-haired college type who I hope isn't following me, I hike Beverly to Drexler and go left, in the dark and all uphill, clear to Mockingbird and back down again, and finally find it tucked in behind some trees away from the road on Stratford. No mailbox I can see, and I interpolate the address from the houses on each side, also without mailboxes.

The drive is faux-earth, and it must have cost a fortune to get the feel of a real dirt drive. I lumber up the path toward the house, and now that I'm here, I feel stupid. I came because I was mad, but now I'm more wired than angry. For the briefest moment, I consider stalking into the first all-night Baskin-Robbins I can find, where I'll demand a fat scoop of Rocky Road from a narrow-eyed Pakistani with marginal verbal skills and call it a night.

The house is one of those semi-rustic, mini-mansions Dallasites are so fond of, designed to look exploded or deconstructed or just plain queer for the sake of queerness. None of the lights are on in what I take to be the back of the house, which faces the street.

I sneak around to the front and see a light at the far end of a curved wall. Skulking to the window, I display all the grace of an earthmover and bang my shin on a garden gnome, a fat little guy with a red pointy hat. The window is high, so I pile some bricks from the flowerbed into a step. I peek inside a bedroom and see Billie Fatso herself and Mr. Fatso having an argument. Billie's seated on the edge of the bed dressed in a puke-green sweat-suit top and panties, her fleshy legs squishing out in all directions, her eyes on the wall of mirrors, shouting and pointing at Mister's reflection. He's still in a pressed dark suit, his tie not quite long enough to cover the hump of his belly.

Billie's worked up, her face blotchy, pacing back and forth in front of the mirror. She says, "I've wasted enough time! That's it. I mean it!"

Mister's got the casual tone of a man who knows a casual tone will drive his wife mad. He says, "What's wrong with wasting time?"

"That's a liberating concept," she says.

"If people didn't need to waste time," he says, "we'd be out of a job. You, especially."

"You have the gall to ridicule my career?"

"You write a hate column," he says, "for wannabe intellectuals who are too lazy to go out and look for themselves. The more venom you spew, the higher your readership."

She says, "What, so now you're an avatar of the Populist conscience?" This triggers a new level of anger and Mister tells her, just one more: one more word that sounds like it came out of her column and he'll smash her face.

"This coming from the self-proclaimed—"

And *bam*, he hits her in the jaw. She bounces off the mirrored wall and drops to the floor like a drunken whale. He reaches out to give her a hand up. Stupidly, she takes it and when she's upright, he slugs her again. This time hard, in the stomach and she lands face down with a *clomp*.

He saunters over to the walk-in closet and stands in front of the belt rack. Says something about the one he got for Christmas. You know, with that hideous buckle. The ugly one he said he loved. Billie's lying in the crease where the floor meets the wall not saying a word. She watches her husband stroll back her way with the Christmas belt. He raises the leather and spanks her across the legs. He catches himself in the mirror and likes what he sees, like a cowboy swinging a lasso. Then another, and another. She doesn't make a peep until he starts in with the buckle.

Now that I'm here, all I want is to run, and as much as I despise Billie Hannah, this ain't right. I look around, spy the gnome with the pointy hat and grab hold of the hat. He's not nearly as heavy as I'd expected, but heavy enough, and I wing him through the bedroom window. And haul ass. Almost immediately, the outdoor lights go on and a dog starts to yelp.

I trip over another lawn ornament—a stubborn little concrete angel—and land face down. At first, I don't move a muscle, laying there in pine-scented mulch thinking, stupidly, that I can't be seen as long as I stay still. I freak when I hear the front door open. I pick myself up and aim for the road.

Within what seems like seconds, Mister has clamped onto me with chubby hands. His stinky sweat's so foul I nearly vomit, and his face is pulsing like an exposed heart. He drags me inside the house to take a good look at me. Makes me stand in the middle of the living room while he pours himself a Crown Royal, neat. The living room is enormous and clinical, done up in shades of white.

Mister is panting like a worn-out dog. "Let me catch my breath before I call the cops."

"I can call while you drink."

He passes behind me and brushes a hand against my ass, says, "Anxious to get to your cell?"

"Your wife might need a doctor. And the police might wanna know how she got that way."

He downs another drink and tells me that little trick I pulled could have killed someone. Attempted murder, seems like to him.

I say, "You want to dial, or should I?"

Mrs. Fatso saunters into the living room wearing a long robe that covers her legs. Her eyes are red, but her face is freshly primped and powdered, so much so she looks her normal ugly self. You'd never know she'd just been flogged with a Christmas belt. She holds the stubborn little gnome in her hand, says, "Any idea how Gadsby here got into our bedroom?" At my look, she says, "That's his name, Gadsby Jr."

"I was just passing by," I say.

"Ruined my bedspread," she says, "There's glass everywhere." There is no emotion in her voice, but I can almost smell it in the air. She looks at her husband, and he is looking at her. She swallows hard.

"Why?"

"It looked like you needed some help."

She bites her lip. "I know you, don't I?"

"You do, yes."

It comes to her and her face flushes. Mister doesn't know what's going on, and he's already into his third Crown, this one a double. Mrs. Fatso goes, "Why are you here?"

I tell her about the shitty review. I get chatty and say I was angry, angry enough to slap her in the face if I got up the nerve. Anything to make her feel as worthless as I felt reading her words. She goes still for a moment and frowns. Her bottom lip curls. She looks away, ashamed, sort of, and tells me this must have made my goddamn day, seeing her like this.

"Enough!" Mister shouts.

Mrs. Fatso says it's all over and ushers me to the door. Her robe breezes open and I see giant welts on her legs. Tomorrow she'll write another review, she says. A good one. A great one, if she can remember how. Actually, she likes my work, but people don't read her column to hear what she likes. Her husband's right, she says, and I can tell she's talking to herself like she suddenly deserves all the lousy shit in the world. At the door, she whispers that she's heard rumors. About my work. I whisper, too. I tell her they're not true. The foyer is all mirrors, and her glance ricochets to her husband. I can see she loves him. And she wants to hurt him. She says, "Your sculptures protect people. It's what some people say."

"You don't need protection," I say. "You need to leave."

In the mirror, she can't take her eyes off him. Mister is lounging, near horizontal in his chair, with the bottle propped on his stomach. She says, "Can they protect me from him?"

"I'm sitting right here, for chrissakes," Mister shouts. "And for whatever it's worth, I'm sorry you made me do that. Now send your little friend home and let's go to bed."

I whisper, "Abandon the piece of shit and never look back."

"Tell me how it works," she says.

"It's not true, whatever you've heard. I already told you."

"Do you use a model, work from a picture, something like that?" She won't give it up. The clincher is when she tells me even if it is true, she doesn't deserve it, which is true, but could I please do one for her? Please. Really. Please.

I tell her I've got a gallery full of unsold work, thanks to her. Come by anytime and take her pick. She stares at me in the mirror. Her eyes go moist and she turns away but there's nowhere to turn I can't see a reflection of her miserable face.

I say, "Listen, lady."

"Call me Billie, please."

My voice involuntarily softens. "You're asking me to do something I don't want to do."

She says *please, please, please* and other things, but I stop listening. I'd rather be flogged with a Christmas belt than hear someone beg. I give it a long, hard thought, because after I do this, it'll never be the same.

I say, "If you want it, then I do it now."

Billie says, "I don't understand."

"What's not to understand? Now."

Mister shouts it's too late for whatever we're talking about.

I say, "It'll take me most of the night." I point to Mister. "He's my model. If you can keep him still, we've got a deal." I read her mind and say, "The mantle above the fireplace." The fireplace is one of those huge, ornate jobs with two fourteen-foot columns each side of the opening. It has two separate mantles—a narrow one for showy little nothings and a deeper chunk of wood with hand-carved edges. All of it oak, probably blue oak or leather oak, large pores and winding grain. I point as I speak. "It's now, with him and that piece of wood. Or never."

Mister throws his half empty bottle at the fireplace. "You touch my mantle and I'll rip your head off!" He bounces up and grabs a poker. I pause here to look at myself in the mirror. And to let Mister's rage fade into middle-aged impotence, which should take all of fifteen seconds.

I've no idea what she told him, but Mister is seething quietly with a fresh bottle of Crown at his side. I can smell his stink, a mixture of nervous sweat and good whisky. I hold the jack in one hand and sweep the showy crap to one side of the mantle. Most of it is glass or ceramic, and Billie scoops the pieces up without a word. I make like the jack is a big rock and take two quick overhead whacks at the mantle before anyone changes their mind. Mister and Billie flinch with each whack, but the mantle doesn't budge.

Mister's in a mood. He's fed up and bitching nonstop. I go into the bathroom and pack my ears with cotton. When I return, Billie is plying him with doubles and triples. She gives him a pill, says, "Take it," and when he does she gives him another. I grab a sturdy chair from the kitchen and stack it with leather-bound books from the bookshelf. I set the base of the jack on the books with the jack's top wedged under the lip of the mantle. Round and round I go, winding the jack handle in tight little circles. I plan to jack the thing off the wall. It takes a while, but it comes free with lots of wall attached. I drag it across the carpet and lay it in front of Mister. By this time, he's out cold, head flopped over the back of the chair. Billie props him upright with some pillows.

I unzip my shoulder pack and pull out a wooden mallet, two chisels, a small ax, and a whetstone. I tell Billie to get the hell out of here while I work.

By morning, it's nearly finished and my arm's a noodle from swinging the ax and mallet. The living room is blanketed in wood chips. The carpet is shredded, glass everywhere. Mister is dead pale and hasn't moved in six hours. I dig through a bedroom closet until I find some black shoe polish that I use for color and sealer. Behind some shoeboxes, I find something I haven't seen in a long time: one of my sculptures from a long time ago. A time when I could afford to work in bronze. I fondle the smooth, cool metal, lift it out of its hiding place with both hands to get a feel for the weight, and then shove it back where I found it.

The wooden Mister is a good likeness of the original, only thinner. It stands as tall as the real thing with a belly and bird legs and a belt dangling from his hand. I cover it in shoe polish and buff it shiny with an arm cover from the couch. "It's done," I say to no one.

I tell myself this isn't why I came, and no sooner do I think it than I know that it is. When I sculpt, I shut out the world. I'm alone with a handful of primitive tools and a forgiving piece of wood, and for those few moments I'm doing what I do best. That my best gets lousy reviews, I realize only now, is something I can live with.

Mister wakes. He looks around the room, says, "Morning," and I'm not sure if he's asking or telling. He's got some color in his face and his eyes are clear. He's different. Like a man you wouldn't mind knowing. His eyes are fixed on the six-foot-tall black carving in front of him. He circles the piece several times, stepping over chunks of wood and glass and pieces of fireplace. Mister says, "Me, right?"

I pull the cotton out of my ears just as Billie eases into the living room. Her face is puffed and powdered in shades of pink, and she's wearing a simple blue dress that falls just above her knees. Her legs are stained with purple bruises a shade or two darker than the dress. The getup looks color-coordinated to show off her injuries. She goes straight for the sculpture, the first to touch it, and as she does, Mister slips his hand into hers. He rubs his forehead, says, "It's hard to remember. I feel good, though."

Billie stands on her toes and rubs her powdered cheek against the shoe-polished wooden cheek. She runs her fingers along the side of the head down the arm and stops at the belt. She looks me in the eye. Mister notices the detail in the buckle and breaks into a horse grin. "That's the belt you gave me for Christmas. I love that belt."

He looks at the hole in the wall where the mantle used to live and back to the sculpture. He reaches out to touch the buckle when he sees Billie's discolored legs. A long minute passes and then he bites his lip as if he's about to cry. He looks up at his wife, says, "Can you forgive me?"

A t dawn, I make my way back to the slummier edge of town. Back home. I walk down Henry and spin onto Canton Avenue. It's a canyon-like alley with a railroad track down the middle and four-story warehouse fronts on each side. My precious lane is pitted and chunked like a war zone. No greenery, no colored trim, no centerline or parking stalls, but I do delight in the half dozen dumpsters angled just so to make life for the trash man a tad easier.

I live in an old Ford assembly plant where they bolted together Model Ts and sold them for $600 a pop. In the late fifties it was sold to the Adam Hats company, which is how everyone refers to the place. Five years ago it was converted to lofts—with an industrial flavor, breathtaking views of downtown, and a spectacular atrium. That's what the brochure says. I was one of the first to move in and got my pick of the lofts, which is how I ended up with a corner overlooking downtown for a whopping five hundred a month.

I trudge up the stairs to the third floor, unlock my door, and see Otto in the middle of my loft at the top of a twelve-foot ladder. Otto's a black man with a bald spot who fixes things around here. He's twisted like a pretzel and apparently asleep. Or he was until I ask what the hell he's doing in here. He says, "You got eyes in that pretty little head? I'm changing a light bulb."

"I didn't know I had a light out."

"Trust me, it was out."

Otto has a habit of fixing things before I even know they're broken. A habit that, frankly, grates on me. I inspect the ten or so other exposed bulbs in the room and wonder which one he'll replace next. He says, "I was to tell you the sun's gonna rise tomorrow morning you'd ask me how I know." He winces when he talks, and he's hunched up knot-tight, clinging to the ladder. "Lady called. Said it was an emergency. I told her you'd be right over."

"Why'd you say that?"

Otto says, "Cause that's what she wanted to hear. It was yesterday some time."

"I was here yesterday and even if I wasn't, why are you in my studio answering my phone and making promises I can't keep?"

"You don't keep your promises, that's your problem. I'm here to replace the bulb, is all."

Ninety-nine percent of the people in Dallas do not know shit about keeping promises or seem to care. Otto is part of the other one percent. His word is all he's got, he's told me over and over when he's trying to sell me on the idea. "Walk the talk" he'll say to me, "or quit yakking." He's one of the faithful, the promise keepers. He squirms, changing his position by a fraction of an inch. It's only now that I see a shattered bulb at the base of the ladder, no bulb in his hand and the light socket empty. I say, "What's wrong with you?"

He looks hurt by my question.

"I was doing you a favor."

"Why are you tangled up like that?"

He tells me he can't get down. It's a spasm in his back. Give it some time and it'll probably go away. He admits he dropped the good bulb some time ago. Got mad and threw the dead one against the wall. "Sorry."

"How long have you been up there?"

"How long ain't important. How much longer is the question."

Tuesday afternoon, I'm lounging in my La-Z-Girl when I hear someone slinking up the stairs trying not to be heard. A habit full of good intentions, but it nonetheless reminds me of a well-practiced peeping tom and instantly puts me in a bad mood. I jerk open the door, and it's Billie Hannah. At least the face is hers; the body I've never seen. It's been weeks since my midnight prowl in Highland Park, and it's hard to believe this is the same woman. She's scrawny, with layers of baggy clothes and clunky red shoes. Her face is gaunt, empty of makeup, and her limp, straw-colored hair lies as close to her head as if it were painted in place.

My loft has a natural stink to it, a tinny fruitiness that I can't get rid of. The smell hits her and she points her nose high in the air like some sort of warehouse-sniffing connoisseur. I'm guarding the door, gaping at her. "What happened to you?"

"What happened is that I used to be a grim unlovely hulk, and now I'm a breathtaking sliver of happiness."

"You promised to re-review my show," I say, "or did you forget?"

"I wrote it. My editor pulled it. I quit the paper."

"Don't tell me you quit over me?"

She gives me a shrug and hands me a business card. I don't read it, just shove it into my pocket. She looks over my shoulder into my studio.

I can't stop gawking at her. "You were hit by a truck, right?"

"Thank you for noticing," Billie says. "I had my stomach stapled. Now invite me in."

She strides through the door and I give it a good slam behind her. I say, "What is it you want?"

She takes in the bleak emptiness. "Homey." Then she lays it on me: "I want to model."

"You want to commission a sculpture?"

"That's not what I had in mind. I want to model. Nude."

"You're out of your mind."

"Because I know what I want?"

"What's wrong with you?" I shout at her.

She stands taller. Her cheeks redden. "That's just it, I'm making choices. *My* choices, and it doesn't make any difference if they're the wrong choices."

"Not just wrong," I say, "bad, rotten, stupid, four-year-old choices. Who cares what you want?"

"You don't have the courage to want, then I can't help you."

"Help me?" I scream. "You've written scathing reviews of my work for years. You hate me. We're enemies."

Her shoulders actually jerk a bit. "We're friends," she says.

"And you started it," I say.

"No. You started it by coming to my house." Confidence oozing out of her. "So let me ask you: What is it that you want?"

I answer without thinking. "To sculpt. Recognition. Other stuff, I guess."

"And I want to model."

She doesn't say it, but I still hear it: *So there!*

"I'm out of wood," I say, partly because it's true and partly because I can't think of anything better.

Slowly, she walks around the perimeter of the room, examining the walls, the wooden window frames, the floors. She kicks at two of the loose baseboards—large, ten-inch-wide planks an inch thick. She tilts her head back and examines the wood-framed ceiling, and then fixes on one of the massive pine columns. She says, "Use that."

She's getting back at me for chopping up her mantle. Billie Hannah has lost it and I'm determined to get as far away from her as possible, so I decide to play along and get this over with. "Over there," I say. I point to a sawdust-free spot on the floor. "Strip. Everything off. Now."

I lift my baby ax and walk over to the column, a chubby, rough-cut, sixteen-by-sixteen about fifteen feet tall. It's a rare piece of heartpine, probably more than three hundred years old when it was harvested. With two deep thumps, I slice out a pyramid-shaped chunk of wood from the corner. The grain is dense, as many as thirty rings per inch. I've never seen anything like it. I'm used to fifty-year old yellow pine, or Douglas fir or soft maple. My heart is racing. I take a deep breath.

I say, "Everything off."

Naked, she's a stick figure with sagging skin, a bluish tint, and a not-entirely-hideous scar across her belly. She's nearly as gaunt as my own sculptures, only this is the real-life boniness of an anorexic who has somehow managed to hold onto a pair of unsinkable breasts. For some reason, she refuses to part with her shoes—a pair of fancy red Anne Klein sandals with extra fat heels.

I tell her to relax and stand away from the window. I get her into a standing pose and pace the room looking for an angle. There's nothing here to work with that hasn't already been pinched tight or squeezed until all the joy-juice is long gone. Then I see it: a tiny bulge of a tummy and a purple scar hidden under a layer of make-up. The area is soft and plump like a water balloon, and I have the urge to give it a spank just to hear the sound it makes. Just then Billie sees that I'm not ogling her jagged shoulders or perky breasts but her belly, and she breaks pose.

"For chrissakes," I say.

She starts blabbering, all of her confidence escaping into the hazy blue atmosphere surrounding her. "I knew this was a mistake," she whines. She mashes on her stomach like it's a lump of clay that refuses to hold its shape. What she doesn't realize is that I like what I see. Belly and all. It's a hint at her vulnerability, a chink in her self-loathing. I walk over and squat on my own widening thighs, my hands reach out with craggy fingers and nubbed nails, and I caress her little pooch. She doesn't know what to think at first, but eventually drops her hands to her sides, fingers curled inward, not quite touching her thighs. Slowly, she stands tall; shoulders lifted a half-inch, chin up, eyes slightly upward. This is the pose, I know it, and instantly I decide on a name: Tummy.

The work goes slowly because I have to stop every three minutes and ask Billie to shut up. I scold her like a spoiled puppy until I think I'm getting through, and then she starts in again. She says, "How did you find your calling? I can be trusted. If it's a secret."

"Billie, you know those people who can't walk and chew gum?"

"I know the expression," she says.

"Trust me," I say, "the world's full of them. And I'm one. Only with me it's different. I can't sculpt while your mouth is moving."

"You want to talk about it?"

I don't answer. She's quiet for almost two minutes. Then she can't help herself, says, "My guess is that you were a child prodigy. Am I right?"

I ignore her and pound away on the column for several long silent minutes. "Okay," I say, "here's the deal. I talk and you listen. No responses, no humming, no whistling, nothing. As long as I'm speaking you don't move your lips. Can you manage that?"

She gives me a tight-lipped smile and I go back to work. I make a series of chops with my ax as I dole out a sentence at a time between flurries. I'm barely listening to myself and I stretch it out with long pauses, sometimes so long that I forget what I'm saying and then I blurt out anything that comes to mind.

I tell her how in high school every goddamned thing I could slap together was scooped up at any price. It had to do with a comment a movie star made on a morning radio show. One of the Dallas shock-jocks calls this actor, some has-been living in University Park, I think. The DJ hounds the poor guy about his latest movie. The film is a disaster and as a segue the actor mentions this hideous sculpture he'd seen in the front yard of a house near Love Field. My house. It was one of my first found-object pieces—made from a bicycle tire and a barstool—which I'd more or less scammed from a book I'd just read. He says sarcastically that it's the most artistic thing to come out of Dallas in the last twenty years. The guy's mocking me, but nobody seems to care because shortly thereafter my work hits the market with all the verve and success of the Pet Rock.

Billie says, "It sounds more like an anecdote than a life. Is it true?"

I tell her no, even though it is. I bark at her to stand tall, to straighten her back and to stop dropping her head to see what her belly is doing.

"Touching story," she says.

I don't let on, but her sarcasm is growing on me. I jerk my head at her. "That's it. Get dressed." I'm not angry, though I let her think it. It's nearly seven and I'm tired. The rough is half finished. Tummy stands four and half feet tall, mouth open, arms to her sides, shoulders raised and square, skinny as a toothpick and not nearly big enough for all the weight on her shoulders. For Billie, I'd sculpted Tummy's tummy as flat as a pancake.

"I abandoned Richard," she says. "That's what you told me; abandon the piece of shit, I think you said."

"Richard?"

"My husband. And before you ask, his new outlook on life didn't last. So I've told you mine, now you tell me yours. Just one little secret. Please, please, please."

I put my chisel and mallet on the small wooden table. I say, "I have breast cancer."

"That's not funny," she says.

"No, it's not." I say it without thinking, and then I order Billie Hannah back on Wednesday.

I don't know why I tell Billie about the cancer. Maybe it's because I've wanted to tell someone for weeks and telling a stranger, an enemy even, is easier than telling a friend, which I'm appallingly short of at the moment. Or maybe it's because Billie has been through a lot herself and managed to survive. All she needed was a splinter of hope. And that splinter was there all along, hidden inside a six-foot length of fireplace mantel.

I sometimes think that my lumpy wooden broomsticks are no more of a cure than a good self-help book; that they don't do anything except give people enough courage to put up a fight, which is more or less what Dr. Novak tells to me when he delivers the bad news.

Novak has a phony but rousing, cheerleader-like quality to his voice. He sits on a low stool in the tiny exam room, says "We can fight this thing." By "we," he means that I lay very still while he slices off my left breast. He asks, "Do you have pain?"

"Only when I work."

He actually cackles when I tell him what I do for a living. Sadly, Novak is a lousy communicator, maybe because most of his patients follow his advice even when it makes no sense. Maybe because anyone who cuts off women's breasts for a living doesn't understand the tender influence of words.

The nurse buzzes him about his next appointment.

He stands and orders me to take a pail full of pills and to quit work until the surgery, which I'm not having. No heavy lifting, no pounding, and whatever I do stay clear of chainsaws. I accept the pills because I can sell them for twice what I pay, but I balk when it comes to the no-work rule.

Novak is beside himself, flipping through charts on the narrow counter, punching numbers on his phone, glancing at the corny posters on the walls while I sit there refusing to budge.

I ask, "Why can't I work?"

"Because I said so."

Billie called a couple of nights ago. Wanted to talk about my "condition," she called it. She says, "I couldn't do it." I'm not sure what we're talking about, but I tell her sure she could. "No," she says. "I'm not like you. I'm not a good person."

I am a good person. I am a good person. I repeat the sentence like a mantra lest I forget and revert to my nefarious self.

It's hard to be good in a city so filled with rotten people. It's no secret that I live in a high-crime neighborhood. Downtown Dallas is bad; Deep Ellum is worse. Drive-bys and run-bys were the rage a couple of years ago. Lately it's walk-bys and the ever popular sneak-up. And I defy you to tell the bad guys from the good. Today's paper has a picture of three-year-old Dalton Cahill. Blond, with ears he hasn't yet grown into. Smart eyes. The police say the 12-guage was less than a foot from his face when his mother pulled the trigger. It happened not far from me over on Walton.

I know it's not a good idea walking the streets at night, but I do it anyway, looking for something to sink my ax into. Commerce Street is peaceful enough around midnight, but even in the dark it's the image of neglect. Gravity is tugging on the facades, bricks are slipping out of joint, metal panels are buckling at the seams, and foundations are giving way. I hope nothing falls on me. It's quiet, I'll give the place that much. Nearly all I hear is the clop clop of my own boots.

I hit St. Crawford and head south. Blocks later, I come to a corner and look left and right. It's dark, but I can see two kids on the opposite corner under an ugly yellow light. One is puking in the gutter. The other glances helplessly across the street at the corner grocer behind me. I know the look. Someone's been hurt.

I turn around and peek through the side window of the all-night market. In the back, next to the Cheez-Its with a racecar driver on the box, I see a pair of skinny legs on the floor. Female legs. No blood, no one else. The legs and feet are dressed in baggy, expensive slacks and red Anne Klein sandals with extra fat heels.

My first impulse is to run inside and see if anyone else is hurt. My second impulse is to run like hell. I don't do either; I half-jog across the street to the kids. A boy and a girl. The one puking, the boy, sees me coming and starts into a sort of confessional. He thinks the woman's death was a gang murder. He isn't sure because no one ever gives him the straight story. I begin to hyperventilate, and I can barely get out the words. I ask if he knows the lady.

The girl barks at him. "You don't know anything." She looks bored, or like someone trying hard to look bored, and stares at the grocer, says, "I'd been to four funerals like this one by the time I was eighteen."

My throat feels dry and cold. "What about the woman?" I say.

"Looks like I have another," the girl says.

I stand still, listening, waiting for answers. She finally looks at me. "Ignacio. It's him was shot. Everyone called him Iggy. It was probably Iggy's stupid idea."

I've waited long enough. I grab the girl by the arm and squeeze. "Tell me about the lady on the floor."

She doesn't pull away, just gives me a melodramatic, phony sigh. "Some shopper, I think, not from around here."

I let go of her arm.

"Should I do something?"

"If you like, but it don't really matter. They're dead." She reads my blank stare. "The lady and Iggy. They're dead."

I slump to the curb next to the boy and begin patting his back. He's nine, maybe, and skinny. He ate spaghetti for dinner, or something that on the uptake resembles spaghetti, and it doesn't smell as bad as it could. The bored girl tells me that Rank and Iggy owned the corner. She glances upward at the street sign.

"St. Crawford and McKee. It was their piece of real estate. That's what they called it: real estate. They owned a piece of Dallas real estate. They'd hang out with other friends in black jeans and silver shoes and hassle some of the customers. Not too many, just enough to show it was Rank and Iggy's piece of real estate, and not the customer's. And not the old man who owned the store. The old man didn't mind so much. He wanted to get along, but his daughter, she didn't like it. Said she'd put a stop to it. She did, too."

I take a deep breath and muster my courage, walk back across the street, and enter the store. I walk straight for the shoes. They're Billie's shoes on Billie's feet. She has a cut across her throat, the same color as the shoes. Her eyes are open and glossy. Hidden neatly behind the counter is a tough guy in black lying face down with a bullet hole in his back and a puddle of blood seeping out from underneath his chest. The scene looks suspiciously bland, nothing like what I think a real murder scene should look like.

In the distance, I hear sirens. I stand there paralyzed, gazing down at Billie's ugly red shoes.

Pop. Pop-pop. I hear the sounds from my bed and hope it's not what I know it is: gun shots. Something small. Twenty-two. I've never held a gun, but I know the sound. I lie in bed for another ten minutes and then dress and rush down to the market to pick up the *Morning News.*

The article is short, to the point. Police are looking for 23-year-old Randall Kowalewski—Rank, to his friends—in connection with a robbery and murder Saturday night. The story doesn't mention Billie by name and it's even sketchier about how Iggy—Ignacio Ongile—got himself shot in the back.

I'm sitting in my La-Z-Girl feeling sorry for myself when the phone rings. It's a girl with a perky, twelve-year-old voice.

"I'm calling from Dr. Novak's office to schedule your procedure."

"This isn't a good time."

"I'm sorry, I'm new at this. It's just that Dr. Novak has a busy surgery schedule, and I thought—"

"Take me off your list."

"I don't understand."

I can tell from her voice she thinks she's done something wrong. Something she'll be blamed for later. I say, "Did you know that Novak wants to cut off one of my breasts?"

"You sound so young."

"I am young, an infant practically. So tell me, would you let that phony bastard slice off one of your tits?"

She hesitates. "Hold please," but I can still hear her breathing. Little hiccup-like gasps, as if she might be crying.

I whisper into the receiver. "I'm scared."

The girl's voice is distant and muffled. "I don't know what to say."

This time I shout it. "I'm scared. Tell Novak the answer is no."

L ate Friday night I climb onto the 11 and head into downtown. I'd spotted it on the way home from Billie's funeral a couple of days ago: a wooden pilaster stuck to the side of a brick warehouse over on Market Street, near the Dallas Convention Center. Sixteen inches wide, ten inches deep and twenty feet tall jimmied under something heavy.

I'm sitting near the front of the bus when the driver notices my outfit: all blacks and grays, with a large black shoulder bag draped across my body like a mountain climber carrying heavy ropes.

"That's the wrong getup this time of night," he says. "Impossible to see."

I go, "Yeah, I know."

The bus makes a sloppy left at Houston. I get off and try to get my bearings. I go right, south I think, and amble along for a couple of blocks until I see the School Book Depository, the same building Lee Harvey used to take pot shots at the president, and it occurs to me that I took a wrong turn. I'm on the edge of West End and nowhere near my piece of wood.

I turn around and pick up the pace.

I pass the Hotel Lawrence, a bland building thrown up in the 1920s, and things are starting to look familiar. I go left at Young and right at Market. I can't find it. Maybe it's

South Lamar or Austin Street, so I try both. Lamar is a wide street I don't remember, so it must be Austin. It's not, it's a tiny street north of Memorial without a street sign. The building is a pots-and-pans manufacturer with half the facade redone and the other half left derelict. That's my half. It's unlit, and I've rigged a funky, lantern-type flashlight attached to a string to slip over my head. On me, it's too bright, shining up into my chin, but there's nothing I can do about it. If I look down I'm blinded, so I look up at my wood.

I shut off the light and hang in the dark across the street, tucked into a stinking crack between two buildings. I spot a few homeless in other cracks and wonder if they're as distressed at seeing me as I am them. For an hour there's little action, and I'm getting antsy. I cross the street and unload my shoulder bag. I pull out a mallet, two chisels, small ax, and a whetstone. I grab four crates from the alley, make a low scaffold, and draw part of a sketch on the wood with a grease pencil. A car with its lights off passes behind me and out of sight.

I'm so damn good with my baby ax it's scary, with chunks flying like popcorn. I can feel the grain with the blade the way a blind man fingers a stranger's face. No bigger than a hairbrush, I had it made with a brutish get-outta-my-face blade on one side and a precious little razor edge on the other. It's balanced and weighted to the strength of my arm and the size of my hand. I gouge with the heavy end, and on the upstroke I flip the blade around and shave with the next stroke. I know how hard to swing, when to twirl, and how much attitude to put on the handle.

What I don't know is when some pervert is on the ambush, sneaking up behind me with a big stick. Not until he jabs me in the side.

"What's it gonna be?" the perv says. He's a black man, a filthy Asian, or the dirtiest white guy I've ever seen. Flattish nose, gaunt cheeks and a bushy Tolstoy beard. I ask if he's Russian and he doesn't answer. I look down and get dizzy from my flashlight shining up into my face. I ask if he's heard of a caryatid. He says he don't know any artists. And he doesn't need a lecture in the middle of the goddamn night.

"It's a woman," I say.

"Like you?"

"Taller. Her name's Billie."

"Why in the middle of the goddamn night?" he asks.

I say something about the building owners and he says I'm full of it.

"It's graffiti, ain't it? You did the one on Munster near Crockett, right?"

He's right, but I don't let on. It's a stupid idea but it's all mine: spread my skinny figures around like a tree-lover plants saplings. Most will die, get crowded out by new construction, torn down, or just plain neglected, but some, I'm convinced, will take hold. I'll start here around the Convention Center and work my way out until I've blanketed downtown in narrow wooden totems. I figure one per block ought to do it.

"Am I right?" he says.

"Go away."

"Police are looking for you."

I swing as hard as I can at the wood. *Thwack. Thwack.*

He says, "That her tits?"

"It's a knee."

"Goddamn tall."

He starts telling me his story before his butt hits bedrock. He's been on the streets three years. Sometimes stays with a friend when it gets cold as hell. It's not a bad life, but you gotta settle into it. Take it one day at a time and not make too many plans you're not willing to abandon. Best not to make any plans at all.

What he actually says is a jumble of words with "goddamn" every third one. His mother worked in dry goods a few blocks over on Jackson. For Higginbotham-Bailey, Founders Square. He says do I know the Founders Square? I tell him I do, and then I hear a low rumble and I slap off the light and listen. We both hear it: a car motor, coming or going, I can't tell which. Then it's gone and I switch on the light and go back to work.

"Momma kept to herself." he says. "Hauling bolts of cloth in the goddamn front and ready-to-wear out the goddamn back. Unload and load."

Some of his words are drowned by the chatter of my ax, but I hear him say that his name is Finger. Born with a broken finger sticking sideways when he dropped from his momma and she thought he was the cutest thing, pointing to heaven with thumb and finger like a lobster with pinchers. He pronounces it peenchers. Definitely not Russian.

"Momma says get the goddamn doctor in here and fix my baby's finger and the nurse says he's busy, so she did it herself. Snapped it back proper, easy as that, even if it don't work so good on cold nights and foggy mornings." He jabs me in the leg with his stick. "Why here?"

"Because this is a dark part of town," I say.

"You think I'm a Russian nigger?"

"This place is mean spirited."

"And you think that's gonna help?"

Finger finds more crates and we pile them higher. I'm up here swinging the ax, in my rhythm, twirling the blade and switching hands mid-air, pruning around Billie's long face. She's got thick hair pulled back, a scarf around her neck and a button shirt. The crates are rocking and Finger has his back to the pile, keeping me from tumbling over.

A car weasels up silent and I think it's a cop and my knees go weak. It's not. It's a couple of street urchins. The driver's window is down. A voice says, "Whassup?"

I can't see his face, but the voice is young and tough.

Finger tells him the workers complained. Sounds like a goddamn woodpecker from the inside, so we gotta be out here all night if that's what it takes.

I get the hint. *Peck, peck* and the guy says, "Bullshit."

I glare at him and the car pulls away.

I wrangle a picture from my pocket. A clipping from the *Morning News* next to Billie's obit. I hold up the picture to see how I'm doing. Looks good, and I go at it again. Billie's got on a black skirt to the knee and I stretch her legs long and shove them inside a pair of practical flats around a knot. By the time I get her roughed out, it's one a.m., and I tell Finger to hurry and get rid of all this. We move the crates back to the alley and I pick up any big splinters and heave them into the adjacent lot. I sweep the chips from the sidewalk into the gutter and down a drain with my foot. I ask Finger if he wants to hang with me in the stinking crack across the street. Just until my arms stop throbbing.

We're there two minutes when a car of lowlifes drives by. Same car as before, I think, but now they've brought back-up. They reach the end of the block and stop.

"Those the ones?" I say, and he knows what I'm talking about. This is their block, their piece of real estate.

He says, "Hard to tell. Probly."

Up the street, all but the driver spill onto the pavement and bleed into the dark. The driver turns the car around and eases it back our way. I want to slink deeper into my hole but there's nowhere to go. He drives with his brights on and angles the car to a stop with the lights on Billie. She stands on a four-foot base and stretches twelve feet tall. Even unfinished, her face is scolding in a quiet way.

The driver gets out of the car carrying an aluminum bat. The only thing I can tell for sure is he's big and goes for baggy clothes. He has a ball cap pushed sideways. He's into some street talk with a lot of language and half-words or non-words that I can't make out. He knows we're here and he's talking to us. He's talking to me.

"That bitch," he shouts.

Bitch on the wall he means, and he ain't gonna take her black eyes prying him in his quarter. The guy telling me now if I did this he's gotta cut me or worse. Maybe worse, he says, accounta the fact I'm a honey. Telling me what he's going to do to me. Saying it like a lover, like I want it.

I'm panicky and repulsed. I shove backward into Finger's chest and foul clothes. He doesn't want to touch me but I can't help it and I pull the front of his coat over my arm and shoulder. I want to crawl inside and disappear, and the guy won't shut up. Says how I'm gonna feel, and I can have all I want 'cause he ain't gonna stop even when I beg, 'cause begging's not a tongue he understands.

Finger whispers something, but I don't understand it.

"Shhh," I say.

My world goes cold, all icy and slick beneath me. Finger grabs my arm and shakes hard but I can barely feel. He says, "Time to cut and run." This coming from a man who's mastered the cut and run. I take a couple of minuscule steps to get my footing. "Run," he says.

Only I don't run. I can't. I don't want to. I'm angry at Billie for dying on me. I'm angry at Novak for finding the lump in my breast. I'm angry at myself. I'm especially angry at this asshole with the bat.

Then me and my baby ax walk into the street. The driver looks happy with himself and I get a glimpse of his buddies in the shadows. They're here to watch. I walk toward Billie but he blocks me. Sees my baby ax and laughs. He drops the bat, reaches under the driver's seat and pulls out a long blade. Then he marches at me with the blade down and the confidence of a Downs baby. He's in my face with bad breath and nasty teeth, and doesn't realize that I can make him bleed with either hand, either blade, across the neck, remove the nose or an ear, a finger, a hand.

I say, "I don't want to do this."

I can see his eyes and there's no understanding. He shows me the blade. Big throwaway piece. He handles it like a ten-year-old with a butter knife.

I inch in the direction of the car lights when he reaches for my jacket. On impulse, I slice the closest leg with the razor, switch hands and gouge the back of his knife hand deep so the hand's no good any more. The knife clanks to the ground. His feet are glued in place and he can't believe it. Big Boy just stands there, a look of surprise on his ugly face, not sure what just happened. He looks down at the knife then at his leg that won't move. His right hand hangs numbly at his side bleeding. His left hand balls into a fist.

I'm angry and pumped with adrenaline. I glare into Big Boy's eyes trying to pick a fight. We both glare. Out of the corner of my eye, I watch the fist. I wait for it to swing at me and when it does I'll slice him deep under the wrist. Deep enough, maybe, to take the entire hand. He's scared, too scared to take his eyes off me. Too scared to back away, even if he could. And too scared to throw a punch.

I feel his boys inching out of the dark, and I finally back away to stand in front of Billie in the light.

It's a long time before I see his boys come into the light, not happy but not unhappy either. These guys don't give much away. At most, I see a little surprise.

Finger shuffles into the street and they tell him to scram, so he scrams. Goddamn. They come at me with the same donkeyish drive their leader had, if he was their leader. They come without making eye contact. They come until they reach the light, but they're not coming for me. They stop at the light and look up at Billie.

I can see that they're just boys, sixteen or seventeen, with clear eyes and lots of tattoos. Then, still facing her, one of them shouts, "Is TK all right, or does he need a hospital?" Another boy says, "Hospital," and they get in the car and drive away.

Finger steps out of the dark, says, "How does a piece of wood make people do that? How does it keep people from killing each other? 'Cause without that," he says pointing to Billie, "you, my friend, woulda been dead."

I'm shaking bad. "I don't know how."

I know what I have to do, and it's now or never, because if I leave now, scared, I won't be back. We re-pile the crates and I grab the mallet and the big chisel. I climb up and take a hard stare at the photo. And then shut out the world.

Two hours later, I hear Finger going on about his momma. She tells him don't say yes unless you mean it and don't make plans you can't abandon. He's repeating himself. He asks me for money and I tell him if I had any money I wouldn't be carving the sides of buildings.

"You're one of us," he says. "A goddamn failure. Get used to it, 'cause it don't wash off."

"I am not a failure. Go peddle your religion elsewhere."

Between Finger and the guy with the butter knife, I'm worn down, beat, and grouchy. I don't ask him, I tell him to toss me the small chisel. He says, what small chisel? We argue for a minute over the difference between big and small, that I'm holding the big one so that leaves the other one in my pack and he tells me the goddamn pack's empty. I tell him to give me the goddamn chisel so that I can finish what I've goddamn started.

We both know where the chisel is. My guess is in his shoe, but the crafty bastard might have woven it into his beard. He needs it to sell or trade, I know that, but I'm furious anyway. I give up and chafe away with the big chisel, which works just fine. From my pack, I pull out a can of stain: a dirty gray mixed to look old and weathered. I smear it on and the job's done.

I feel him watching me and I don't care, because I'm still pissed off over the chisel.

Finger says, "You embarrassed him in front of his crew."

"Tough shit."

"It's not over."

"It's never over."

We clean up. and I relent and give Finger some money for his stories and his company.

"It's a marker. isn't it?" he says. "A grave marker?" Then he asks what kinda range she has. "You know. What's her zone of protection?"

"I have no idea."

For some reason, I ask where he's from. Originally. He says, "Jackson, near Founders Square. Do you know it?" I switch off the light and wait for my eyes to adjust to the blackness. Finger doesn't move, says, "I might just sit in the zone for a while. Maybe till daylight." He reaches in his pocket and hands me the chisel. "Won't need this, I guess."

I wake to see Otto standing in my doorway with a newspaper in his hand, saying, "You still in bed?"

"You ever heard of knocking?"

"I been knocking," Otto says. "You don't answer, I figure you're out. Cause I'm a gentlemen, I was planning to leave this here story on your divan."

"I don't have a divan."

"I'm not sure I like you in the morning." He saunters across the room to the bed, drops the paper on my legs. "C2, about the middle," Otto says.

The headline reads: "*Graffiti Artist Tags Area Buildings:* Uunknown artist takes it upon herself to make Dallas a more livable city." It doesn't say that, of course. What it says is that some heinous serial vandal is destroying property by carving on the sides of local buildings. The carvings are described as artistic gang-style tags—tall, skinny figures of unknown origin, possible Egyptian—with Anne Klein footwear. The story softens near the bottom, describing the culprit as a graffiti sculptor—a marginal upgrade from heinous serial vandal, in my opinion. What has authorities stumped isn't so much who's behind the sculptures as why they're drawing such large crowds.

Otto says, "I went and had a look for myself. Had to stand in line, take my turn to get close. This latest one, near Austin, a lady. She looks a lot like your new buddy." Otto stands there, waiting to say something, but doesn't.

It's after lunch when I step onto the 11 and get off at Young. I walk to Austin and hang a right. From a distance, I can see that Billie's hemmed in by a handful of office workers and a gaggle of pot makers. Couple of cops. The mood's festive. A news van double-parks and jacks the antenna. More cars park, more people get out. A covey of homeless hovers to the side.

I reach the fringe of the crowd and hear an engineer in khaki with a clipboard shout numbers to a man in matching khaki on the roof. He ambles over to an executive in a dark suit and tells him it can't be removed without major work to the building.

"Structurally, it's sound," he says. "So much as give her a nose job, and no guarantees."

The suit tells a ruddy-faced cop he's disappointed but the cop doesn't say anything because he's focused on Billie.

I mingle with the mob in the middle of the street and I can smell him before I hear him. Finger is in a small crowd off to the side, telling a younger cop he saw what he saw. "Movie people with trucks and vans. Goddamn lights to blind you. First thing I wonder about, goddamn, I ask myself, who are all these people?"

The cop says, "Name please."

Finger ignores him but likes the attention he's getting from the herd of looky-loos desperate for a story. He says, "A dozen people go at it with saws and all kinda power tools. It's so noisy I can't hear myself. An hour, maybe, and it's done. They pull out the cameras and some movie-type stars, and *action!*"

The cop wants to know the name of the stars.

Finger says, "Ashley Judd before she got famous, she coulda been here."

The cop roles his eyes, but writes the name anyway.

I stand on my toes and look at the congregation of bobbing heads between me and Billie, people crowding into the zone whether they know it or not. Each time I move closer I get snared by a cross current and end up somewhere else. I'm a twig in a mean current, and I accidentally elbow a sheepish man in the gut. He tells me he gets the headaches. Paralyzes him, he says, and he winces hard like one just bit him. He's tried everything and they're getting worse. Look at him, he says embarrassed, now he's taken to rubbing an old piece of wood.

The tide changes and I'm shoved closer to the wall behind an older lady with a neck loaded down with beads and crystals telling another lady it's as natural as rocks in a riverbed. She says, "Anybody can see that, just look at her. Over the years it splinters away until you've got what's left. I've been watching this one for some time."

The other lady says, "Really?"

The beaded lady nods, says, "The process is faster now, acid rain and all. It's happening all over town. They're holy. Beacons of light in this godawful city, pardon me for saying."

The beaded lady gets close and reaches up to touch a leg. Her friend grabs an ankle. It's infectious, and on the next surge, I wedge between them and do the same.

I stretch high and clamp onto Billie's skirt like a little girl greedy for attention. It feels good and I'm no longer afraid. The fire in my breast eases off a couple of degrees. It feels so good that I don't remember letting go.

L ate that night, I zigzag up and down streets near the convention center—past Harwood, St. Crawford, Ervay—looking for something to carve. City Hall's on my left, a giant inverted pyramid of concrete and glass, mostly concrete, and it's foreboding as hell at this time of night. The whole shebang's surrounded by a ten-acre plaza made from, you guessed it, more dingy gray concrete. The plaza's saving grace is a Henry Moore sculpture—a sixteen-foot tall, triangular metal blobby thing that doesn't make me gag.

Naturally, there's not a stick of wood in sight. When I do find a wooden pilaster or an old thick post, which isn't often, I jot down the address in a small note pad. I'm looking for something tall, wide, and with enough depth to swing at without falling on me. What I need is a fat wooden column, soft and not too many knots, holding up nothing.

I angle around the back of City Hall where it's dark and find a couple of small columns that will have to do, one near Browder and Cadiz and a second not far away around Evergreen and Marilla.

Walking home, I think of Billie. I met the woman all of three times. And in those three meetings, I felt something strange: I liked her. And because of that, those few moments where we connected, I feel responsible. She left my studio last Sunday at five, so why, seven hours later at midnight, was she only a dozen blocks away? And even if she was just sneaking a box of Twinkies in the corner grocer, why do it in the one of the roughest areas of downtown? What I really want to know is why she's dead, and the only person I can think of who can help answer that is Randall Kowalewski—Rank.

When I enter my studio, Otto's standing next to the fridge with the door open, taking a big dumb gander at what's not inside. He says, "You got nothing to drink."

Invited or not, his presence is oddly comforting. I scan the room looking for anything broken that Otto might be fixing. "I didn't know I was having company, but I'm glad you're here. I need a ride."

"It's late," Otto says. "What's wrong with your ride?"

He knows damn well that my truck is sitting idle in the parking lot next to the building and has been for weeks. What's wrong, I've no idea. It won't start and I can't muster the courage to have it diagnosed for fear that it's something serious and unfixable. I'm developing a not-entirely-irrational fear of mechanics, doctors, dentists, and especially gynecologists—anyone whose job it is to look inside before telling you what's wrong, the parts that need to be replaced or, worse, the parts that just need to be torn out. I'd rather just leave things alone, in one piece—whole, in other words, even if it's broken—and hope that they fix themselves. I believe in miracles.

I tell Otto where I keep the vodka and I grab the phone book, find four numbers and addresses, and dial the Kowalewski closest to the Seagar Grocer where Billie was killed. When someone picks up, I speak slow, friendliness oozing out of me. I say, "Is Rank around?"

"Here?"

"Yeah."

"Why would he be here?"

Bingo! At least, she knows him. "Is this his mother? It's important that I get a hold of him."

She says, "About what, and no this isn't his mother. Do I sound old to you?"

I want to ask how old she is, what she looks like because my impression is early forties and attractive, sinewy, the type of women who looks you in the eyes when she's lying, and I'm usually not far from the mark. I'm wasting time, so I decide to just lay it out there and see what happens.

I say, "I was a friend of the woman who got killed. At the little market near Ervay, a couple of blocks from you. A girl from the neighborhood told me that Rank hung around the market. It was his corner, she said. I want to ask him if he knows how it all happened."

"Assuming he was there."

In the silence, I listen to a faint monotone of laughter in the background, a sitcom probably.

"A friend huh?" she says.

And then she lays it out there. Saying if I'm just a friend, like I say, then I want to find out who did it. But if I'm more, like family or a real close friend—insinuating that Billie and I might be a couple of lezbos, though she doesn't say it—then I might want to do something about it, and she's clearly afraid that Rank could get hurt.

She says, "Randall had nothing to do with it."

"Probably not," I say, "but I still want to know what happened."

"What happened? I'll tell you what happened. We live in an angry world, in an angry city, and that little market is located in a very angry part of town. Your friend got hurt because someone got angry with her and didn't have the self-control to walk away, which is what I'd suggest you do. Walk away. You think you can do that?"

I tell her no and she says she thought not. Someone screams fire, she tells me and I want a closer look. Maybe even a sneak inside, see who got burnt. I'm the type, according to Mrs. K., who runs into burning buildings.

"You got me all figured out," I say.

"And you never get burnt?"

There's an especially long pause as we both listen to the laugh-track on TV.

"What's your name?" she says.

"Susan...Ross."

The Susan was easy. The Ross came out a little slower. I've been walking the streets so much lately that I can't get the names out of my head—Live Oak, Bryan, San Jacinto, Ross Street. So much for laying it all out there.

Mrs. K. says, "You sound like an honest person, Susan Ross. I'm Randall's mother. Be good to my boy, you hear me? Twelve oh two Gano."

The line goes dead.

It's the same address I have sitting right here in front of me, and I would have found him sooner or later.

Otto has poured a finger of vodka in each of two glasses. He slides mine in front of me, and I down it in one gulp. I wince from the little jolt it gives me.

I say to him, "Are you going to give me a ride or not?"
I want to get there before Mrs. K. changes her mind, calls her son, and gives him a heads up. We hustle into Otto's car and I throw my black canvas bag in the back seat. It's got a couple of chisels, mallet, my baby ax, in case I need to do some carving.

Otto's car is big and dark and old. Buick, maybe, or a Pontiac, if they still sell Pontiacs. We pull onto Gano Street, spot the house near the corner, and park on Wall for no reason other than it seems the prudent thing to do. From here we can see the house and the street, and suddenly I have to pee. I mean, I really have to pee, and it might have to do with all the medication I'm not taking. I grab my bag and hustle to the door. It's a dump from a distance and worse up close. Before I get there, a young guy opens the door. Dark clothing, ring in his nose, tattoos.

He says, "What do you want?"

"Rank?"

"Who are you and what do you want?"

"Susan, a friend of your mother's. Mind if I use your bathroom?"

He rolls his eyes, says, "I don't know anything about the lady was killed because I wasn't there. My word, I wasn't there. I should have been, but I wasn't."

"I really have to pee."

"You're not getting inside my house."

Until two seconds ago the last thing I wanted was to get inside his house. The *last* last thing I wanted was to get inside his bathroom and put my butt in contact with anything that his butt has touched. Now, however, I want inside the house.

I sort of buckle at the waist in what I think of as a universal sign of a woozy bladder pain. I say, "You got a bucket, a bowl, anything I can use?"

At this I get a laugh.

I say, "Come on. I just gotta pee." Men are so stupidly gullible. I can sense it, I've got him. Then he takes two quick steps back and slams the door.

Back in the car, Otto and I sit there for a moment trying to think of a place to get a cheap drink. My vote hinges on several things, but at the top of my list is a clean bathroom. Otto suggests the Club Clearview, where it's too damn loud and I counter with the Angry Dog, where I can get some good wings. Clean bathrooms in both. And both within walking distance of the loft. We sit there in the car and chatter for a couple of minutes about anything but my stunted conversation with Rank. Otto doesn't press. He's a man who doesn't get involved unless he has to, and I'm sure he just wants to end his tour as chauffeur.

Otto didn't even know Billie. Doesn't really know she was a friend. Doesn't know she's the woman I found dead in the market. Doesn't know why we're here watching a house on Gano. Doesn't even know me, really. What he knows is that I asked for a ride and he said yes.

A huge SUV zips down Gano and pulls into Rank's driveway. It's got to be one of the biggest they make, extra wide, sitting high off the ground. The horn blows, lights in the house go out, and Rank bounds out of the door and climbs up into the SUV.

"Follow them," I say.

"Thought you wanted a beer."

"You wanted a beer, I wanted a vodka."

"What say we go get us a beer and a vodka, then?"

There's no convincing a man that he wants anything, and Otto's more stubborn than most. He's got to want it himself. Life's easier still if he comes up with the idea. I look from the corner, where the SUV just eased out of sight, to Otto. Back and forth. Forth and back. I don't say a word, giving him time to come up with the idea. Back and forth.

"He's not the guy," I say.

Otto says, "That what you think?"

"He doesn't know anything. He wasn't there."

"Then why'd you want to follow him?"

"He's innocent," I say

Otto says, "Huh. Nobody's innocent."

I can't think of anything clever to say so I stare at the corner squeezing my bladder.

He says, "Nobody's innocent." This time to himself. And to prove it he says, "Let's go."

We hustle to the corner and up Akard and I spot the car waiting in the left-hand turn lane at Elm. After the turn, the guy drives fast and Otto lets several cars get between us.

On my side of the street we pass the Bank of America building, Renaissance Tower—big glass boxes of reflected light—and some other buildings I can't remember the names of.

The traffic is unusually heavy, rocketing up to forty between lights. At Market, everything comes to a halt. I stick my head out the window and look ahead. I see lots of cars in our lane—the middle lane—and the right turn lane but no big SUV. It must have changed lanes.

I say, "He's on your side, right?"

Otto tilts his head out the window. "Two or three back from the crosswalk. Shit, the guy's getting out."

The light changes and the mass of cars surge ahead. As we get closer, I can see Rank on our left, standing in the road between lanes. His hands in his pockets, hopping foot to foot like a fighter between rounds. Traffic is tight and fast, everyone rushing to get somewhere. It's dark. Cars race forward, all of them not seeing Rank in his dark clothes until the last second and then involuntarily braking or jerking the car left or right.

When we reach him, Otto jams the big Pontiac to a stop in order let Rank safely by. This wasn't planned and I wonder why he did it at all unless maybe he just wanted to get a look at his face. Instead of a thank you, Rank glares at Otto like he's being an asshole. His stare shifts to me and he's confused, pauses in front of us, the cars behind us honking now, and turns squarely to face me for a long moment. His lips move, either cussing under his breath or confiding in me. In my mind he mouths, "nobody's innocent," though it's an unlikely thing to say in this situation. Besides, those are Otto's words and it strikes me as odd that these two men have even two words in common.

Rank pulls a hand out of a pocket and at first I think he's holding a knife but he's not. It's only a hand. He pushes the palm out as if to stop oncoming traffic and steps confidently further into the street. He's next to me, not ten feet away when a green pickup hits him flush-on and bounces him into the middle of the intersection—changed him from an innocent man to a collection of arms and head and legs clumped on the pavement.

Our car moves quickly by, the light red, but Otto plowing ahead, weaving us around cars. My heart is thumping, cold sweat seeping through the pores of my face. In my side mirror I see Rank's motionless body in the road. A half block later, I look again. The green truck has pulled to the curb, and a figure rushes back up the road. I see a group of gloomy people, heads down, huddled out on the pavement around the body and I recall the last words Mrs. K. said to me. "Be good to my boy, you hear me."

I catch the 8 at Ervay and go north. At Mockingbird, a woman from the front of the bus gets up and comes directly at me. She doesn't rush. She pauses next to my seat, close enough to bump my shoulder with her hip, and glares down at me. "Are you the sculptor?"

I tell her it's me.

"Stop what you're doing," she says, and throws a newspaper in my lap. It's the article about Billie. The headline reads: *"Art Critic Killed During Robbery,"* and someone has circled the words "art critic" and written next to it: Willamina (Billie) Rosaline Hannah. I look up at the woman: dark skin, full lips, Mexican-American probably, and she smells terrific, like a double shot of fabric softener.

I say, "Are you a friend of Billie's?"

No answer. The bus squeaks to a halt, doors open, and people push and shove to get out. The woman steps down and out the door.

I yell at her. "What exactly am I doing?"

She turns and looks both ways like what she's about to say is top secret. "You're getting people killed."

* * *

In the last couple of months, I've memorized several of the bus routes—the 11, parts of the 10, the 12, the 19 I learned the hard way. I fell asleep one night and ended up ten miles south of downtown around Ledbetter and Marsalis, lost and confused. The 8, the bus I'm on now, takes me up on the map towards Billie's people in the Park cities—Highland Park and University Park. Mr. Billie—Richard Hannah, though I can't get myself to think of him as anything but the asshole that Billie married—has wooed me into having lunch with him.

He wants to talk, though about what he won't say, and he apparently wants to do it on neutral ground. When I suggested he meet me around the corner at Adair's, or the AllGood, or the Angry Dog, even, he laughed. Persuaded me to come up his way. Fine, his way it is, so long as it's along the bus route. I'm in no mood for a long, goose-pimply stroll in the cold. It's November, for chrissakes.

I tell him where I catch the bus in downtown and where it loops back on itself up around Westchester and Northwest Highway. Richard Hannah is sharp and he figures the straightest line between here and there is Preston, so he suggests a couple places on Preston. The problem is the bus routes, and especially the 8, weren't designed to get me from Deep Ellum to my lunch date. They were designed, I suppose, to meander through the neighborhoods where the little people who actually use busses can flag one down without hiking the Chisholm Trail to get to a bus stop.

Mister knows just the place, the Rosa Ravioli. It's on my way and impossible to miss, he tells me. Just look for the big yellow sign. I do miss it, and the sign isn't big it's small, and it's not yellow but ochre, if that.

When I arrive, Mister is guarding the door in a gray double-breasted suit covering his big belly, looking much like a lawyer though I know he's in advertising.

I reach out to shake his hand.

He says, "I'm still pissed at that stunt you pulled with my fireplace mantle." His voice is extra gruff, nothing like on the phone. He's holding a long package wrapped in brown paper. "Here."

I reply with extra syrup. "A present. How thoughtful."

It's heavy, and I know what it is by the heft of it. How he got it and why he's giving it back, I'll figure out later. Right now I'm famished. Mister is buying so I'm ordering one of everything. What I don't eat in, I'll take with me. I move to open the door, but he blocks me.

He says, "We're not eating."

"Why the hell not?"

Mister says, "I was asked to return this. I have. So now you and I are done."

"Why make me come all this way?"

"Because I'm important and you're not."

His frankness shocks both of us. He laughs a little, grows embarrassed, says what else did I have to do, as if this is any less pompous.

"Who asked you?" I say.

"Who's not important?"

Before I can argue, a young couple in business outfits hustles down the sidewalk aiming for the door behind us. Mister lets them squeeze by, and when the door opens I'm smothered in a gusty wind of warm sour dough.

There are lots of things I could have said. But I'm hungry, so I say, "Billie talked about you."

He finds that hard to believe, he says. Mister begins to say—and then looks away and sighs, not one of those good sighs, but the kind where he resigns himself to bad news; where he admits that yes, confidants, who include his wife, probably have been blabbing his whole goddamn miserable life story to strangers behind his back. And at least some of that story is pretty damn ugly.

I say, "I couldn't get her to shut up, in fact."

He can't help himself, he has to ask. "So what'd she say?"

"Are you buying lunch?"

The Rosa Ravioli is small and sprinkled with people in dark business suits. We get directed to a booth against the back wall. I open the menu and see too many options, most of them ravioli. I pick something from the bottom of the list, wild mushroom ravioli, grab the closest waitress and order. As an afterthought I ask about appetizers. She's in a rush and rattles off a list from memory. Calamari salad, gorgonzola cheese ball, balsamic roasted asparagus—she gets that far when I stop her and tell her one of each. Oh, and a bottled water. Mister unbuttons his suit jacket, lets out a big breath of exhaust, and orders a nice slimming plate of fried jalapeno ravioli in sage butter, a side of meatballs, a loaf of that big puffy bread (our waitress nods knowingly), a bowl of zesty arrabiata sauce for dipping, and a Coke because they don't have anything stronger.

I put the package in my lap and tear away a piece of the paper just to confirm what I already know. It's the bronze sculpture that I found hidden in Billie's closet.

I ask, "Where did Billie get this?"

"Pastor Sammy," Mister says.

"The guy on TV? He gave Billie a sculpture that I cast over five, six, years ago? That doesn't make any sense."

"He was a client of mine, couple of years ago. He and Billie hit it off."

"What exactly do you do?"

"Is this really necessary?"

"Just until the puffy bread arrives."

He hesitates, says, "I tell people what to think."

"Like which laundry detergent to buy?"

At this his face goes red. "Advertising is too damn valuable to waste on commercial products."

"So you're the champion of good causes, then?"

In fact, these are Billie's words, and I'd just remembered them. She told me once that Richard was an advertising rebel, that he believed in causes, the more hopeless the cause the more passionate the ad campaign.

He says, "I've been called worse."

When I ask what he considers a good cause he's reluctant at first, but then leans forward, places both hands on the table, and inhales like a man who knows how to get messages across. "The Giant Panda, the Dallas Symphony Orchestra, the Sierra Club, cancer research, teenage alcoholism, AIDS in Africa, I can go on for hours."

"So what'd you do for Pastor Sammy?" I ask.

"I gave him something he didn't deserve, a new reputation."

"And you consider that a good cause?"

"You're spoiling my lunch."

"Okay. Okay," I tell him, hands in the air like I'm giving up. I look around the room—at a couple of guys yaw-hawing about the Cowboys, at three secretary-types complaining about a coworker with a low-cut top and too-big tits, at our waitress running between tables and the kitchen, at Mr. Richard Hannah—thinking about how different we really are from our reputations. A reputation is like a scorecard or a bad credit rating—abbreviated, absolute, unfixable. The life itself, well, that's a whole lot more contradictory and hopeful.

I ask, "What was wrong with Sammy's old reputation?"

"Christ, when was the last time you picked up a paper? Look, if you're a televangelist, a popular one, especially, it's easy to think you're made of titanium, and that your reputation is equally unbreakable. But it's not. Just misquote the Bible a couple of zillion times, pilfer millions from the collection plate, play sugar daddy to a secret girlfriend who's tired of being a secret, and claim to heal people that were never sick."

"Sounds like you don't like him."

"Sure I like him," Mister says. "About as much as I like a good old-fashion prostate exam."

"Then why work for him?"

"Do I really need to answer that?"

The puffy bread arrives and Mister goes at it with all the zeal and grace of a starving walrus.

After lunch, Mister goes quiet and sullen. He's got a chunk of red sauce on his gray suit jacket, but I don't say anything. And he's no longer in a rush to get rid of me. I say, "Who asked you to give me the bronze?"

"I told you, who's not important."

"Was it Billie?"

He's getting a kick out of this. He knows something I don't. He says, "I'll tell, and then you tell what Billie said. Then we're done here."

"Sure."

"Pastor Sammy called me this morning and suggested that I return the bronze. That's it. Now you."

This has me stumped and I can't think of a thing to say.

Mister says, "It's not an easy adjustment."

From the red eyes, I assume he means living without his wife, though I could be wrong. He could be a man adjusting to lots of things. And he seems to be angling for something. My guess is that he wants to know what his wife thought of him without actually hearing the words spoken aloud. Not what she told him, but what she'd tell a outsider like me—the truth. Or, at least, that's what I think he's thinking. And Billie was a talker, we both know that.

What she told me in her own bookish way was that Mr. Richard Hannah used to slap her. Mostly when he was drinking, but sometimes not. And not so much to hurt as to humiliate. Oh, and the kicker, she tells me, is that she deserved it. By way of explanation, she hinted that Mister learned his trade from his father, a man who believed that a well-timed open-handed slap helped keep everyone in the family on the same page. What she'd had to put up with, she assured me, was nothing compared to what Richard had had to endure.

Mrs. Billie Hannah told me in great detail how he did it—open-handed, palm forward, mostly striking her with his stubby fingers—and how often—quarterly, as far as she could tell. What she did not tell me was what she thought or felt about the experience; what she thought or felt about Mr. Billie Hannah. Either she had long ago locked her emotions away so they wouldn't get trampled, or she simply wasn't telling me.

Mister has slumped in his chair, the back of his suit collar riding up at the neck. He says, "So what'd she say about me?"

"That you are a crusader," I say, and this part is true. "You crusade against cigarettes because they kill people, against billboards because they make the world ugly, against boxing because it turns men into vegetables. You want me to go on?"

He nods, looking hopeful.

I say, "You crusade for integration, for religious tolerance, for human freedoms of all kinds."

"That's it?"

"And," I say, "that no man on earth made her happier," and this part is a lie. Why I say it, I don't know. Maybe because I can. Maybe because Billie's dead. Maybe because I believe the fat, rich executive in the gray suit sitting across from me still has a chance to become a better person, and telling him the truth will only make becoming that person a whole lot tougher.

"She said that?" he asks.

"Yeah. One last favor," I say, "and you'll never hear from me again."

"What is it?"

"Give me a lift to Pastor Sammy's."

"Not on your life."

"Billie said one other thing."

"What's that?"

"You giving me a ride?"

Mister says, "Let me give you some advice. Learn when enough is enough, 'cause this thing you're doing, it can get pretty fuckin' tiresome."

The Global Healing Center is a twenty-minute freeway ride west. In the car, Mister is talking, his eyes glued to the road, the cars all around us weaving in and out of lanes doing eighty or better. Mister saying that why God wanted the Center built in Irving isn't clear, though it's rumored it had something to do with lower taxes. Then he starts giving me directions I didn't ask for.

"Just take the Stemmons freeway north to the John Carpenter west to Storey north."

I suppose to a man like Mister, this is a worthwhile give-and-take, but it means nothing to me.

I say, "That's very helpful."

Mister nods, like he knew it would be.

"So how do I get back into downtown?" I ask.

Mister looks at me—my hair's a mess, my sweater's too thin, it's chilly, and my nipples are poking out. He says, "Try that thing you do on Pastor Sammy, see how far it gets you."

Off to my left, I can see Texas Stadium wedged inside a huge triangle of freeways. A minute later, we exit and Mister scoots down the street a couple of blocks, drops me at the corner of Century Center and Century Drive. He points a fat thumb back at the rear window and tells me it's on Century. I can't miss it. He's not going near the place, but doesn't say why. My guess is that there's some bad voodoo between Mister and Pastor Sammy. I hoist the bronze and giddyup down the road.

Standing in the lobby, I get a tour of the 150-acre park on a super-sized TV set built into one wall. On screen, a very dapper Pastor Sammy is telling me what's what. He walks me through the Healing Cathedral where his television program is shot, the Healing Tower, the two-story Healing Hall of Faith, and of course the Healing Gardens.

Next to me a couple is watching the TV, oohing and ahhing with every mention of the word healing. Mom is holding a cute little girl, four-ish, with braids and a frilly pink skirt that I wouldn't put on a puppy.

Pastor Sammy closes by making us—me and the couple next to me—a solemn promise: if we can see it in our hearts to come up with another $15 mil in the next year or so, he'll install an IMAX theater and several rides, maybe a healing roller coaster.

More oohing and ahhing from the thrill-seekers next to me.

The little girl wants down. Mom says no. She still wants down. No. She tries wriggling. No. Shouting. No. Whimpering turns into crying that grows into a full-scale, throat-scratching bawl. The bawling lasts only a couple of seconds until the girl gives up, quietly sobbing, her face sunk deep into Mommy's fluffy sweater. Mom finally caves and sets the girl on the marble floor like a piece of unsteady china. The girl takes a couple of wobbly steps and it's obvious that her legs don't work, or at least, not the way they're supposed to. Mom shuffles along behind her, flinching with each awkward step, her arms poised to catch her baby when she falls. Dad stands his ground, his face hard, watching his little girl stumbling away from him. He shoots me an embarrassed glance, the tiniest tear forming in one eye.

I do a 360 and see two more groups—a man and a woman, and two women—mother and daughter, is my guess—and all of them have that same broken look about them.

The Healing Center is several connected buildings, but all I can see from the entrance lobby is an expanse of marble floor—large enough for the Ice Capades—and an enormous barrel vault overhead that makes me feel very small. Lots of glass, lots of dark wood, lots of stone.

A receptionist stands behind a high counter, vigorously pecking at a keyboard. She's older than me, though not by much, and by the scowl on her face I get the feeling she's having a bad day, like she'd take anything you said the wrong way. I amble up to the counter.

Head down, she starts speaking before I open my mouth. "There's no service today. Sunday, come back then if you like"

I'm still holding the bronze Mister gave me. It's heavy, so I set it on the counter. I crane my head around and up, taking in the room and the ceiling.

I say, "Wow. Reminds me of Vegas."

Now she looks up. "Seventy-five a show…service, I mean. I get in trouble I call it a show."

"I have to pay to attend church?" I ask.

"This isn't a church," she says. "And no, you don't *have* to pay. Stand in the lobby all you like. You want to attend the service, the one's on TV, then we gladly accept your donation. Seventy-five dollars. MasterCard, Visa, cash. No American Express, no personal checks. You can pay now and come back Sunday, avoid the lines."

Miss Happy is shuffling from foot to foot.

I say, "Bet this job can be tough on your feet."

Her shoulders drop a half-inch, and I'm sure I scored a point just for noticing. "Yeah."

I say, "What's it like working here?"

She glances past me to the little girl in the frilly pink skirt tottering her way across the lobby, then to a man in a wheelchair coming through the entrance doors, a woman behind him struggling with the door, the wheelchair, and an oversized purse all at once. Tells me in a quiet voice, the guy could have used the handicapped door. All you do is push the button. I look to the way in, to the extra wide doors on each side of the entrance—plastered with blue handicapped signs—but say nothing. She tells me lots of people don't use the doors that should. Pride, she supposes, people too stubborn to admit they need help.

There is a silence.

"Working here," she says. "It's a real joy."

"And Pastor Sammy?"

"What about him?"

"What's he like?"

At this she stands taller, her body rigid, like she just figured me out. I'm either a heartless auditor with the IRS, or worse, part of a sting operation with *60 Minutes*.

She says, "Who are you?"

"Your fearless leader," I say. "I'm here to see him. Tell him it's about Billie Hannah."

She hesitates, picks up the phone, mumbles into it, listens, puts it down. "Someone'll be here shortly."

She goes back to pecking at the keyboard.

A few minutes later, I hear faint footsteps behind me drumming across the marble. I look, and it's the bus-lady from this morning. The one who politely told me to stop what I'm doing. There's still thirty feet between us when she sees me, stops for a beat, and then picks up the pace.

On the bus, she was wearing jeans and a worn sweater. Now she's in a tailored business suit, a pale goldenrod with a V-neck jacket, notched collars, hidden buttons, and a below-knee length skirt. It looks good against her brown skin, but might be a touch tight in the hips.

She reaches me, grabs my hand, and shakes without me having to contribute much.

"I'm Pilar."

I say, "Miranda—"

"I know who you are."

"You remember me?"

"I'm good with faces. And yours I saw just this morning. And," she says, pausing, "I've seen your work."

"Where?"

"This way, please."

She walks fast and talks faster, pointing out spaces and rooms and hallways as we meander to wherever we're meandering to. She's got a brochure in her hand, and it's got a floor plan on the back. She doesn't look at it, but she's not giving it to me, either. We take a couple of turns and the hallway widens. We approach a set of double doors. She uses her card key to open the door and ushers me inside.

I'm supposed to be wowed, and I am. It's a huge, octagon-shaped room topped with an ornate dome large enough to cover a small mountain. The Healing Hall of Faith, she tells me. It's connected to several small theaters that show re-creations of services of famous evangelists—two theaters just for kids. Next we come to the Healing Chapel, where adults can pray 24 hours a day, followed by the Healing Prayer Tower, where, no doubt, prayers are shot straight to heaven like out a giant cannon. She mentions but doesn't show me the in-the-round repertory theater, the combo zoo-Kilimanjaro safari experience, the Mary Magdalene aerobic workout room, and the healing pools, mud bath, skate park, and coming-soon 18-hole golf course.

I say, "You're like my own personal tour guide."

"I'm not your personal anything."

When she mentions the healing sculpture garden, my ears perk up: life-size bronze statues showing scenes of healing from the Bible, some piped-in dialogue, and even some mood music for a little added ambiance.

"The sculptures," I say. "Do they actually heal people?"

"Believers."

"And non-believers?"

"Faith is important here, Miss Tate."

"Miranda," I say.

"Miranda, you should keep that in mind."

"Can I see it, the sculpture garden?"

"No."

I've got the bronze in my hand and it's getting heavy. I shove the thing at her and ask if she minds. Confused, she takes it in one hand as I snatch the floor plan out of her other. I look for anything green that might indicate a garden. I'm not so good navigating Dallas by the names of old dead guys, but I can read a floor plan just fine. I turn and take one step, when Pilar surprises me. She latches onto my shoulder with her free hand and spins me around. Now we're standing face-to-face, both of us waiting for the next move.

There's really nothing she can do, and I want her to understand that without having to prove it. Pilar is strong, but I'm stronger. It's one of the benefits of a lifetime working with chisels and hammers and chainsaws and chunks of wood as heavy as some cars.

"This morning on the bus," I say, "you told me to stop what I'm doing."

"I was trying to help."

"I don't understand."

"No, you wouldn't," Pilar says.

"What do you do here?"

"I'm Pastor Sammy's executive assistant."

"And you run his errands."

"Of course, but this morning was something else. I was trying to help you."

I feel suddenly, unexpectedly distant and lucid, and now I really want to see what's in the garden.

I take two quick steps back and hurry down the hallway, go right at the first corridor, left at the next, and see another lobby with glass doors that lead out onto an open space.

I open the glass doors and involuntarily catch my breath, first because of the colors, then because of the smells. The tiny green shape on the map is, in fact, a 20-acre arboretum in something less than full bloom, and a regular leaf-peepers paradise. Some of the colors I recognize—climbing winter jasmine; lion's ear with its long, hairy-tooth leaves; densely planted river birch in beds of blue pansies. The smells are tougher to figure, but no less overwhelming: the balsam scent of witch hazel, the tangy tongue of apricot, and mint, I think.

Pilar is scampering along behind me in her hip-hugging skirt, mumbling about rules and restricted areas. She catches up and just stands there watching me, enjoying the look of awe on my face. She doesn't exactly smile, but if she had, it'd be the first smile I'd seen since entering the Center.

Wide brick paths, roomy enough for maybe twenty people shoulder to shoulder, lead me through the gardens. I stroll into the topiary garden—large shrubbery trimmed to look like people and animals. There's a mean old guy with big hands pointing; a naked man laying on his side, one arm on his knee flashing me his tiny pecker; a couple of poor souls nailed to crosses, and lots of semi-overgrown pieces I can't figure out.

Then I come to the sculpture garden.

Pilar promised scenes from the Bible, but there's none of that. The way it's laid out, it's a sort of shrine to famous faith healers of the past, a regular Holy Ghost Mayo Clinic for the lame and afflicted. It's not hard to imagine wheelchair-bound parades shuttling from DFW Airport to Irving like pilgrims of Mouseketeers pouring into Disncyland.

Adjacent to the sculpture garden is an area under construction. So far, nothing but teeny concrete pads.

I point at the concrete footings, say, "What's going in here?"

"Ask Pastor Sammy."

"Top secret, huh?"

Pilar has her arms crossed, the bronze gripped tightly in one hand, one foot in front of the other, posing, looks like to me. She's good at it, and really quite beautiful. She's staring at the concrete pads.

I look from Pilar to the pads and back to Pilar.

I say, "Come on, what gives?"

"You're not supposed to be here."

"Here in the gardens, or here next to whatever this is?"

"You know what, I'm starting to like you. You have a way of asking the right question."

I stare at the construction area, at the nubbly little gray pads, at some of the wooden forms showing where the walkways will be poured, and try to think of the right question. I look at my floor plan then glance between trees to my right. I can make out the two Olympic-sized pools and I know from the map that they're surrounded by a dozen bubbly jacuzzis.

Pilar lifts her arms and does a sort of Vanna White half-turn gesturing to the gardens, the cathedral, the tower, the pool area. She says, "So what do you think?"

"It strikes me as sort of a healing theme park, or maybe a new-age miracle spa."

"If you mean that as a compliment, then, yes, it is."

I say, "I'm not sure how I mean it."

Pastor Sammy Gann has a doughy face and a bad toupee or the worst comb-over I've ever seen. It kills me the lengths men will go to hide a bald head. On TV it looks silly. In person, it's hysterical. The hair sort of cantilevers off the side of his head four or five inches and then sweeps up and back, where it's plastered in place over the hairless parts. I feel for him, the guy not knowing the do makes him look stupid. Somebody ought to tell him, and then scram.

He greets me at the door of his office, reaches out as if to shake my hand, gives me an awkward little wave, and then quickly turns and sprints back down the court ready to score. At least, that's how if feels. The office is echoey-big with a hardwood floor, high ceilings, and cone-shaped light fixtures hanging down, spotlighting the floor like a small gym. The architect did a bang-up job here: more dark wood, more tiny-paned windows at one end, more expensive frames and crappy pictures nailed to the walls and balancing on the bookshelves.

"Mr. Gann—" I say.

He doesn't look up. "Pastor Sammy, please."

"Pastor Sammy, then. You gave this to a friend of mine." I hold up the bronze sculpture, peel away most of the brown paper, and give him a good look. A pointless gesture because he's now forty feet away, and the sculpture is small. I ball up the brown paper in my free hand and look for a trashcan. I say, "Would you mind telling me where you got it?"

Pastor Sammy says, "First things first."

I'm ready to bet anything that we have to run through a little prayer before we can get down to any business. But I'm wrong. Pastor Sammy has to be seated on his throne before we can get down to business. He settles into an over-sized chair behind his over-over-sized desk with the windows behind him. A dull gray light streams through, making him look thinner, more angelic, with a glaring, headachy aura about him.

Pilar is behind me, keeping quiet. Five large men, goons in sloppy, loose jogging suits, stand off to my left looking dumb. Bodyguards, or the on-stage catchers who pick up the newly healed after Pastor Sammy has blown his supercharged bad breath into their faces. I've seen the circus on TV: some people fainting, most politely falling backward in a way that doesn't break any bones, a few convulsing like a stuck pig. The catchers always have round arms and rounder bellies. It's their job to keep the newly healed from falling on top of the not-yet-healed in the row behind them. And collectively, this bunch looks as if it has just the IQ to handle the job.

On my right, a shorter man wearing a sporty blue Dallas Mavericks button-front jersey is sitting on a leather couch in the corner. I give them numbers, one through five, left to right. Number Six for the Mavs fan on the couch.

Number One moves close, puts a hand on my arm and nudges me to a seat in front of Pastor Sammy. I jerk the arm away, but then sheepishly hand him the brown paper and mumble a thank you. I don't take the seat, but stand stubbornly behind the chair.

On Pastor Sammy's desk are three large, white, stiff-paper bowls, like a bucket of popcorn comes in, but white. All of them stuffed with cash. No offering envelopes, no checks, no credit card slips, just the green stuff. Pastor

Sammy settles his angelic butt deeper into his chair. He's ready to begin.

He says, "Let me see what you have there."

I set the bronze on the edge of the desk. There's no way he can reach it from where he's sitting, and he doesn't bother.

"I see," he says.

Enough niggly-pigglying around. I tell him why I'm here is, I'd like to know how he got a hold of my work and why suddenly he wants to give it back. There's more, he's sure, he says and there is. I want to know what happened to Billie Hannah. I want a lot, according to Pastor Sammy. The glare coming through the window is painful. There's that, or maybe it's looking at that ugly rug, thinking the guy who made it should be reported to whoever you report bad rug-makers to.

Pastor Sammy leans forward. "Let me tell you a story?"

Pilar has moved to a chair next to Pastor Sammy's desk, but she doesn't sit. She nods, almost imperceptibly, coaching me along. I know a stall when I see one, but what the hell. I scooch around to the side of the chair and fall into it, one leg draped over the side like an unruly high-schooler. It's this place, this man with his big swooshing hair, and now the stall. It's put me in a bad mood.

Pastor Sammy says, "It won't take long, I assure you. And I think it will help."

I finally nod.

"When I was a boy," he says, "my father entered into a pact with the man upstairs. Father took a knife from the kitchen and made an incision on his wrist. Not a big cut, but big enough to draw blood. Father was large, or at least that's the way I remember him, and proud. I can see his face. He wouldn't ordinarily let a little cut on his wrist bother him, but it did. It's one of the things I remember about him."

I'm half listening, looking around but seeing the little girl with the legs that don't work, the frilly pink dress getting dirtier each time she falls, the little girl thinking maybe this is the way it's done, this is how everyone learns to walk. Her four-year-old mind giving a logic to it—the legs are spongy until you get to five or six, and then they stiffen and you get to walk like everyone else.

"The other man did the same," Pastor Sammy says, "and the two men rubbed their wrists together until the blood mingled. To look at them, you might have thought they were good friends, just shaking hands the way they stood there with their backs straight, holding each other's hand."

I see the girl in the pink dress, older, sixteen maybe, standing between her mother and her father like in a quickie backyard pic. She's done something to make them proud. She doesn't move, just stands there. That's the way I see her in my mind: just standing there, not really drawing attention to herself, nothing to say there's anything wrong with the legs. No way to tell from this shot if the legs work, because she's not in motion.

Sammy says, "Then father let the blood drip into a glass of wine sitting on the table. Table wine, something my mother always kept in the house. Then both men sipped from the glass. Where I come from, this is the strongest bond there is between men."

I look over at Pilar, seated now, but she's not giving me any help. No subtle clues how to respond to this one.

"Where I come from," I say, "that's a good way to get AIDS."

Number Two, I think it is, giggles.

Pastor Sammy is dead serious. It's an act, but he pulls it off like a trouper.

"If you'll permit, I'd like us, you and I, to enter into a pact."

"You don't even know me."

"I know all I need to know. I've seen your work. It's charming, really, in a primitive way. You're good at what you do. And with the help of the Holy Spirit you can be better."

I ask, "Did the Holy Spirit tell you to enter into this pact?"

"In a way, yes. And I always obey Him."

Pastor Sammy, so sure of himself it's nauseating, gets up and comes around to my side of the world. Pulls a chair close to mine and sits. Puts his hand on my arm, and for a flash I think we might be making a pact, the man ready to slit my wrist whether I like it or not.

"Miss Tate, I can tell you don't like me. Father and the man upstairs, they didn't like each other either. You see me as...well, I'm not sure how you see me, but it's not good. Television has helped bring my ministry to millions. And now television is ruining me. You've probably seen some of the shows, so called 'investigative journalism' has taken me down a peg or two. And maybe it should have. I'm human; I've said lots of things on air, spur of the moment that were stupid. Done things I wish I hadn't. But these shows, the producers, they've gone too far." Anger in his voice now. "They've come into my office, sat in the chair you sit in now and criticized my ministry, the construction of this Center, my home, my car of all things. So what I drive a BMW, you think I should drive a Honda?"

I hear papers rustling behind me, Number Six on the couch rifling through a magazine, asserting himself without asserting himself. Signaling Sammy to keep a lid on it. Sammy gets the idea, looks into my eyes, calming himself, a trick he learned in TV land: gaze into the camera and think happy thoughts. Raising a hand now, motioning the guy to knock off all the paper shuffling.

Pastor Sammy moves closer, says he's not concerned for himself, but these kinds of attacks are unfair to the body of Christ, portraying members of this ministry as a group of nut-cakes, morons who come to his crusades for the same thrill you get from a nightclub hypnotist. Telling me, with venom it, that the people who come to his crusades are intelligent, geniuses practically, for seeking him out.

"These are not fools," he says, gesturing around the room--I suppose at the pictures on the walls, though he could mean the yobs in jogging suits. His tone softens. It's almost pleading and boyish. "All evangelists go through this," he says, "like Christ Himself. I know that, but it still hurts."

Next I expect him to tell me nobody understands him. My first year at UT, I had a ChemE major tell me the same thing. Then he slipped his hand under my bra and was suddenly a lot less concerned about being understood. Maybe I should offer Pastor Sammy a feel.

More paper shuffling from the Mavs fan. This time Sammy raises a finger and the noise stops.

"So now I preach and, God willing, I heal people who have no other place to go, no other hope. I tell them to see a doctor. We have a doctor on staff, here to help when she can. Listen to your doctor, I say to them, but they don't listen. They don't want to listen, they want to be whole again, free of pain. I've spent a lifetime as a faith healer, and I know these people. You've just begun. You don't know a thing."

"You see me as the competition, is that it?" I ask.

"No, of course not. But we have things in common. Ways we can help each other."

"You and I have nothing in common."

"Billie Hannah. We were both friends of Billie's." Sammy saying it like there is more to it.

Billie was my friend. The kind of friend you don't like, but keep finding excuses to be around. The kind you make fun of right to her face, because she can take it and send it right back at you with a kinder, gentler spin on it. The kind you tease for being a dumbass because she's one of the smartest people you know. A friend you look to as a mirror— when she shows a little gumption, does something courageous or just plain decent, you feel better about yourself.

All that, sure, but Billie and Sammy and me in the same club? I don't buy it.

Sammy hops up and goes to the window. "It's raining, and I want you to stop what you're doing. Stop with the healing art. Do you understand what I'm telling you? Stop the graffiti sculptures."

"And why would I do that?"

His back to me now, looking out the window, hands behind his back like something he'd seen in a movie. Telling me that his program, *The Healing Hour*, is seen in over 200 countries. And China, he's reaching out to the 100 million Christians in China. Think about the $240 million a year in donations his ministry takes in. "Two-thirty eight," Pilar says. Sammy's going on again about an 18 percent increase in domestic revenues this year. Who knows the jump in international? Millions, probably, lots of millions, big numbers. Sammy turning from the window to deliver his message. Do I understand what's at stake here? Can I even imagine how much good this money does?

Men, in my experience, are the master counters of the human race. They count anything—the distance from here to anywhere you can think of, horsepower, home runs, dick size, Christians in China. Oh, and money. They love to count money most of all—net income, net wealth, net anything, dollar cost averaging, ROI, churn rate. And when they're done counting theirs, they start counting yours.

All this begins a conversation that meanders through my lackluster college years, my yet-to-begin career, my miniscule bank balance, my broken truck, and my somewhat shabby wardrobe. Pastor Sammy wants to know how many pairs of shoes I own, thinking, I suppose, that this is the most truthful, if imprecise, measure of exactly which rung of the achievement ladder a woman like me is now standing on. One, I tell him; the pair I have on.

What he's doing is putting me in my place: big numbers for Pastor Sammy, little numbers for Miranda. Three popcorn buckets full of cash for him, no popcorn for me. Once I'm in my place, I suspect that he'll offer me something to get me to stop the graffiti art. And in his mind, that something means a number.

Only I don't want a number. I want to find out what happened to my friend. And I think Pastor Sammy knows.

I say, "Your father and this man upstairs. What was the pact? What exactly did they agree to?"

Sammy says, "It doesn't matter."

I tell Pastor Sammy in my most let's-get-down-to-business tone that it's time to talk about Billie Hannah, how she got hold of the bronze, and why he asked Richard Hannah to give it back to me. Sammy ignores me, showing me that he can, going on about God's people dying to see his whimsical landscapes, his connoisseur's vision of the Garden of Eden—which I apparently missed—his topiary display, his sculptural retrospective of famous evangelists, when I say, "What about the bathrooms?"

He says, "What?"

I say, "The women's bathrooms. Are they as spiritual as the rest of the place? You know, faucets shaped like cute little cherubs peeing in your hands, woven straw hiney cushions on the toilets, that sort of thing."

That gets him to shut up. His eyes wild, Sammy looks to the Mavs fan on the couch, then stares at me for six long seconds. He knows *nothing* of the women's bathrooms, he shouts at me, nada, zero, zilch, the guilty shit, thinking he's been found out for some past indiscretion in the lady's room, but not sure.

"The bathrooms are fine," he finally chokes out.

"Fine, huh? Can I see one?"

He ignores me, tells me I might be interested-- when I interrupt again, telling him I'm interested in seeing a bathroom. Or in talking about Billie Hannah, he can take his pick.

I stand, glance at the door of the office, at the man on the couch, wondering what's up between these two, the guy not bothering to look at me.

Sammy speaks quickly.

"Two minutes, please. Can it wait, Miss Tate? Two minutes, that's all I ask. My mission here is to bring the gospel to as many people as possible. To be touched, not by me, but by God. He wants to reach out, to give people what they want. And what they want—" Here he pauses just waiting for an interruption that never comes. "Is you. What they want is you."

The guy says it with such charisma that I almost believe him.

I say, "Is that so?"

Pilar escorts me to and from the executive crappers, a big let-down, in my opinion—cold, hard seats, lighting that makes you look pale, mirrors that make you look fat.

Sammy, back in his office, now looking every bit the performer, wants to show me something, he says, just the two of us, which gets a rise out of everyone in the room. Pilar looks hurt, starts pouting, Numbers One through Five shuffle around mumbling but basically stay quiet, and the Mavs fan coughs, says he thinks not, his voice three times bigger than he is. The accent's back east somewhere, and he says it like it's up to him. Pastor Sammy waves him off, grabs my wrist—again—and shuttles me through a side door that leads into a small office. Furtively, he looks over his shoulder and quickly shuts the door. Then he tugs me to another door that leads outside.

The rain has stopped, though the sky is still dishrag gray. It's not cold, but I'm already thinking ahead, hoping we get back inside before my nipples make an appearance.

We circle around a leafless thicket of red oak and pin oak planted close to the walkway. The path is wet, curvy, and tunnel-like, snaking underneath dense, mature evergreens—

tall white pine, Christmassy Scotch pine—and some live oak with canopies that make me think of giant raisin muffins, which means I must be hungry and I am.

When we stop, we're standing under Pastor Sammy's office windows, with Numbers One through Five and the Mavs fan, noses to the glass, ogling us. I hadn't noticed before, but the view--the one Sammy's boys are now taking in--is beautiful. The green-space is carved out of an old pecan grove and landscaped to look natural, almost scruffy, and even in winter the vision is gripping: a private paradise for Pastor Sammy's eyes only.

Squinting, Sammy looks more devious than usual. He says, "I know a lot about you. I know, for instance, that you were in Africa. That your work has an African influence."

I've been, yes. Influenced, no. My work is void of anything African, unless you consider Alberto Giacometti's bushy haircut an Africa influence. Giacometti's Swiss, which is as un-African as you get, a great painter, an even better sculptor, and the person I most want to come back as when I die. The thing is, nobody ever says, 'Gee-whiz Miranda, that looks an awful lot like a Giacometti.'

This because Dallasites are more interested in the latest 'stang chili than obscure sculptural influences, and rightly so. And second, I'm not good enough to be recognized as a copycat. Every time I honestly try a blatant Giacometti knock-off—like the one of his brother, Diego, which I've copied oodles of times—it turns out a skinny Sandra Day O'Connor. Or it looks like somebody's grandmother, or mother, or the babysitter, for chrissakes, and I'm pegged as a reluctant savant. What's that? Reluctant is unwilling; a savant knows a lot. Unwilling to know much?

I swivel around and catch the sneak looking at me. "Tell me about Africa," he says.

I say, "Thirty percent inflation, poverty, diseases we used to have here a hundred years ago and got rid of with a ten-cent pill."

"Blessed are the pure in heart: for they shall see God."

"I don't know about pure, but the people I loved. Want to hear a story?"

Sammy says, "Please."

So that's what I do. I tell him about this little girl and her family, lived in a village about three hours south of Harare. One of those villages that should be a commercial for famine relief. I'm there, visiting I guess you'd call it, and late one night I have to pee. I go out to the outhouse, this small concrete box with a hole in the floor, and there she is. The girl, the littlest, five or younger, curled up in a corner with her baby goat in her lap. This goat looking right at me, not making a sound."

"A goat, huh," Sammy says. "If his offering is a goat, then he shall offer it before the Lord."

I wait a beat, let this gem sink in, and go on telling him. Inside the outhouse I can't see a thing, and at first I can't see the girl, so I light a match and all I see is the goat's head and some dark skin, no arms, no human head, nothing to make me think it's a little girl and not some goat-headed African monster. At the sight of the goat I freak, bang my head on the low ceiling and nearly wet myself, when the girl finally speaks. I can't remember what she says, or said, but my heart starts beating again. She tells me something is chasing her. Not some one, but some thing. Her and her little goat friend, which is why she's hiding in the shithouse. She's crying, she's shaking she's so scared, squeezing the goat so tight I think it might pop. I tell her it's just a bad dream. I know all about bad dreams and they don't hurt, not in any way that counts. Don't worry about it, I tell her. Besides, I'm here to protect her.

"These people, were they Christians?" he asks.

"Sort of."

"The Lord says, for them that honor me I will honor, and them that despise me shall be lightly esteemed."

For chrissakes, it's like Trivial Pursuit for evangelists. I say "multitudes"; he says, "went up the mountain."

Pastor Sammy leads me away from the windows and the brain-squad, now chortling away, a private joke, no doubt, and I can guarantee it has a priest, a little boy, or boobs in the punchline. We stop at an area where the ground is torn up. I hadn't noticed before, lurking behind the Scotch pines, but now I see more nubbly concrete pads.

"Go on," he says.

This is five years ago, I tell him. I'm twenty-four, a college grad—UT, mind you, where most grads leave with enough confidence for nine lifetimes. I'm healthy, strong-- invincible in other words. Hell I'm from Texas, where any *thing* chases you you don't want, you just shoot it. I actually believe what I'm telling this little girl I hardly know, and the best advice I can come up with is, "don't worry about it." She believes me, or says she does, and we fumble in the dark back to the sleeping huts. We snuggle up together on the floor, and the next morning she's gone. At this point, I consider her-- Sekai her name is; it means laughter--I consider Sekai my friend. And I promised to protect her, which I didn't do.

"So what happened?" he asks.

"It takes me a day and a night to find her. She's stuffed in the crease where a rotting tree is lying on the ground. And she's missing one of her feet. Some heartless bastard has chopped off her foot, plans to sell it to a bush doctor."

I pause here, just thinking about it.

Sammy says, "And you wanted justice. I can see it in your face."

"I do, or I did."

"You must learn to trust in God's grace and mercy."

"Sammy, I don't mean to be rude, but will you please stop doing that? I found the man. I talked to him."

"You were alone, the way you tell it, and you talked to this African who had just severed a little girl's foot."

"He wasn't African, he was an old white guy, tall, balding on top, kind of reminds me of you. And he didn't chop off her foot, he had his boys do it."

"And you talked to him, that's it?"

I say, "That, and I cut off one of his feet."

"Interesting story. Is it true?"

I look directly at him, say, "It doesn't matter."

It starts to drizzle. We don't move, just stand there staring at the concrete pads. Sammy asks if I know what they're for. I do. It just came to me. I'm slow sometimes. I tell him they're footings, designed to hold up something big, several big somethings, by the look of it. Not big, he says, but heavy. Tall and heavy. Tall, skinny, heavy somethings.

"Care to guess?" he says.

"Sculptures. Bronze is heavy, probably bronze."

"And the artist?"

I say, "Enlighten me."

Pastor Sammy raises a hand and snaps his fingers several times. The boys in the window jump and seconds later Number Three, the one with the goatee, comes jogging out the door, looping around the wet walkway toward us. He's got a sculpture in his hand, tall and skinny, not bronze, hoisting it over his shoulder like a spear.

Sammy says, "Recognize it?"

"I do."

It's one of mine. It's wood, light as a feather and way too short and slender for outdoor artwork. I'm fond of dark, earthy colors, but I'm too cheap to actually buy dark wood, so I smear my work with good old-fashioned Kiwi shoe polish. Brown sometimes, black mostly. And while shoe polish is cheap and exudes a certain starving-artist charm, as a protective finish outdoors, it's next to useless. What the rain doesn't wash away, the sun will melt into an ugly puddle at her feet.

"Put it there," Sammy says to Number Three.

One of the footings has a six-inch metal dowel sticking up out of the center of the pad. Number Three sets the sculpture on top of the dowel. Someone, not me, has apparently drilled a hole in the poor girl's feet and she slips neatly over the dowel. Without it, she'd likely fall on her face in the monkey grass.

Sammy says the pact he mentioned earlier, this is it: this private area, the glorious Garden of Sammy, he calls it, the footings, the sculpture garden--it's all for me. He'll buy them as quickly as I can make them, and that fast I go from artist to assembly-line worker. I have visions of myself back at the old Ford plant cranking out Giacometti knock-offs for twenty-five K a pop. This is the reward for all my hard work, Sammy says. Twenty-five thousand each.

"Imagine," he says, and it works because I do imagine it. I picture fixing my truck. I picture buying this new chisel I've had my eye on for some time, and that's when my imagination runs dry. Eight footings, he says, now pointing and counting, very slowly, all part of the pitch, part of the show, like we're back in kindergarten, six, seven, and eight. That makes two hundred thousand dollars. All for me, he says.

"Why me?"

"I asked the Lord for guidance in choosing an artist, and the answer was you."

"God asked for me by name?"

"He has called us to do great work together. I asked Mr. Hannah to return the bronze to you because I hoped it would bring us together. The Lord has guided you here today, Miss Tate, to this Center, to this path, to this garden. Be careful with the power He has given you. Don't play games. And don't misuse it."

I say, "Eight sculptures for two hundred thousand. That's the deal?"

"And you agree to stop the graffiti art."

"Oh, I see. Is that part of His plan, as well?"

"Think about it," he says.

"I have. I'm not interested."

Sammy pauses, tilts his head, thinking before he speaks.

"How about this, you do just one, and I'll tell you all I know about Billie."

I ask, "Who is my model?"

Sammy shrugs.

"Well?" I say.

"Does it matter?"

"It matters."

"Then do one of me."

Big surprise, "do one of me," saying it like it just came to him, though it sounds like something he and the Mavs fan cooked up while I was taking a tinkle.

"I've got a better idea," I say, "I saw a little girl in the lobby. Something wrong with her legs. I'll do one of her."

"You think you can heal the little girl?"

"No. I'll do a sculpture of the girl. It might brighten her day."

Pastor Sammy thinks about it. "I want one of me."

"Fine, but let's do the girl first."

"Me first, then the girl."

"The girl."

"Me."

Me first. The simplicity of the two words gets to me. It's what we all want, really: me first, God; make me pretty, make me smart, make me healthy. Then you can do the rest of the block, but me first.

I say, "Let me think about it."

P astor Sammy and the brain-squad are huddling outside in the glorious Garden of Sammy in the rain, ya-hooing about secret pacts and God's wants. I wasn't invited. Sammy asked me to wait inside, so here I am sitting in his office in one of those big chairs, tempted as hell to put my feet up on the desk. Nudge the bronze to one side; maybe accidentally kick one of the popcorn buckets. Punt it right off the desk and onto the floor, see what all that green looks like spread out on the fussy Oriental.

A door opens, and here comes Number Six in his snappy Mavs jersey, a heavy gold chain I hadn't noticed before around his neck, and one of those gaudy, '80s gold-nugget pinky rings. The kind of ring that does not inspire wide trust.

He doesn't take a chair, but weasels up between me and the popcorn buckets and puts his bony thigh on the corner of the desk. Then he throws that bottomless voice at me. "The name's Roe. I know who you are, so now we've been introduced. The way this works, I put you in a taxi—"

"I don't have enough cash for a taxi."

Roe reaches behind him inside one of the popcorn buckets, grabs a big wad of cash in one hand and pulls me to my feet with the other. He stuffs the wad into my jeans pocket, deep, and it won't all fit without more cramming. I jerk away, but his grip on my arm is strong, so I look off, feigning absolute cool. Besides, I could use the money, but this feels too back-alley even for me. It's some kind of joke or straight-up, harebrained intimidation, and I'm not playing along. He wants me to say, "Oh, my, I really couldn't…" So I don't.

Roe stops, thinks about it and takes another handful out of the bucket next to it, this one all hundreds, looks like, and stuffs this wad into my other pocket. The pinky ring gets caught a couple of times and tugs my pants into the slinky low-rise look. He picks up a hundred from the floor and stuffs it in the pocket as well. When he's done, he steps back and looks at my crotch, at my plump pockets.

"Think that'll cover the fare, Sugar?" he says.

Out in the hallway, we move quickly, just the two of us, aiming for the lobby. The place is busy: sightseers and Pastor Sammy groupies gawking at the lushness of the place, hoping to soak up a stray miracle. We pass an old man and woman, holding hands, hobbling in our direction. The old guy's hunched, his head bent forward, the eyes aiming only a short distance in front of him. Call me paranoid, but when he gets close, I imagine him staring at my hidden booty. I've got the bronze in one hand, and I swing it out in front of me trying to deflect his attention.

Roe hustles us along, in a hurry.

"Just Roe?" I ask.

"John Roe, but everyone calls me Roe. It used to be longer."

"What, one of those names nobody ever gets right?"

"Roebling. I changed it because, being from Brooklyn, people kept asking if it was my family built the Brooklyn Bridge. John Roebling designed the bridge, no relation, but sure, I'd tell them, that's us, and I'd go into the story. Now it's just Roe, and I don't have to get into to all that."

The guy is sure of himself. It's in his tone of voice, mild, sociable, giving me the feeling he's in charge and knows it.

"The story?" I ask.

"The bridge, what happened to Roebling."

"Tell me, I'm interested."

"Maybe some other time."

"What do you do around here?" I ask.

"This is it; you see me doing it."

I ask what he did before and he tells me three years with PTL, as in "Praise the Lord," as in the TV show. I ask why he left, and he says because the boss got into a jam that even he, meaning Roe, couldn't un-jam.

"The man was a thief," he says, "but one you could trust."

I let loose a self-righteous snort.

Roe stops, looks me up and down. "Sugar, is that sanctimony I hear? Because if it was, I might ask if Pastor Sammy is aware your pockets are full of his money? Big pockets, I might add."

I say, "You're the one put it there."

"How it got there isn't my question. Does Pastor Sammy know? Because if he doesn't, that's stealing, making you a thief. See that little camera up in the corner? Now let's move it along. I don't have all day."

We reach the lobby and are nearing the front doors.

"Look," he says, "I go into all that, my name, a little history, because now we've talked. We can be civil to each other. We know we can, because we just did. Now I want you to leave the Center and not come back. Take what you've got in your pockets with you. It's yours, I mean it. If I see you anywhere near this place, you won't like it. I mean that, too."

This is Roe with a different tone, sounding like a tough guy and no patience, and it rubs me the wrong way. Shit, thirty seconds ago all I wanted was to leave and never come back. Now, I don't know. I look away; see another camera high on the wall. Roe notices my gaze and slides over, puts his ugly mug between me and the camera.

"Are we clear?" he asks.

"Can I ask why?"

He moves close, so close that I feel his breath on me, each mouthful of air dense and stringy, a fishy breeze to it. He has a long, slender neck pitted with acne, which might explain the clunky gold chain: hoping people stare at the gold and not his rutted skin. We're unnaturally close now, and several gawkers watch, see what's going on. His eyes move from me to the bronze in my hand. He says, "I see you as stubborn *and* dumb, so let me put this to you in a way you can understand. You come back here, and this guy won't like it."

I lift the bronze, turn the face to me.

"This guy?" I ask.

"What, you think I don't know? I'll bet you put me in the same category as the five stooges, back there. Stay away and we won't have any trouble we'll have to work our way out of later."

I turn the face of the bronze to Roe.

"This guy. You know him?"

"I know who he is, who he is to you. Where he lives, where he works, his phone number, I need to get a hold of him."

I say, "I don't believe you."

Roe giving me that "you-really-are-too-dumb-to-be-believed" stare. Then he gives me a name—Handy Cavander. My husband. The man I sent packing, he says, which isn't true, Handy being a man keen enough to do his own packing, if that's what's called for. Yeah, Roe knows who he is, now poking the bronze in the chest with his finger. Switching to his sociable tone, he tells me that if I come back asking more questions, then Handy Cavander will pay for my sins. Always saying both names like it's not him unless you put them together, and me wishing that I had my baby ax in my hand. I don't know what I'd do, if I'd actually swing the thing or just wave it around, get the conversation moving in a new direction, but I'd feel more comfortable if it was near.

Roe slides back a step. "It's best you get going now, Sugar." He turns, and ambles away.

My eyes are still focused forward, gazing up at the tiny black camera lens.

I met Handy Cavander almost five years ago. I'm twenty-four, traveling Europe and later Africa by myself, and I meet this guy who listens more than he talks—and when he does open his yap says something kind or funny or oddly insightful. It's a rare quality, listening more than talking, even rarer in travelers, kids in their twenties with stories bottled up in their heads, some pouring out of their ears, most of them whoppers. Handy told some whoppers, but mostly he'd listen and follow me around the countryside like a stray puppy. In fact, when I'd finally tired of wandering the sub-Sahara, he followed me home.

We married a year later.

The bronze was a wedding present—me to him. He wasn't sick, nothing like that. It was just a sculpture for the man I loved.

Handy never believed the rumors about sculptures that heal, anyway, which was fine by me. He was a non-believer when Dr. Smith said the lump in my breast was nothing, besides I'm too young. He held firm when Dr. Bloom said it was "most likely a cyst, it'll probably go away if we leave it alone," now talking to me, "and quit mashing on it." Handy flat-out wouldn't budge when Dr. Lee, acupuncturist and Tai Chi master, said my previous doctors were a covey of quacks, that it's as clear as Chinese crystal that I'm bloated. Nothing but water retention, according to Lee.

Then when Dr. Novak diagnosed early stage breast cancer, Handy did an about-face. It didn't bother me that Handy now believed. It didn't bother him that I did not.

What killed our marriage was that I refused to do a sculpture for myself. That, in Handy's mind, I refused to get better, that I was committing suicide by omission. Weeks went by and I resisted. Then, in secret, and in a moment of pain or weakness or pity, I suppose, I whittled a little something out of a scrap of alder. The lump in my breast didn't go away; in fact it felt larger each time I kneaded the area, making little circles with the pads of my fingers—following the nurse's instructions—probing until I found the lump again. I did more sculptures, tried again and again, but the lump and the swelling and the pain didn't go away.

I didn't tell Handy any of this because I couldn't. Weary of doctors and misdiagnoses and god-awful treatment plans, he'd come to believe it was our only hope, my only hope. Telling him the sculptures didn't work was squelching his hope, and that I couldn't do. So I lied, told him I refused to do a sculpture for myself and if he didn't like it then go pester someone else.

He did and took a job in Boston working for an insurance company. That was four months ago. We still talk, but it's been weeks since I've heard a peep.

I stare at the bronze in my hand, at the green slate floor and muddy-gray grout. Funny how your mind will focus on the irrelevant when something important is going down. But the gray grout makes me think of Handy. Almost everything I see makes me think of Handy. I need to give him a call, and now seems a better time than most.

I swivel around looking for a pay phone and spot a security guard in formal blues spying me, speaking softly into a walkie-talkie. His eyes peek down a corridor, in a direction I can't see, talking to other men in blue, no doubt, planning a sneak attack. I should have seen this coming: Roe filling me up with green, thousands maybe, pilfered from the collection buckets, and then parading me, posing me really, in front of the cameras.

The guard takes several tentative steps toward me. Another guard rounds the far corner of the lobby. He looks to the first guard and then to me. A third guard steps out of a door behind the receptionist. There's no question they'll catch me.

The question is how to get rid of the money before they do.

I see myself playing out the next ten minutes, watching it happen scene by scene: a dozen people spread out in the lobby in small groups, some eyeballing Pastor Sammy on the widescreen, kids craning their necks to get a view of the ceiling; watching the three guards in cookie-cutter uniformity whispering into their walkie-talkies; watching Ms. Happy at the ticket counter, her head now swiveling side to side, from one guard to another to me, then doing it all over again; feeling an impulse to run, or at least create some chaos, reach into my pockets and fling handfuls of cash into the air, realizing, *shit, coming here was a bad idea,* one more bad idea in a string of sorry ideas that started about the time—if you listen to Roe—that I sent Handy packing.

I march over to the ticket counter and plop the bronze on the speckled granite. I say, "Here, watch this for me, will ya?"

Ms. Happy says, "I will not."

Guard number three, with a thick chest and a buzz cut, moves out from behind the counter. Before he can open his gob, I tell him I want to talk.

Guard number one, a pipsqueak, arrives beside me, says, "Hold your position, ma'am."

"Who's in charge here?" I point to Buzz Cut. "You or him?"

Buzz Cut says, "You can talk to me."

"You first," I say.

"Me first, what?"

"Why are you following me?"

Pipsqueak says, "Pat her down."

"Down boy," I say.

Pipsqueak snarls at me. "Most women thank me afterwards."

"Let me do you, first," I say. I lunge at him quick, my hand moving for his crotch. Pipsqueak stumbles backward, trips over his own feet, and nearly does a face-flop on the marble floor, lands on a knee and then catches himself. The other guard snickers. Pipsqueak rights himself, face red, and walks up to me, says, "Don't make this harder than it needs to be."

Ms. Happy says, "What's going on here?"

Pipsqueak to me says, "Resist and you won't like it." Sounding like something I heard not five minutes ago. Roe saying to me, "If I see you anywhere near this place, you won't like it."

"How'd you like to bite my ass?" I say.

"I'm on duty or I—"

I talk over him, say, "I've been dying to ask, is it true one in three men in uniform are impotent?" I swivel my head from Buzz Cut to the other one to Pipsqueak. "Of the three of you, I was to guess, I'd say it was you."

Pipsqueak's stubby arms, stuffed like bratwurst into his short blue shirtsleeves, make me suspect that he's spectacular at breaking collarbones and deadly chokeholds. The little asshole standing there in his blues, he'd like to clamp a chokehold on me now. If not for Buzz Cut, he probably would.

Buzz Cut gives me an embarrassed smile, like this is all fun and games, and motions me to the office behind the ticket counter. He says, "Please step this way, Miss. I'd just like a moment of your time. To talk."

"Talk? This guy wants a strip search."

Ms. Happy is on the phone now, droning away in a low voice.

"I'm on your side," he says, hesitates, and then motions me not to the office, but out into the middle of the giant lobby, where we can talk in private. Reaches up to the walkie-talkie clipped to his shoulder and turns it off. "Let's start over. I'm Officer Sean Harris. I'm sorry about my partner over there."

I glance back at Pipsqueak, and I'm this close to sticking out my tongue.

He says, "That move you made, getting him to back up, unpredictable. Nice."

Over his shoulder, I see a sign that reads, "Gift Shop."

"Sean, I don't feel well." It stops him, me using his name so easily. "I need something to eat, a candy bar, anything. What say you and I walk down the gift shop, then I'm all yours."

Officer Sean Harris says, "Mind if I ask one question first? You promise not to get mad?"

"Since you asked nice."

"What's in your pockets?"

I like this guy, Mr. No-Nonsense. Looks you right in the eye and says what he wants to say.

I say, "It's a surprise."

The Global Healing Center's gift shop is the mother lode of spiritual healing accessories. Teaching cassettes, books, audiobooks, music, candy, cookies, cookware, makeup, toys and movies and clothes, every piece of it showing off Sammy's logo—an overweight bird with a halo—and all of it more or less promising to heal what ails ya.

There's an entire wall of collectables with a line of Sammy figurines—the Temptation of Sammy, the Song of Sammy, the Sacrifice of Abraham, though even Abraham resembles a young Sammy. There's a birthday aisle, a business aisle with leather briefcases, an aisle of nothing but luggage, where I spot a three-piece Sermon on the Mount set for kids.

It's dizzying, not to mention the place reeks of moolah.

Shoppers are prey to ravenous forces aimed at coaxing just a few more bucks from the family unit. The place is jammed with Pastor Sammy devotees. It's impossible not to bump hips with mothers and fathers and kids and slow-moving grannies, or to get your toes nipped by crabby people in wheelchairs. I move quickly between racks of Easter dresses with irresistible springtime blooms and ultra-comfy stretchy jackets, all the while Officer Sean Harris is sticking to me like spandex.

A half dozen surveillance cameras blanket the room.

I stumble onto a U-shaped wall of athletic shoes, Nike and Reebok look-alikes, mostly, all with the same flabby bird logo glued to the outside of the shoe. The frenzy is contagious and I get down on my knees and pull a box from the stack, open it and yank out the extra tissue paper. I pull more boxes, upend more shoes, more tissue piling up around me, creating a mess.

Officer Sean Harris is impatient but doesn't rush me.

"Sean, see if she has a ten. In this," I hold up a running shoe with blue mesh.

He looks at me, at the pile in my lap, not sure how to take me. He says, "You could get me in trouble, you do something stupid."

"I'm trying on shoes, Sean."

He says, "Now, but I let you out of my sight, who knows what you'll do."

"I promise not to run away. That make you feel any better? You remember the size?"

"Ten. In that one," he says, giving my size eight feet a good stare. "Do you mind me asking why you came? Here, to the Center. You don't seem the type."

I ask, "What type is that?"

"Desperate."

I draw a breath, the guy getting serious on me. I say, "I'm desperate for a ten, and a candy bar, nothing with chocolate."

"Fine, you don't want to answer, I have another. What are we doing here, because I'm not as dumb as I look."

"Sean, I look at you, I don't see dumb. I see a man who wants to help. A Samaritan is what you are. It's inside of you and you know it. All right, you want me to say it, I will. I need your help."

Officer Harris says, "But you're not sure you want to tell me about it."

"Ever feel the gods frowning down on you? That's how I feel right now. I'm a good person, Sean. I am. You go ask that lady for a ten and I owe you."

"It sounds to me," he says, his voice low now, "like you're asking me to turn my back."

Here he is again, a man with nothing phony about him, can't even pretend phony. "I'm asking for help," I say.

"And you want me to believe you."

"People believe what they want."

He says, "I'm not people. I do believe you, if you're telling me straight."

"Are you gonna help or not?"

When he's gone, I pile even more shoes and tissue onto my lap and then reach under the mess and shove all the green from my pockets into the toes of a pair of ten and a halfs. At the last second, I keep two hundreds and a fifty to pay for the shoes. I'm good with numbers and I guess that each of my pockets holds fifty bills, minimum. The left, the one with all hundreds, makes five thousand. The right, fifties and one or two twenties, comes to twenty-five hundred, at least. That's seventy-five hundred dollars, easy, tucked inside my spanky new Sammys.

Officer Harris returns. "No luck," he says, looming over me.

I hold up the shoes. "What do you think?"

Yeah, he tells me, the blue'll look good on me. The flirt.

On the way to check out, I grab a blue ball cap with the chubby bird logo embroidered in gold, and a tee shirt, a black job with the words EXERCISE YOUR DEMONS in big block FBI yellow on the back, which I think is adorable. I throw the pile on the counter. The checkout girl starts ringing me up and puts everything in a large, logoed Sammy satchel. The rack behind her is bright with batteries, film, and toenail clippers, the one next to it filled with Cajun peanuts, wasabi peas, soybeans, sunflower seeds, flax seed and good old-fashioned trail mix with coconut and raisins.

I ask for a package of sunflower seeds, a flax seed, a trail mix and one of those eye-tearing wasabi peas. The extra hot, if she has them. I lay two hundreds on the counter and lift the satchel, holding it against me, covering my now empty pockets. The checkout line is crowded, and Sean watches me as I squeeze up to him so close he can't see my waist, though he could kiss me if he was in the mood. What he can see is the snacks disappearing from the counter, as I casually shove them in my pockets.

Officer Sean Harris, all business now, stands politely behind me in the lobby, directly in front of the ticket counter. Pipsqueak and the other one are off to the side. When the phone rings, Ms. Happy jumps, tells the caller, "Standing right in front of me...I'm positive."

I hand her the box.

"Here," I say. "For you."

"What's this all about?'

"This job can be tough on your feet. You said so yourself. Open it."

She does, isn't impressed, and tells me they're too big. I say try them on, please, and give her a look like we're on the same team and these lugs in uniform are big time rivals. Tentatively, she lifts a shoestring, like it might be wired, and a shoe slowly makes its way out of the box.

"What's the joke?" she asks.

This is a woman not used to getting presents. I say, "It's a gift."

She squeezes the sides of the shoe, the heel, the toe. "There's something in the—"

"Just put it on. See how it fits."

She looks inside the shoe, into the toe, hesitates, then dips down behind the counter and slips the shoe on. She stands, her face flushed.

"I don't know what to say," she says.

I hand her the other shoe, and she slides it on. I say, "How do they feel?"

She bounces a few times on the balls of her feet. "Expensive."

I say, "You're worth every penny."

Officer Sean Harris has maneuvered behind the counter and is now standing in the doorway of his office, waiting for me. He says, "If you're ready, let's do this."

Pipsqueak and the other one are moving inside, anxious to get on with the show. Pipsqueak leans in and says something to his buddy and they both laugh. I step into the office and right away he barks at me to empty my pockets.

Before I do, Pilar storms through another door and glares at Sean and me. She says, "Where have you been?" and I'm not sure if she means me or him.

I say, "Officer Harris was kind enough—"

"Harris," she says, "what exactly is happening here and why wasn't I notified that we had a disturbance, if that's what this is?"

Officer Harris says, "I assumed that you were."

"Meaning?"

"The call came from your office," he says, and to me, says, "Go on, let's see what's in the pockets."

From my right, I pull out the sunflower seeds and the wasabi peas. From my left, I come up with the flax seed and a fat bag of trail mix. I toss the whole shebang on the desk. Pipsqueak grimaces like he's just been groined. To be mean, I raise my arms and shake my hips at him, do a little hula dance just because I can. Give the pale-skinned little tyrant something to dream about at night.

"I'd still like to pat her down," Pipsqueak says.

Pilar, still trying to put it all together, is pissed off, ready to backhand someone, near enough to backhand Pipsqueak, which always seems like a good idea.

I offer him the package of wasabi peas, hoping he'll have a meltdown, but he's not hungry. The other one says no to the wasabi but wants to know what's with the flax seed. He's seen it around, but never tried it. Good for the cholesterol, I tell him and leave out the part about giving him the runs. I toss him the package.

Sean looks amused, like maybe he saw it coming, says, "I apologize for the inconvenience."

P ilar ushers me outside, where it's raining and the sky is a delightful purple-gray. She pulls an umbrella from her purse and commands me to stay while she gets the car. I give her an obedient look. Waiting, and still lugging around this goddamn bronze of Handy, I notice a half-dozen fat wooden columns holding up the portico. I go over to one of the columns in direct light and give it a closer look. I can't tell the wood, something hard with lots of knots and a couple of deep crevices big enough to slip a finger into. What I wouldn't give for a chisel and mallet about now.

In the seven years since I got out of college, I don't think I've gone a day without sculpting. Occasionally, if I'm out of wood, I'll leaf through a book of some sculptor I admire, but even then I get the pang, put down the book and go play with my chisels.

I stare through the glass doors, back into the lobby, and see the little girl with the legs sitting in a chair with Mom. Dad sits in another chair by himself. I swing open the door, scan for Pipsqueak, Roe, anyone who doesn't like me, and mosey across the lobby, veer by the ticket counter and ask Ms. Happy to keep an eye out for the bad guys, and finally pause in front of the little girl.

I look at Mom.

"I'm a sculptor," I say. I lift the bronze, as if to prove it. "I'd like to do a likeness of your little girl. Maybe something from about here up."

Mom gives me a big leer and rolls her eyes. She's one of those women comfortable with making snap judgments, like hanging up on telemarketers, slamming the door on well-groomed men selling vacuum cleaners guaranteed to swallow up dust mites and pollen grains. To me, she says "Not interested."

I tell her there's no charge. Dad seems okay with the idea, almost flattered, looks at his little girl in her pink skirt, at the bronze in my hand. He wants to know, what can it hurt? And Mom says the kid can't sit still for fifteen seconds. I've been standing here for fifteen seconds and the girl hasn't moved a muscle. She's staring up at me, giving me a fretful look, and I want to ask what's on her mind, but she's four and probably couldn't put words to it.

Dad says he's fully aware the kid's a wriggle-worm, but so what? He reaches over and pokes her, softly, at which moment the she lurches forward out of the chair and grabs hold of the bronze in my hand. She hangs there, Mom and Dad watching but seemingly unbothered, used to seeing the kid hang on things. Those unsteady legs of hers aren't much help, and the only thing keeping her upright is the bronze, gripping it like a lifeline.

I'm tempted to let go, but it's heavy as hell, and when she drops it, it could break someone's toe, maybe the whole foot. Dad looks over at the child who looks at him smiling, hoping to hear a "yes"—a "yes" in her mind equating to ownership, it's hers now, she can keep it—knowing intuitively that to look at Mom is asking for a "no."

The kid has her face pressed against the rough body of the bronze, rubbing her cheek up and down on the bumpy surface. I know just how she feels. Whenever I visit the Dallas Museum of Art and no one's looking, I routinely fondle the artwork. Hands mostly, but I once got cheek-to-cheek with a Nigerian ceremonial spirit mask. It felt good.

Mom says, "Emmy, it's Emily, but we call her Emmy, has to be held or she's off exploring."

I say, "Yeah, well, it's what kids do, I guess."

"You have children?" Her voice hopeful.

"I did," I lie for reasons that even I don't understand. "No, no kids, not really."

I expect her to pounce on the "not really," but she lets it slide. "Then you don't know beans about children. Especially kids like Emmy."

I take a quick look around, ready to be blindsided by Pipsqueak or Roe or assailants unknown.

Bending, I whisper into Emmy's ear. She lets go, falls backward against the cushion and then scooches up and into the wedge between Mom's hip and the side of the chair. Once she's settled, I set the bronze in her lap.

"Give that to me," Mom says, but Emmy's already got a never-let-go grip on Handy's legs.

"That's not necessary," I say. "It's a gift."

Mom says, "I don't want it."

"Good," I say, "because I didn't give it to you."

Mom stands. She's shorter than me but wide, reminds me of a momma bear. Dad stands, too. He's all teeth and smiley face, but it's an act. He's cranky, impatient; sitting around here waiting for a miracle might be a waste of Dad's time, for all I know, though I doubt it. To me, Dad seems the more hopeful of the two.

I swivel to face him, tell him I can work from a picture. He reaches into his wallet and pulls out a crumpled snapshot, takes a pen from his pocket and writes a phone number on the back, reaches out to hand me the photo.

"I said no," Mom says, grabbing the photo. "What's gotten into you?"

Dad glowers at her until she looks away. His decisions come slower then Mom's, but once made, they're final.

She gives me an antagonistic glare that might be ready to slide into sarcasm, asks where it is, where I do what I do?

I've flaunted the bronze, and she might logically get the idea that I cast metal, that I have a well-equipped shop somewhere with a kiln, molds, sandblasters, and welding equipment. I don't. And I don't have the heart to tell her I plan to immortalize Emmy in cheap wood on the side of some building in a seedy part of downtown.

I say, "I'll let Pastor Sammy know you're not interested." I turn and stride for the doors.

Mom calls for me to stop, but I don't. Hold on, please, she begs, but I keep up the pace until I feel her hand on my elbow. Amazing, the power of a slightly skewed message from the divine.

She presses the photo into my hand. She says, "Here. Take this, please."

Pilar pulls up to the curb in a red Nissan Maxima, old but squeaky clean. I jack the heater to the max, and lickety-split, we're on our way. Out on the highway, we're silent for long minutes as I sulk over my exchange with Emmy and Mom and Dad. I can't help feeling the brunt of a cosmic joke that goes like this: *I want to be left alone, and people come knocking on my door, pleading for a sculpture. I want to give them away, and nobody wants one.* Ha-ha funny. That is until I mention Sammy's name, and then they gobble them up whole, and that makes me angry in a way I can't get my arms around. I did it to myself, I was the one who mentioned Sammy, but that doesn't even begin to make me feel better.

Pilar says, "Did Pastor Sammy tell you?"

"Tell me what?"

"That he and Billie were having an affair, that she wanted to leave him and go back to what's-his-name, her husband? Sammy wouldn't have it, so she threatened to raise a stink. Get it in the papers. Lot's of publicity."

"Why are *you* telling me this?"

"I have a favor to ask."

"What'd Sammy do?" I ask.

"What he always does. Talked to his accountant, figured a way to pay for it that was in the ministry's best interest. He offered to buy her a home in Highland Park, not too far from her old house, if that's what she wanted. One million cash to buy the house."

"Did she take it?"

"I guess. Roe was sent to deliver the money the night she died."

"So where's the money?"

Pilar says, "Roe says the robbers must have it. It's why they killed her."

"And you believe that?"

I catch a whiff of pine-scented deodorizer. Pilar takes great care of her car, so it surprises me the mess the windshield wipers are making—a terrific blurry sweep across the glass. Rain is hammering the car and I can only hope that visibility is better on her side of the ship.

We sail south on Central Expressway to exit 284C, then a soft left on Good Latimer, bypass the heart of Deep Ellum, and another left at Commerce. I point to a quick right on Henry, a short, final block to Canton, and it's right after I tell her this is it, that's my building, that she asks if they work. My sculptures, she means. Do they heal?

I tell her the same thing I tell everyone. The long answer is, "How the hell do I know?" Sometimes when I'm not in the mood, like now, I shorten it and tell her "No."

"What does that mean?" she says.

"If you have something to say, just say it," I tell her. This is the favor. I give her credit for waiting all of twenty-five minutes before easing into it. But now we're there.

She says, "Why are you so rude, all of the sudden?"

"Because I know where this is leading."

This slows her, but she can't stop herself. "It's about my husband—"

"I've heard it all before. He's ill, it's not fair, you love him, you'll do anything. Save it. Anything you have to add only dilutes the message."

She says, "Why are you doing this?"

"I'm taking your advice. This morning you said to stop what I'm doing, so I'm stopping."

"I meant stop asking about Billie, not stop your work. This isn't like you."

"It's just like me," I say. "Ask anyone who knows me. I'm cold, self-absorbed, and mean."

"He's gotten to you, hasn't he? Pastor Sammy or Roe or one of the others, they got to you. You were so confident, so sure of yourself, I thought you might stand a chance, but whatever they said or did, it worked."

When I enter the loft, Otto is standing by the window, his back to me, looking out at the Dallas skyline. The most prominent building from this angle is the one with a seven-story hole in the middle near the top, the J.P. Morgan Chase Tower, what the yokels call the keyhole building. It's not the tallest, but it's lit up at night, making a glass tower with a hole in it look all the more impressive.

Otto says, "A guy down there. He followed you home."

I waltz over to the window and take in the view. It's dusk, just after five; the rain has stopped, but it's still gray. On the sidewalk opposite my building I see a toothpick-chewing stubby man with a dark coat, blue pants, and a ball cap with a logo on top. I can't make out the logo, but I know what it is: an overweight bird with a halo.

"Pipsqueak," I say. "He works for Pastor Sammy."

"You didn't see him behind you?"

"I didn't look."

Otto shakes his head, disappointed in me. "I made coffee."

"I'm not even going to ask why you're in my loft."

"How is it I always choose to visit and you're having a bad day?"

I stare down at Pipsqueak. I say, "Or Pilar told him where I live."

"Who's Pilar?" Otto asks.

I tell him and he says, "She'd do that?"

I t surprises me that Pastor Sammy or Roe or whoever's calling the shots wants to keep an eye on me. Surprises, but doesn't shock me. There's a pattern to Sammy's need to mimic God, to Roe's need to threaten and scare. There is likely a larger pattern that connects one to the other, and a thread that connects me to them. That I don't see the pattern doesn't mean it's not there. Of this, I have absolute faith.

As for Pipsqueak watching me, my guess is that someone wants to make sure I don't do any more graffiti, which makes me all the more determined to do just that. I hadn't made up my mind about Pilar—whether or not to do a sculpture of Hubby—but now I'm in the mood.

I wait until after midnight, slip on my all-black outfit, and gather my tools. I make sure my chisels are sharp. Inspect each one—the wide-swing gouge, the spoon gouge, the fishtail, a few others—and slip each into its slot in the cloth roll-up pouch. I grab the heavy wooden mallet--the big one, not the little one--my baby ax, whetstone, and flashlight, and place everything inside the black canvas bag. I throw in a rain poncho, just in case.

At the last moment, I grab the biggest gouge I own. Rusty, I call it. Something I designed myself—a twelve-inch long, fluted blade, two inches wide, with an extra long handle, leather wrapped tightly around the handle like a tennis racquet. The end, the butt, flares out like a mushroom, heavily padded and covered in leather. The whole thing's close to three feet long and won't fit into my bag without poking out the top. It's so big it takes two hands. I grip the handle and then lean into it with my hip or my stomach, or use my knee to kick Rusty in the butt. A couple of strong knee kicks and this thing will slice through the hardest knot on the planet.

Pipsqueak has been out there for hours, now sitting in his truck around the corner on Henry Street where he can keep an eye on the front of my building. Here's a guy, give him a uniform, a walkie-talkie, a hefty flashlight to swing around, someone to intimidate, and he's in heaven. He's accustomed to having power—if you think keeping sick people and devoted crazies clear of Pastor Sammy as having power.

What little I know of him tells me the guy's a hothead, likely to do something stupid if no one's around to stop him. That's the part that scares me. He could surprise me some night, catch me alone, in the zone, pounding away on the side of some building, and I could get hurt. But take away the surprise, on my turf and face-to-face, he doesn't stand a chance.

After hours in the truck, he has to be hungry, bored, tired. Hell, he could be asleep. I can see that both Henry Street and Canton are vacant, some cars but no late-night amblers, no drunks, no one else spying on me. I could slip out the back, unseen, that's not a problem, but I decide to go at this another way, a way that Pipsqueak will understand.

I charge out the front door of the building onto Canton and go straight for the truck. I'm twenty feet away, directly in front of it, when the lights go on. Then the brights. I'm blinded, but don't hesitate. I drop the bag, yank out Rusty and run forward directly between the lights. The truck is huge, with large tires, and sits high off the ground. I get up close between the headlights, where the glare isn't so bad, my eyes adjusting to the darkness, and place the tip of Rusty's blade against the grill.

The horn blast is so loud, I'm momentarily dizzy.

I can't hear, can't see; the sheer size of the truck has me disoriented. The goddamn grill is a gigantic rectangle of chrome, shoulder high, and I'm staring right into the hood ornament: a mean-spirited ram with long, curving horns. I get all ten fingers wrapped tightly around the handle of the gouge, set my feet, and quickly knee-kick the butt punching right through the plasticky-chrome grill and into something harder, probably the radiator.

The kick is so hard that the entire truck shudders.

Pipsqueak is screaming, though I can barely hear him. The driver's door cracks open with a solid *thud-clunk*, and his shrill voice gets louder. He doesn't get out, content to sit there on his perch until he sees what's what. The coward.

I rush around to the driver's side and place the tip of the gouge against the middle of the door.

"Push on the door and you won't like the mess it makes," I say.

I'm unnerved by how high the doors are. The little asshole put lifts on his truck. I'm holding Rusty out in front of me like a spear, ready—if Pipsqueak does something stupid like come down out of the cab—to poke him a couple of times, get his attention.

The window slinks down, his face surrounded in a haze of spicy cigar smoke. He says, "You bitch. You so much as touch this truck and I'll kill you."

I lean into the butt of the gouge, the blade pressing on the soft metal, creating the slightest dimple.

"Too late," I say.

Pipsqueak cranes his head out the window trying to get a good look at the damage, his face awed by the size of the gizmo in my hands. He's a heavy breather and I get a lungful of his hazardous breath.

"What are you doing here?" I ask.

"What did you do to my grill?"

"You first."

There is a silence, not long, Pipsqueak and I looking at each other until he says, "Roe says you're blackmailing Pastor Sammy."

"And what do you think?"

"I agree with whatever he says."

"Just do what you're told, is that it?"

Pipsqueak says, "Sammy never sees people, outside of his show, but he saw you, didn't he? Why was that? You must have some bad shit on him."

"Suppose I told you I'm a sculptor and Sammy likes my work."

"I don't care what you are. Another bitch tried the same thing, got a little something on Sammy. Some shit nobody cares about. I had a talk with her, too."

I say, "So that's what this is: one of your talks. This other woman, you know her name?"

Pipsqueak getting up his courage, takes a draw on his cigar. Blows smoke at me, telling me to back away from the truck. He means it. I lean on Rusty, this time digging into the metal door, and ask if her name was Billie. He tells me this other girl, way prettier than me, he followed her. Snuck up on her one night and convinced her to rethink what she was doing.

He puts a stubby arm on the window, showing off the muscles in his forearm and bicep, and makes a fist.

I say, "You hit her."

"What do you think?" he says.

"You sound happy about it."

"Shouldn't I be?"

Without thinking, I knee-kick the butt of the gouge and send the wide blade through the outer metal and past one or two inner layers of truck door. Pipsqueak opens his mouth but nothing comes out and for a moment I think Rusty may have gored him. I wait but he doesn't make a sound, still not sure what he's seeing. I yank the gouge out of the door and look for blood. Nothing. I move quickly to the back door and knee-kick Rusty hard, clean through the metal skin and the inside door panel, and jerk the gouge free. Pipsqueak bangs open the door, shouting and screaming, so loud and high pitched at times I can't hear it but feel it. I'm waiting for him to jump me, to beat on his chest, break down and cry, something, curious to see just how stupid he can be, a pumped up loud guy with a tiny little brain. Instead, he just sits there.

"Are we done with our talk?" I say.

Pipsqueak's mad as a bulldog, the veins in his wide neck pumping away, the skin stretched as tight as a drumhead.

"One more thing. The woman you asked about. It's to do with her." Now, warily agreeable. "Get in. Give me five minutes. Then I'll take you anywhere you want to go."

I say, "What about her?"

"Look, I know you're not afraid of me. Bring your stick along. I've seen what you can do. I'm not gonna mess with you."

"You got something to say, say it."

"It's better if I show you."

Every molecule in my body is telling me not to get inside the truck. Another part of me, the part that has nothing to do with molecules, the part distinctly separate from my body, the critical, willful part, says *what am I waiting for?*. I've started down a path and the path leads where it leads. Get off the path anytime I want, but do and risk slogging through life ankle-deep in regret.

I say. "This thing you want to show me, how far?"

"Less than a mile. Half mile, maybe."

"Billie Hannah, did you know her?"

He pulls the door shut, reaches out the window and down the side of the waxy door. Finds the dent, the gash in the metal, and runs his fingers around the edge.

Pipsqueak says, "You can be a bitch when you feel like it. You keep asking me about this lady; you go crying to

Roe, Pastor Sammy. Only now I've got something to show you and you don't want to see it." He issues me a savage-eyebrow look that comes off clownish. "I got to go. Last chance. You coming or not?"

"Let me get my bag." I zip around to the front of the truck, pick up my canvas bag, and move to the passenger door. I open it and heave myself up and into the cab. I put the canvas bag on my lap. Rusty, I set on top of the bag with the blade pointing at Pipsqueak.

He starts the engine, takes another drag on the cigar, exhales. It's not so bad, a mixture of toasted bagel and wet leather. He glowers at the canvas bag, says, "What do you got in there?"

"None of your business."

Pipsqueak does a U-ey. At Commerce, goes right. Instinctively, I reach for the door handle and give it a tug. It's locked, and the lock knob has been filed down to a nub too small to get my fingers around.

He says, "Cool, huh? I had it rigged that way. Once you're in, you're in till I let you out." He pulls out a cell and presses a button, says, "Meet me out behind the Cotton Bowl, on Nimitz."

We take Commerce all the way to Fair Park where the road Ts and we have to go left or right, choose left and then a quick right into the park. Almost immediately, we veer onto Admiral Nimitz Circle and I can see the stadium, first between buildings and then up close. We're at the back, the building in deep shadow, gray and old and immovable. Lots of history. Lots of tradition. Looked at another way, a good place for a crime.

Pipsqueak pulls to the side of the road and leaves the lights on and the engine running. The road curves slowly around the stadium, and just where it disappears, I see a car parked on the opposite side of the street. Pipsqueak flashes his brights and three men get out of the car. No other people on the street, no other cars. Neither of us says a word until we see the men.

Pipsqueak looks pale and grim and hostile. He's fuming over the scratches in his truck. Peeks over at me, tells me I'm not gonna like this. I try the door handle again. Nothing.

"This other girl," he says, "the one better looking than you, you got kinda crazy when I mentioned I hit her."

"Yeah, silly me."

He says, "You like boxing? I like boxing, seeing those guys, especially the ones about my size, welterweights, beat the shit out of each other. It turns me on, you could say." The truck has a dense log-fire smell to it. The ashtray is open, jammed with the dark, turd-like stumps of three cigar stubs. Pipsqueak mashes out his cigar and places it next to the others.

I say, "You ever empty your ashtray?"

"I like the ones hit hard," he says. "Hard and fast."

"What is it you wanted to show me?"

"The ones know what they're doing, they get in close, a clinch like, and stay there. I've seen fights, all ten rounds the guys're no farther away than you and me."

I say, "You want to box, is that what you're telling me?"

"I've done some boxing."

"You any good at it?"

There is a hidden flap in the end of my black canvas bag. It's something I came up with, just big enough to slip my hand inside and get a good grip on the mallet. The big mallet, the one I'm holding, is a smooth, wooden cylinder, like a rolling pin with one handle.

Pipsqueak glances at Rusty, at my right hand resting on top of the bag, at my left arm buried under the bag.

I watch him staring straight ahead, watching the three men coming slowly at us. His neck tense, arms extended, hands gripping the top arc of the steering wheel. Strong hands with dirty knuckles. He says, "The girl I was telling you about. I did more than just hit her, and she didn't even fuck with my truck."

I tighten my grip on the mallet, get ready.

His right fist balled now, pumping the muscles in the hand, fast. Pipsqueak says, "Bitch!" Turns his head and strains against the seat belt, cocks the arm just as I bring out the mallet and whip it fast and hard into his mouth, knocking out teeth. His head bangs against the headrest and bounces forward into the steering wheel.

A pause, then he swings at me backhand to club me with his fist. I spring up and back trying to take the blow with my shoulder and not my face. The punch lands solid on my left breast, the one with the spiteful cancer killing me from the inside. The pain is intense, and the swelling is almost immediate. The whole left side of my body is on fire and the pain shoots to the right like ten thousand fire ants mad as hell and biting their way across my body, left to right. I'm out of my seat belt, on one knee with the mallet as high as I can get it and swing down on his leg, close to the knee, with all I have. A bone snaps, the leg pushes down on the accelerator and the engine momentarily howls.

Outside, the men stop. They're sixty feet away, crossing the road directly in the headlights. They can't see us, but I can see them, at least one of them. Roe.

Pipsqueak is toast, both hands gripping his leg, his head propped up by the steering wheel, his face to me, his mouth a giant bloody hole. I show him the mallet, then rest it on the top of his head. I lift it, holding it there like a guillotine and ask, "This woman you mentioned, was it Billie Hannah? Yes or no."

"No," he begs, blood spattering the dashboard. Some teeth fall out. His words coming out thick-tongued and garbled. "Jethica thomething. I thwear."

I ask, "Is she alive?"

His forehead wrinkles. "I thcared her, ith all…"

He says other things I don't understand and probably wouldn't believe. I tell him not to move and reach over him and unlock my door, yank on the brights, making it even harder for Roe and his thugs to see. I shove the mallet inside my bag, switch the dome light to off, open my door only as wide as I need to climb down, grab my bag and Rusty, and shut the door. I tiptoe to the back of the truck, and then run.

A dozen blocks away, I'm still shaking, and what I need more than anything is to pull out my baby ax and swing.

I make my way to the corner of Wood and Ervay. Several nights ago I spotted a nice, plump, free-standing, wooden column—a sort of fattened up American version of the slimmer Greek Doric column—in front of what looks like an accountant's office or a law firm. Ervay's a small street and the lighting is for shit, the streetlights casting heavy shadows every which way. I hook up my flashlight, the one that hangs around my neck, and I go to work. The sketch of Pilar's hubby takes only a few minutes.

She'd given me a crummy snapshot of the guy standing in front of a spanky new car—what I recognize as Pilar's Nissan Maxima way back when it was hubby's car. The guy's giddy with himself, feeling at that moment that life would never get better than this—though I imagine him a couple of years later telling Pilar it's merely a damn good car, perfect for her, while he needs something sportier, something with a little more zoom-zoom.

All of that taking place before he got sick. Before he started hoping for miracles, satisfied now to drive a wreck, or to keep his shitty job, or to live in his shitty forty-year-old two-bedroom, one and a half bath. Satisfied just to be alive. The carving takes most of the night. I'm back in the loft before dawn.

I feel bad for Pipsqueak in a way that doesn't make any sense. Bad about the teeth and the leg, bad because I started it, really, and once started, it couldn't be stopped. Twenty seconds of this starts a spiral of dolorous self-assessment—what I'm good at is swinging an ax or a big mallet. What I'm bad at is people, holding a meaningful conversation, holding on to a friend or a lover for more than a season. I'm mouthy, uncompromising, too raw-boned. My teeth are crooked and I'm pretty sure I have a cavity. I know I have breast cancer.

I know what Mother would say, if she were around.

I'd tell her I feel lost, put on a dispiriting frown.

She'd say, "Every face is a self-portrait of the person inside."

I'd say, "Oh, for chrissakes."

Her voice loud, trying to hammer some sense into me, she'd say, "Listen babe, some women dream while others get off their ass and do. Which one are you?"

I'd laugh at her, ask her where she gets this stuff. Tell her she's been watching too much daytime TV. She'd come back with a, "Look at me." I would, and she'd tell me in a softer voice, "You're not lost, Miranda. We both know where you are. So why the sad face?"

I wouldn't answer right away because there is no way to explain what I feel: that these are the final days of an old life playing out, the one where I was married and healthy and anonymous; that something is happening; that pretty soon it would be over, and I'm resigned to it, waiting impatiently, sad face and all. Right here in downtown Dallas in the Adam Hats building. How do I explain that kind of feeling to anybody? Even Mother. Especially Mother.

So instead, I'd tell her about Pipsqueak, about Roe, about Pastor Sammy. I might even throw Handy under the bus, the son-of-a-bitch. I might just call him a son-of-a-bitch.

Mother'd like that. She could be scathing, acid-tongued at times, and she got a real kick out of thinking she'd passed this sterling trait on to me.

I'd tell her how Pipsqueak hit me, how I knocked out some teeth. She'd go quiet for a moment, giving herself time to breathe it in, put herself in my place, feel what I feel. Then she'd say, "Good for you. Don't you ever stand by and let anyone shit all over you. I'm proud of you, Miranda."

It's the way she talked, like a tough old broad. It's the way she spoke even when I was young and she was a long way from being old. Lots of "shit this" and "shit that." When I'd tell her about some trouble I'd wangled my way into, she'd pause, let it sink in, and say, "Well, fuck me," as in "No kidding."

She didn't talk like other mothers, and it's one of the things I loved about her.

"Don't let anyone shit on you." It's what she'd say, because it's what she'd said hundreds of times. That and other things just like it. The point—I think, though Mother was never big on simplifying life's lessons to a single point— was to stand up for myself. Even if standing up meant making an ugly mess. Even if it meant doing things I didn't want to do.

S unday morning, I wake around ten. I got four hours sleep and, still sandy-eyed, I sit up and nearly yark on myself. Last night, I felt a mixture of pain and numbness, but now all the numbness is gone. What's left is a tug-o-war—the left side of my body fighting a dull, prolonged hurt, the right side still stinging from ten thousand gluttonous fire ants. I lay back, give my right breast a squeeze. Do the same for my left. It feels big and swollen and sore.

I don't want to think about it, will myself not to think about it, and then can't stop thinking about it. "It" being any of several things: my little problem; the surgery I'm not having; whether a hard smack on the breast can make my little problem any worse, in which case I can blame the whole thing on Pipsqueak.

Last night, I felt sorry for the guy. This morning, I've changed my mind. Fuck him. He's lucky I didn't kill him.

The pain in my chest isn't so bad if I move slowly, inch my way upright and pause, let everything settle. Standing is trickier. Walking I can stomach if I hobble in short granny-steps. I do just that all the way to the bathroom, take three Advil, and stand there, wait for the healing to begin.

* * *

I'm staring out the window, the Dallas skyline staring back at me. It's gray and ugly outside, even for November, and I'm thinking that the day looks angry, when someone taps on the metal door to my loft, not loud, almost polite, in a funky jazz riff. I hobble over, the concrete cold against my bare feet, and check the spy hole. Otto is standing there, his back to me, showing off his bald spot. I open the door and he swivels around, scowls at me.

"This morning," he says, "I'm out for my Sunday drive. I see a commotion up the road on Ervay. Police, reporters everywhere, some church people in their Sunday wears. Not happy church people, either. The other kind. I get close, and I see it's your handiwork. You got to cut that shit out."

"I can't do that," I say.

"You can, you just won't. You mind telling me why?"

"You tell me why everyone wants me to stop, and I'll have a better idea why I can't."

At noon, Otto and I meet for lunch at the AllGood Café on Main. The place is busy, filled with locals, mostly. Youngish kids with too many tats and old people with long graying ponytails. We luck out and get one of the booths next to the window. Otto sits across from me and leans his shoulder against the glass. I face him with a sort of glary light in my eyes.

He and I are friends, sort of. Since I sent Handy packing, he looks out for me, finds reasons to drop by—like today. It's Sunday, for chrissakes. I know of him only what he's told me: a four-year hitch in the Army, a nickel with Liggett working tobacco near Hillsborough, North Carolina, and after, a ten-year stretch with Philip Morris in South Concord. It's all tough talk with Otto, his story unfolding like a prison sentence.

The coffee comes and we tell her we need more time.

"You don't look so good," he says.

"The guy out on the street. From last night. We had a talk."

"A talk," he says.

"About Billie."

I give him a short version of yesterday—my lunch with Mister, my meeting with Sammy, Roe's threats. Billie and Sammy doing the nasty, according to Pilar. Billie wanting out, Sammy coming up with a million reasons to keep her in. Pipsqueak and me last night.

Otto focuses on my eyes, trying to see the bullshit in my story, asking me to slow it down. Way down. Pastor Sammy, I tell him, slowly, is into something. What, I don't know. Roe's in it for the money. The way it could have happened, Roe delivers the money, only he changes his mind and kills Billie—has her killed, I don't know—and keeps the money.

Otto says, "Tell me again where you fit in."

"I found her in the market, lying there with her throat cut. I want to know why."

Otto sits there thinking how to say whatever he came here to say. Me squinting at this thin, old black man with the window behind him making him thinner and blacker, looking mean when he wants to, but now not trying to look any way at all, just trying to find the words. He says, "You getting into that truck last night was plain stupid."

"Otto, I'm not asking for your approval. What I want is a couple of buttermilk pancakes, not advice."

"Listen to me. I owe you, but you get yourself killed, and I don't care how—shot, cut, beaten to death behind the Cotton Bowl, whatever flavor it comes in—and I'm not putting myself in danger just to find out why."

There's no logic to it, exactly, but his words hurt. I ask, "Why not?"

"Two reasons: cause you're dead, and why's not important."

Outside, we can hear the thump-thump of sound coming from a slow-driving Honda with can't-see-me windows. I flip open the menu, change subjects. "What are you having?"

He says, "You're not hearing me. *Why* is not important. *Who* is important."

All I can think to say is, "Who."

He says, "When you find out who, what then? Think you can stop there? Because if not, then it's time you let it go. It's time you let Billie go."

I look up at him. Not past him like I've done a zillion times in the last four years, but right at him. He's got deep horizontal creases across his forehead and little black spots high on his brown cheeks. He's sixty. I'm twenty-nine. He's got thirty-one years on me. He's a guy I should listen to.

But I don't.

Monday morning, I open my eyes, rock up into a sitting position, swing my feet over the side of the bed and stand. It's a slow process. I hobble to the closet, grab something nice to wear, something to put me in a good mood: pants with a wool blend and a silky blouse. I shower, think seriously about shaving my legs, and change my mind.

When I come out of the bathroom, I'm surprised to see Otto standing in the front doorway, the door open and a shiny new lock in his hand.

He says, "This guy you say you hit in the mouth, he the type to come back and finish what he started?"

"Not for a while."

"Maybe he has a friend might want to stick up for him."

We look at each other and I realize he's right.

"Cause this," he says, holding up the glossy new industrial-sized dead bolt, "will stop almost anyone."

The headache is on me in seconds, a constrictive band of tiredness running from my forehead up and over my head smack into the base of my skull. I wince, shuffle over to the bed in my uplifting outfit, and sit.

Before he starts mothering, I say, "I'm fine. I see the doctor this morning."

"You want to invite me to come along, I don't mind."

"It's six blocks. I can walk."

"You want to walk, I can use the fresh air. You want a shoulder to lean on, that's okay, too. Some people have a way of not hearing bad news. Why I bring it up, I'm offering an extra pair of ears. Sit there with you and the doctor and me. Help you remember the parts you forget."

A spunky nurse leads Otto and me to the door of Novak's office. Points us inside and tells us to sit. There's a fusty, weighted clubbiness to the room. Dark walls and heavy furniture; air thick with false promise. It's a man's room used, as often as not, for meetings like these, with women.

It's a man's job, cutting off tits. Not at all something a woman would do. And if she did get roped into it, it's not something she'd enjoy. With P. Novak, MD, however, it's a different story. The P is for prick. The prick who hacks off women's tits because he loves it. Adores these torturous little conferences before the main event where he lays it out in three or five or a zillion easy steps. Where he assures people like me, just stick to the program and everything's gonna be okee-dokee.

Only I'm not sticking to the program. I'm uncooperative. I'm stubborn. I'm stalling. Everyone knows I'm stalling, and why shouldn't I? You put Handy or Otto or Novak, even, in my place and they'd back-peddle a-plenty. A woman doctor tells any of these schmucks the only fix is to cut off his jolly and I'll guaran-goddamn-tee you the guy does not whip it out and tell the good doctor to have at it. He does not say, "By all means, whatever you think is best, ma'am, doctor." What he says is, "Not on your fucking life." Let's just slow things down a bit and think this through. Because there's no way around it, it takes time to get used to the idea of life without the equipment you started with.

I've tried, but there is no talking to Novak. Not in the examining room; not out in the hall, him pointing me that-a-way to radiology; not even here in his angst-thick office where the old heart-to-hearts are supposed to take place.

When he gets here, I want to tell him, look, there's got to be another way to go at this thing. He's a surgeon, so naturally he sees the beauty of a nice clean surgical way out. Snip-snip and I'm on my way. I understand that. All I'm asking is a couple of more options, make me feel like I've got a say in things, like an active participant and not an old truck with a hundred and eighty thousand miles and no horn.

I'll flatter him, mention the Czech Republic or Slovenia or Slovakia, wherever he hails from. Get him to talking apple strudel and sauerkraut soup, maybe debate the current political economy of Central Europe. If I could just think of his home town, pick the right country even, I'd tell him that I've been there, loved the place, loved the people, loved every goddamn thing about it, and get him to lighten up. Take that Central European scowl off his face and work with me here.

Forty minutes later, Novak hustles in carrying a handful of x-rays. He drops into his tufted, burgundy-leather chair behind the desk and looks at two of the dark x-rays with ominous white splotches, at his cutesy-pie family snapshots in front of him, and finally, at me. Doesn't bother to acknowledge Otto.

Novak is a thin man with a gaunt face and bad breath. He's a smoker and doesn't bother to hide it, probably thinks of himself as a tobacco-puffing maverick. He says, "Since your last visit, there has been some increase in breast density."

"Some?" I say.

"That's right." He reaches for his planner and flips to the middle.

"A lot or a little?"

Novak says, "Remind me again where you got that bruise?"

"Why?" I say. "Can it make things any worse?"

Otto reaches over and puts a big mahogany hand on my arm above the wrist.

Novak doesn't know how to take me. He squints at the x-rays. I watch him stare back at me with a cold look, meant no doubt to remind me that he's a serious man and this is serious stuff, and he tells me things can always get worse. He reaches for his planner and flips to the middle, finds what he's looking for and tells me that I missed my last two follow ups. Says it like a question and waits for me to explain. When I don't, he pages forward, puts a bony finger in the middle of the planner and tells me I cancelled surgery a day before post op, too late to fill the schedule with another patient. He taps his finger on the page.

"How big is it?" I ask.

"How big is what?" Novak says.

"Whatever it is you plan to cut out? What's it weigh? I'm just wondering."

"Inflammatory breast cancer grows in sheets. You know this, or you should. It's not a tumor, exactly. There is no solid mass."

"You don't know. Is that what you're telling me?"

"It's the reason we take the entire breast. It's the only way to be certain we get it all."

Otto looks at me, not sure if this is a good time to join the fray, and removes his hand from my arm. To Novak, he says, "Tell me about treatment, if you don't mind."

Novak looks up, stares back at Otto defiantly, extends a hand, but doesn't rise. "And you are?"

Otto doesn't extend a hand, doesn't rise. "Otto."

"Mr. Otto, I normally restrict these meetings to family, but since you're here, you may stay." There's an edge to his voice that wasn't there five seconds ago. "I've been over all this with Ms. Tate. Maybe she could fill you in, at some other time. I have patients waiting." No one moves for a long moment and then Novak drops the x-rays on the desktop and leans back in his chair. "We're looking at IBC. It's rare. It's aggressive. It's a beast. and the only way to keep it from killing you" he says, looking at me, "is to cut it out."

"IBC," Otto says, "like the root beer?"

"You and Ms. Tate share an odd sense of humor."

Otto says, "Say you don't cut it out. You do nothing."

"Mr. Otto, forty thousand women, this year, will die of breast cancer. Many of those women did nothing. Look, I'm the first to appreciate a healthy cynicism. Normally, I would suggest you take some time, do your own research, read what's out there, get another opinion, all of that. Given Ms. Tate's refusal to follow my instructions, I would insist she find another surgeon. No doubt, she's tried, but like it or not, I'm the best there is. What you and Ms. Tate refuse to understand is that there's no time. With IBC, you treat it and you treat it fast." Novak flips a page of his planner forward and then back. "We can start the chemo day after tomorrow."

"I know people who been through that," Otto says.

"Not this. Not likely. If you were paying attention, then you know that IBC is rare. Therefore the treatment is somewhat unorthodox. Three to six rounds of chemo, before surgery. Several more rounds after, high-dose. Followed by radiation, something for hormones, Tamoxifen, something like that. Look, that's all the time I have. If you will please excuse me."

Otto looks over at me, waiting for something, a question, a comment. Wants me to perk up, but I'm all out of perk. To Novak, he says, "About this surgery you do."

Novak says, "What, how long it takes? What are you asking me?"

"Not that. About how many operations you do last year? About, say."

"Forty-two, about. This year, forty-six through October. Now, if that's all, I really have to go. I feel I've been more than fair with my time."

"How many died? On the table, I mean. You keep numbers, right?"

"Yes, yes, of course, but now is not a good time."

"You don't remember?" Otto asks. "Forty-six in ten months, you don't remember if one or two died? I'm you and a woman dies, I'd remember. Me, I'd know her name off the top of my head."

"You're not me. You know nothing about me."

"That's what I'm saying, doc. We don't know and you're not telling. Answer me this. More than one?"

Novak stands. "That's none of your concern."

Otto stands. "It is if I say it is."

I like watching these two go at it. My doctor, the impatient prick, and my maintenance man, the protector of stubborn white girls with breast cancer. Otto's doing what I want to do. What I've wanted to do the moment Novak delivered the bad news. Get in there and slug it out. Stop pretending everything is hunky-dory and scream and bite and insult the only face I have for what's happening to me—P. Novak, MD.

I understand now what Otto is doing. Allowing me to step back from myself; watch the fight without being involved. It's not about me anymore; at least, this part isn't. It's about a couple of guys that distrust the bejesus out of each other. And maybe it's about other things, too, but whatever it is, I'm not at the center of it. In his own Otto way, he's letting me know that someone cares, that he cares enough to fight for me even if it's a fight he can't win, that no one can win. He's right there beside me. Me and Otto on the same team. Us against the bad guys.

I look up at Novak, an asshole but otherwise a good man with some baggage of his own. Behind him, I spot a diploma from Palacky University, the Czech Republic.

"Prague," I say.

Novak lights up. "Yes. You've been?"

"It's beautiful," I say. "You're lucky to come from such a lovely place."

W hen I get back to the loft there's a note stuck in the jamb of the door. The note's handwritten in quick jerky strokes on the back of an envelope. It reads: *We had a deal.* The note's unsigned, but I know who it's from—John Roe. The guy's on my mind, now more than ever, and it wouldn't surprise me if I willed the note into being.

Thanks to Otto, I've got a new angle on things. I no longer care about why, only who. And the who in my life right now is John Roe. My little problem, I've decided, is no longer Novak's fault. It's Roe's. My crappy career, Handy leaving me, that's Roe too. About Billie, there's no question Roe is involved.

Inside the envelope is a news clipping. No date. The headline reads:

Vandals Hit Law Office

Vandals struck the office of attorney Michael C. Barr sometime Saturday night. An ornate wooden column, located at the entrance to the firm, was partially destroyed as vandals gouged graffiti-style images into the face of the column.

Mr. Barr announced this morning his firm is offering

$5,000 for information leading to
the arrest and conviction of the
person   or   persons   who
vandalized his office…

Officer Andrea Caci of the
Central Division confirmed that
the investigation is still open…

There's more, but not a word about the work itself.
What it looks like; nothing about the composition, the
texture, the skill of the artist. Nothing about me.

Thanks to Pipsqueak, I've got an ugly purple-gray
bruise on my chest. No telling how the bruise will affect my
swing until I try. Alone in the loft, I dig out my baby ax and
move up close, say three feet from one of the wooden
columns that hold up my building. I swing the ax slowly at
first. Aiming at the column but not actually touching the
wood. What I'm doing is sort of like shadow-boxing for
woodcarvers, and it looks just as stupid.

My right side, the arm, the hand, feels good; even my
fingers feel strong. I swing harder and harder, extending the
arm, twisting my body and at the same time letting my free
arm swing wide to counterbalance the weight of the ax. When
I get into the rhythm, I can go sixty, seventy, swings without
a break. The trick is to use my whole body: swinging my hips
ahead of the shoulders, ahead of the arm, ahead of the ax. Do
the same thing on the up stroke: hips first, shoulders, arm, ax.

I'm a natural right-hander, but I can switch hands
without interrupting the rhythm. I swing the ax high
overhead and switch hands, right to left, and just as I do a
pain shoots through my left shoulder so sharp that I let go of
the ax. It flies across the room and clanks against the wall.

That's a first. I've never, ever dropped my ax.

* * *

My idea is to get in and get out. Get some information, if there's any to be got, and keep moving. Only problem is when I see the sign, Seagar Grocer, I freeze, stand there in front of the store and look up at beer posters and cigarette ads and a yellow Western Union sign. I turn and stare across the street to the corner where I talked to the girl and her little brother, the one throwing up in the gutter—what, last Monday, only seven days ago. Christ.

In the back of the grocer, next to the Cheez-Its with a racecar driver on the box, I expect to see stains on the floor, dried blood, the outline where the blood had been, something. I look harder, searching for a faint chalk outline of Billie's body like those I remember from TV shows. There's none of that.

The old black guy behind the counter asks if he can help me find something.

I say, "This is where the woman was killed, right?" I say it loud enough to be heard across the small store. I'm pointing to the floor, but he doesn't know that. All he can see is my head and shoulders above the low shelves. I've got my small black bag with me and I bend over, momentarily out of sight, and set the bag on the floor.

"What, you with the health department or something?" he says.

"The cops have any idea who did it?"

"None of my business," he says. "You want something, or you just stop by for the conversation?"

I ask, "Are you the owner?"

"Sixteen years."

A door opens in the back next to the bathrooms and a girl, eighteenish, comes out, a small towel and a bottle of Windex in her hands. She sees me, eyes the counter man, and moves to the front door and sprays the glass window, begins wiping it down. I can smell the ammonia from here. I look over to the girl, now standing in the doorway looking at me, holding her towel and the Windex down at her side not bothering with the glass.

I say to the owner, "I came into your store that night, after what happened, but before the police. I saw her on the floor. Another one, a young guy, I saw behind the counter. I didn't see you."

There is a silence, not long, me and the man looking at each other until he says, "You just happen in here that time of night? I tell you what, get yourself a soda, on the house, and take yourself back whichever which way you came. I got nothing to say to you or anybody else hasn't already been said."

I point my chin at the girl. "Was she here that night?"

"I'm asking you politely, lady."

I'm about to say something mean or stupid when the girl turns her head. It's just a little thing but it stops me. She's pretty with light brown skin and wavy, reddish-brown hair. Her eyes are on me and I sense a question, like *What are you doing here?*

"Who did it?" I say to the girl, "That's all I want to know."

The man says, "Saran, don't say nothin."

I lift my bag and ease my way to the door. A wire stand holds newspapers. On the front page is a picture of Pastor Sammy Gann. Standing beside him and sort of to one side are John Roe and several of the bodyguards. The headline reads: *TV Evangelist Sammy Gann Inspires Thousands in Dallas.* I grab the paper. Show it to the old guy; ask if he's ever seen him. He glances at the photo. Shakes his head.

The girl comes over to the counter and takes a look, tells me, yeah, she knows him. From TV. The old guy says, "Girl, not another word." She says, "Daddy," in that long drawn out way that little girls learn to get things from their daddies. I can see now that the two look alike. The set of the eyes, the bridge of the nose. She tells him it's a picture is all, what can it hurt?

I tell her, not him, "This one," and point to Roe. She takes a long look. Glances up at Daddy, asking for permission to speak. Daddy, shaking his head, says, "You don't know nothing will help those people."

Saran says, "Not them, me."

"I'm all the help you need. You know that."

"That night, Daddy," she says. "I needed you then." Daddy turns and looks across the store. Saran says to me, "I saw him. Just that once, if it was him. He was arguing with the boys. The ones out front all the time."

"Rank and Iggy," I say.

"That's them. He got into a tussle with Iggy, I think."

"When was this?"

"The night it happened," she says.

"And Rank?"

"What about him?"

"He was here?"

"I said he was."

I lay fifty-cents on the counter and put the newspaper inside my bag. I move to the glass doors, still inside looking out at the curb when I get an idea. I turn and ask if she knows what the man in the picture was driving. She starts to smile, then lets it go. Maybe, she says, coulda been a Cadillac Escalade. Black. Big shiny wheels. Maybe.

"That's enough," Daddy says. "Go on now."

Rank was there when it happened. It's all I can think about. On the sidewalk or in the store, it doesn't matter. He was there. I can almost see it: Rank with his dark clothes, ring in his nose, tattoos, pretending to be tough. Rank and Iggy hassling Roe when he tries to enter the store. Roe giving it right back and then pushing through the door, already pissed off at having to deal with these punks. His temper short, nervous, thinking only about himself and that he's better than this: running other people's errands, fixing other people's screw-ups. With all this on his mind, he finds Billie in the back of the store, threatens her. She tells him to go to hell and he cuts her throat.

It could have happened that way.

I'm not a block from the grocer when the girl comes jogging up behind me. She says, "What you said back there," she says. "About who did it, I think I know someone can help."

I tell her if she means Rank, I already know where he lives. What I don't tell her is that I watched him get bounced off the hood of a green pickup five nights ago. That he's probably still in the hospital, or dead. Either way, I'll find him and I'll ask him why he lied to me.

She says, "No, not him. A boy, Thomas. I don't know the house, but I know the street."

She leads me to Beaumont Street, three blocks away. On the corner, two men are in a driveway leaning against a car like a couple of sentries. They've got on baggy clothes and knit caps. They're watching us.

The houses along Beaumont are old and run down. Some of the oldest, prairie-style two-stories, are built up close to the road. Big, foreboding monsters in their day that are now sway-backed and crumbling. The newer homes, say built in the 1930s, are smaller and pushed to the back of each lot, leaving square yards of dirt and patches of brown grass. The real junkers seem to come in threes, as if the house in the middle got sick and infected those on each side.

There's hardly any traffic, but plenty of spiritless cars on the street and in the yards. The entire neighborhood needs a long, heavy rain to wash away the neglect: in some places, a deluge strong enough to lift old cars and boats and discarded appliances and ferry them away.

It's late afternoon and cold, and it surprises me how many kids are outside playing. The one we're hoping to avoid, Saran tells me, is Thomas's sister, Neisha. Anybody says, "There's Neisha," she tells me, be ready to duck. The kids closest to us, six of them, come up to Saran, curious what's going on, and she talks to them in a sort of practiced, singsong voice. There's a salesy tone to it, telling them she's on secret business. She could use some help, if they promise not to tell. They jump and tug on her arm and tell her Come on, what is it? We won't tell.

Saran says, "You know Neisha?"

Lots of head bobbing. One of the kids points to a house four doors away on our side of the street. Out front, a man wearing sunglasses, his arms folded, sits in a lawn chair in the middle of his dirt yard. I glance at him and he stares back. A little boy beside me sees the man, picks up on the vibe, turns his scooter around and rides away.

"Is that her daddy?" Saran asks.

The kids are losing interest. A couple more back away, thinking now that Saran and I might be trouble.

"Thomas around?" she asks. That does it. The last three glance at each other and then run, playfully, but nonetheless a run.

A kid with his back to us, not a part of the curious six, is working on a rusty bike in the middle of the street. He's small but coordinated, tugging on a wrench to tighten a bolt on the front wheel. He peeks over his shoulder at us. Done with the bolt, he stands, but doesn't pick up the bike.

The man four doors away also stands. Stares at the three of us, Saran and me and the boy. The boy takes a tentative step toward us. The man waits a beat, and then frantically begins waving his arm above his head. At first I think he's waving at us or at the boy, but he's not. He's waving to the two men behind us on the corner, the two men now sprinting down the middle of the road.

The boy says, "I'm Thomas," and instantly I recognize the face.

The men in baggy clothes are twenty yards away, still running hard, when I slide the canvas pack off my shoulder. Drop it on the ground. Unzip it. Pull out my baby ax. There's a leather sheath covering both blades and I unsnap it and toss the sheath. I need room to swing, so I step away from Saran, past Thomas and his bike, into the middle of the street with the ax at my side, pressing against my leg. It's small, seems almost invisible sometimes, because nobody ever feels threatened when they see it, if they do. Nobody's ever stopped running.

These guys are different. At ten yards or so, they stop, fast and hard, staring at the ax. One reaches for his waistband, and the other mumbles something, gets him to rethink whatever he had in mind.

I'm so focused on the men in baggies that I don't notice the man wearing sunglasses sneak up behind me. He says, "You're cool under pressure, I'll give you that."

I half turn, the ax still at my side. "Are you Thomas's father?"

Isley, he tells me in a soft voice. Casually introduces me to Shep and CJ. Tells me these guys, and others on the block, are part of the neighborhood po-lice, out to combat social disorder and such. There's a pause, like it's my turn to introduce myself. Then Isley says, "What I don't get is, two Sinbad-looking brothers coming at you and you don't scream, don't run, nothing. You don't look scared at all. What you do is reach into your bag and pull out a shank no bigger than a pancake flipper. Even then, you don't point it at no one. Don't even let on what you've got. Waiting, the way I see it, till they get close."

I say, "Mr. Isley—"

"What do you call that thing?"

"I'm not here to hurt anyone. Or to get hurt."

"I ask because I heard a rumor, maybe you heard it too, about an Indian dude with red hair and a hatchet. Attacked some punks downtown. Cut one of them. It's why Shep and CJ pulled up short. They heard about the dude with the hatchet."

Shep and CJ stare at the ax.

"I'd like to talk to your son," I say. "About what happened in the store."

He says, "This Indian dude, you understand I mean an American-type Indian, from the old West, not the other. Rumor is he's big, I think now, because it wouldn't look right, turns out he's a small dude. Or a girl."

"I'm not sure what you're telling me."

"The thing is, the punk was cut, you ask me, he got what he deserved. Like that boy, Iggy, he had it coming, messing with people the way he did. This mystery dude with the hatchet, I see us on the same side of things."

I look from Thomas to Saran. Both seem unusually calm, and I'm starting to think this is a big put-on—scare the panties off the white girl. Or maybe it's one of those things dads in rough neighborhoods do to all the kids who come to the house, in this case, all the strangers that happen down this street; let them know the street is po-liced; people here looking out for each other. Let these strangers know to take their funny business, if that's what they have in mind, to another street.

Isley and Shep and CJ, all three of them now, are staring at the ax. I give it a flip so that I'm now holding the metal blade and offer the handle to Isley.

"My baby ax," I say. "That's what I call it."

He stares for a moment, not saying a word, then takes the ax by the handle, inspects both blades but doesn't touch the metal. Grips the handle like I do, way out on the end, getting the feel of it. Treats it with the same respect he might a loaded gun. He waves Thomas over to stand beside him. Lets him look but not touch. He motions with the ax toward his dirt yard and three lonely lawn chairs. "Why don't we sit down and talk," giving me a smile. "What do you say?"

It's the kind of yard that has knee-high stumps showing where the old oaks used to live. One dying, leafless red oak still stands. Many of the yards don't have a single tree left: some stumps, some overgrown holly in clusters, but none of the old oaks and maples and elms. Not a pecan tree in sight. I realize now it's what's been bugging me since we angled onto Beaumont. Even though porches are sagging and eaves rotting and siding falling off in patches, it's the stumps that unsettle me: an ugly reminder of what the neighborhood used to be.

The earth beneath the red oak is tramped down and shiny like polished concrete, the air mildly reminiscent of stale beer. Saran and Isley and I sit in unsteady lawn chairs under the tree. We face the street, and I can see Shep and CJ still ambling up the road to their post.

Thomas stands next to his father. He's small for seven or eight or whatever age he is. He's a small kid, period, and far too trusting for this neighborhood. His eyes are filled with hope, believing, no doubt, that telling the truth, the whole truth, will make things right again. Maybe, a long time ago, his father was small and hopeful, but not any more. Now Isley is strong and purposeful and, when need be, intimidating. He leans forward when he talks, using his soft voice when he wants to get his point across.

Isley says, "Whatever happened, it's got nothing to do with my boy."

I say, "I think I know who murdered the woman in the store. I'd like to hear what Thomas has to say, what he saw, if anything."

"My boy couldn't have seen anything, because I've told him a hundred times not to go near that store after dark."

I don't mention that I saw Thomas and Neisha that night, across the street from the grocer. Thomas barfing in the gutter, a reaction to something bad, maybe something he saw.

"Just two questions," I say.

"Not even one."

I pull the newspaper from my pack and point to the photo. "Can I show him this?"

Isley takes the newspaper, holds it at arms length focusing on the grainy picture. Thomas edges close and peeks at the photo. He looks at his father sitting in the chair, the two eye to eye, and Thomas sort of cocks his head. It's hard to describe, but it looks pleading to me. Like a thing he does when he wants something, and his father says no. The way kids get back at their parents; get into their heads without saying a thing. Some kids pout. Some accidentally spill their cereal. Thomas just cocks that narrow head of his and opens his eyes wide. He wants to talk. Dying to tell his father what he saw. Dying to prove to the neighborhood that he's more than just the kid who pukes in the gutter when he sees something bad.

Isley sees it too. Shakes his head, not even pretending anymore. Ready to give in. Knowing that I know this is the reason we're sitting here. He pats his boy on the back. "Go on."

"That's him," Thomas says. "I saw him cut that woman."

Isley looks from Thomas to me.

Thomas says, "It's true. I don't care what Neisha says. I saw him."

"Where were you?" I ask.

"When?" Isley says.

"When my friend was getting her throat cut. A minute ago you said he didn't go near the place. He says he saw it. So where was he?"

"I can hear you, you know?" Thomas says. "You're talking like I'm not here."

"Okay, Thomas," I say. "So where were you? Hiding somewhere, right?"

"Go on," Isley repeats.

"In the cooler. I went into the store to pee. I heard shots and I hid in the cooler. One end of it, about where they keep the orange juice and stuff. This one aisle, I could see through the glass. A man comes in and cuts the lady on the throat."

"Did they argue or fight in any way?" I ask.

"I told you," Thomas says. "She didn't do nothing to him."

"How many shots? You said you heard shots."

"One. That's all the shots I heard." Sounding innocent saying it that way, a disconnect between the words and the meaning. Thomas, looking at his father, at first proud that he had something to tell, something no one else could tell because no one else was there. Now feeling defensive, realizing that he might not be believed.

"A single shot?" I ask.

"That's what I said." Thomas is close to tears.

Isley reaches over, pulls his son close and hugs him, says, "So what now?"

"What would you do?" I ask Otto.

"You figure it's time for some getback, huh?"

"I'm asking you."

"For this Billie lady? A rich lady I never met. Her and me got nothing in common, live on different planets, her way up in Highland Park and me down in South Dallas. Me, I'd let it go."

Neither of us says another word until we cross under Highway 75 where it changes to I-45, the old Pontiac sailing down Elm and then zigzagging north and west, aiming somewhere near the aquarium. Otto stares straight ahead. There's a faster way to get just about anyplace, but Otto's not into fast. He's for taking his time, and my time. Tall, dark buildings line the streets. Lights on in some of the windows, but most this time of night are black rectangles of glass.

I say, "She was a friend of mine."

"So you keep saying," Otto says. "Like you got one friend in the world and now she's gone. It's a big world, Miranda. You get out of your studio a little more, socialize some, you'd know that. Give it a try, I bet you make another friend."

"Turn and walk away. Is that it?"

"I'm not turning you in any direction, 'cause when I do, you go the other way. Your problem, you can't accept anyone telling you what to do. Even suggesting it. It's got to be your idea. Yet here you are asking what I think. And I tell you I would let it go. So now you want to argue. Getting me mad in that quiet way you do. Ruining my evening, cause that's what's you're doing."

I turn and look through the glass out the passenger window. I say, "You can drop me anywhere."

"There you go."

I pull my black bag off the floor and put it in my lap.

Otto says, "It's time you think about yourself. How about you do what Dr. Novak says for a little while, till you get better? Get some rest and stop all this nighttime nonsense."

There is a long silence.

I pull the picture from my pocket and hand it to Otto. He flips on the dome and stares at the photo. It's the one Emily's mother gave me. Emmy, the little girl in pink. "Cute," he says. Asks what she is to me, and when I don't answer he comes at me another way, asking if I got wood, meaning have I found a site for the sculpture. I have but I shake my head no. Tell Otto where I'm working and he's likely to roost in a dark alley for most of the night watching over me like a mother hen. He knows I'm lying, asking me if this wood, the one I don't got, is big or little. Wants to know if I plan something life-size or bigger. Bigger is his vote, shoveling up more free advice, unable to stop himself, though I doubt he tries. A lot bigger. Cute kid, he tells me again, and hands back the photo.

A whole two seconds pass and Otto says, "About Roe, what are you gonna do?"

"Only what I have to."

He says, "Don't let this turn you into something you're not. You're a good person."

"I'm not a good person. I keep telling people."

"It's not what you say, it's what you do. What comes outta your mouth ain't always good, but what comes outta those hands that's something else. You won't listen, but I'm saying it anyways. Trust those hands."

I'm looking at my hands, head down, a little sleepy even, when a car or a truck, something big, rams into the side of the Pontiac.

I don't hear anything at first: I feel it: the seatbelt digging into my shoulder; my head snapping left, then right, banging hard against the side window; a pinching in my lower back as the car hurtles up onto the curb. The muscles at the base of my neck stinging when we finally come to a stop. Then the noises: a dull ringing in my ears, a throbbing on the side of my head, like someone's knocking to get inside my skull; the *thwopetty-thwop* of my heart, metal scraping, glass breaking. I hear Otto say, "Shit." The weight of his body hits me on the shoulder, his head slouching on my arm, not making an effort to right himself.

The radio spits out scores, "…Mavs over the Clippers 90-76…"

The car is vibrating in a clunky rhythm, the engine still running. Barely.

I push myself upright and look out the windshield. In the dark, it takes a minute for my eyes to adjust. The glass is cracked in places, and between the cracks, I see what caused all the pain and noise. A truck hit the old Pontiac on the driver's side and up front. I see the glare of the truck's headlights, its bumper—one of those extra heavy-duty jobs—like a big mouth with metal lips.

The driver is a dark shape, thin, wearing a ball cap. In profile, he's all chin. His hands on the steering wheel, his chin now pointing at me, watching. He jams the truck in reverse and backs up fast, stops, opens his door as if to get out and then changes his mind. The dome flashes on and off and I recognize the face.

I shake Otto hard. "We gotta go. This wasn't an accident."

"Shit. It hurts to breathe."

"In the truck," I say. "It's Roe…"

I wake, feeling hung over and headachy. I recall the dream, if it was a dream, and wonder what I'm telling myself. It's a goddamn life lesson, I know that. But what's it mean? And why does it hurt so much? And when does it end, because this one's not over. I hear tires squealing, turn in time to see the truck come at us again. Pull Otto into my lap, lean over him, and grab hold of his giant body. The truck hits us at an angle and careens off the driver's door.

The fucker backs up and rams us a third time.

Roe tries to back away but we're stuck, the old Pontiac and the truck in a clinch, not letting go.

I take a quick look around to see where we are. Make sure this isn't all part of the dream. Ervay and Federal, a corner of the old post office. It's after midnight and dead, not a car on the street. Everything shut up tight as Tupperware.

I open the door and pull Otto onto the passenger seat. Open the back, jump in and climb headfirst into the driver's spot. I try to get the old piece of shit moving forward, get us unstuck, but nothing happens. I glance left, see the big truck rocking back and forth trying to get unstuck. I do reverse, pedal to the floor, and the car crawls, metal screeching, until we're free. Stop, jam it into drive, stomp on the gas, and pull a hard right onto Federal. At St. Crawford, the road zigzags right, then left, into the tunnel where Federal passes under the Harwood Center. Roe in the rearview. I rocket into the tunnel, get about half way, jerk the wheel left and skid to a stop partially blocking the road.

This is a place I know. I even know some of the residents, the homeless that sleep here at night. Not their names, and most not even their faces. What I recognize, what I'm good at, is the shape of their bodies—if they hunch, favor one leg, shuffle or stomp when they walk. Some of the time, I tell them apart by the crap they cart around with them.

The tunnel is dark, wide, and with the road partially blocked, there's only one way to get at me: head on. The mood Roe's in, it's likely he'll ram the car just for fun. I throw my black bag over my shoulder and help Otto to his feet. He can walk with some help, and I lead him into an even darker tunnel, up the exit ramp to the overhead parking.

We don't get far. Otto collapses on the cement floor with his back against the wall. I drop my bag, pull out my baby ax.

"Don't make a sound," I whisper.

"You, don't do nothin stupid."

I creep back down the ramp. At the bottom, I look back up at Otto, can't see a thing, and hear what I believe is Otto sliding down the wall on his side. He's well hidden and not going anywhere.

Roe stands outside the mouth of the tunnel, his truck behind him, silhouetted against the massive concrete opening. A dull, bluish light shines down on him. The light's a long way off and weak, a puny glow that barely reaches the top of his head. It makes him look small and pointy, like a stick figure.

The scene is all shades of gray, as if the tunnel itself has somehow swallowed up all color. Hiding here in the dark, it's easy to believe there is no color, that everything within eyesight is just as it seems, gray or black or an inky, unnamed non-color. It's easy to believe the color's not just hidden under a blanket of darkness, but has actually disappeared or died. What's left is only variations of blindness, a blindness that once you get used to, once you stop squinting, stop searching for the color, isn't so bad. A good place to do things you might not do in the light. Things you would never do in bright sunshine. Things, no matter how right, just never get done if you have to look at the fleshy color of skin or eyes or of blood.

I don't belong in a place without color. Roe does.

I'm a dozen car-lengths, away pressed into a cutout in the wall, hidden in the blackness, my back against a door, the door locked. It's one of those charming places that vagrants call home for a few hours each night, and I'm surprised there's a vacancy.

I can see Roe, but he can't see me. He's mumbling at first, talking to himself, wondering how to come at me. Wondering why Otto and I won't just lie down and let him roll over us with that big truck of his. I hear him say a few more garbled words and then, "…the goddamn Clippers." I got it all wrong, he's not wondering about me. He's grumbling about a basketball game. A game his team won and still, he's bitching about it. He reaches into his pocket and comes out with a knife, casually pulls the blade open and holds it down by his side.

He looks into the tunnel and sort of yells, "We had a deal."

"I want to know about Billie," I shout back.

He turns in the direction of my voice.

"Okay." His manner is slow and measured. "Your visit to her house, she told Sammy about it. Said you snuck up on her, threw a brick through her window. I like that part, if it's true. Said you were mad at her, something she wrote about you, maybe about your work. Billie was a talker, hard to make sense of her stories sometimes. But I guess you know that. Said she talked you into doing that thing you do. Tore up her living room and came away with skinny black stick looks some like that asshole husband of hers. Hey, you still in there?"

"I'm spellbound."

"Okay, smartass. You know what she did with that stick? She sold it to Sammy."

He says it to hurt me. Like this little deception of Billie's, even if it's true, is the last straw this poor camel can take. What a dope. I move out of my hole, across the street, staying in the shadows. I know my way around, know where the security cameras are located, how to move without being seen. I ease into another cutout in the wall, one closer to Roe. It's wider and deeper, room enough for those noisy metal roll-up doors.

"Go on," I say.

"Huh," a voice says. It's a deep voice and close, on the ground next to me.

"It's okay," I whisper. "Go back to sleep."

"Huh? What?"

Roe turns into the sound. Takes a step in my direction. "She bragged about you. Couldn't get her to shut up. Said you could heal people, really heal them. Not that Sammy couldn't, she told him, but he still didn't like it. Didn't like hearing it one bit. Didn't like to think about it, and now you got Billie, Miss Never-Shut-Her-Mouth, reminding the old man that he's not so special any more."

The homeless guy, if it is a guy, still lying on the cold concrete, uncoils himself and kicks at me a couple of times. Not hard, and he doesn't come close. I'm standing five, six feet away. He doesn't look at me, doesn't even turn his face from the metal door, just kicks and grunts like a giant dirty baby.

Roe hears the noise and takes a step closer. "She said she got one of her own. One with her face on it. Look at her, she tells Sammy. Happy all the time, not so fat anymore. Whatever else good can happen to a person, it's happening to her. So she says. By this time Sammy's tired of hearing it. Tired of Billie, you ask me."

"She had her stomach stapled."

"Yeah, but Sammy didn't know about that. You think about it. This all started with you. Didn't like what Miss Never-Shut-Her-Mouth had to say about you, and the way you are you had to do something about it. Not so different from the good Pastor Sammy, you want to look at it that way."

I want to say I'm not the cause. That I'm not anything, not even a very good sculptor, but that's never mattered to me, and I'm pretty sure it shouldn't matter. It's about doing the thing you do well as well as you can do it, or better. About finding that place where it all comes together—muscle and mind and meaning—and then staying with it until that place fades away. And then you do whatever you do until you find it again. I want to tell him that I don't know what to make of the sculptures, that I'm just like everyone else, an outsider. I've never been sure if the healing is a gift or a curse, or if it has anything to do with me.

Roe says, "You have no idea what I'm talking about, do you? Neither did Billie. Her problem, she wouldn't shut her mouth."

I say "You killed her."

"I didn't," Roe says. "I told you."

"There's a witness says you did."

Roe doesn't say a word. He tightens his grip on the blade, inches forward, standing taller now, coming into the darkness, feeling his way along, aiming for my voice. The knife's out in front of him.

I kick the homeless guy in the back. Not hard. Not hard enough to get through the twenty layers of clothes, but hard enough to wake him. Hard enough to get him shouting in that deep, gravelly voice of his. "What's going…Get away from me, you bastards." A voice loud enough to give Roe a clear heading, maybe thinking that it's Otto's voice and that the two of us are cowering together in the dark.

I kick the guy again and quickly move along the concrete wall to the next cutout.

The guy shouts. Roe marches into the voice only a couple of feet away from me. I step out of the doorway and scrape the ax on the wall. The noise gets him to turn. We've changed places, me in the light, him in the dark. I no longer see a face, a body, a man even. What I see is a colorless stick figure, and I swing hard slicing across the neck. The one swing is all it takes.

I get Otto into the car and get the old Pontiac moving in the right direction. It's taken its time, but the pain is finally on me, my shoulder, neck, my lower back. My chest is one big bruise. The rush of adrenaline is gone. A trickle now, just enough to keep me moving forward, put some distance between us and the scene, get Otto to a hospital, get me into bed where I can sleep it off and pray that a nifty bout of amnesia sets in by morning.

Otto is slumped against the passenger door, a grimace on his face and droopy wrinkles under his eyes. He's not cut or bloody. Take away the ugly grimace and he looks okay from the outside. It's the inside that's broken.

I maneuver us past Bryan Tower, the shapeless glass box that looks dated in among the newer high-rises. I can see the car's crumpled reflection in the glass as we drive by. I listen to the sounds of scraping metal and wonder if the old Pontiac is gonna make it. The sound isn't loud, and after a few blocks it's almost soothing, a sort of high-pitched whine blocking out the hush of the city.

"I didn't have to kill him," I tell Otto. "I wanted to." The words in my head want out. Lots of words, and I'm just waiting for the right moment, a sign, something.

He looks at me, reading my face and says, "Don't tell me."

The only guy I think I can tell, and he says don't.

"Aww, Jesus."

Otto says, "Me and you were never here. Not together."

"Oh, so where were you?"

His eyes open wide and then he looks up, like he's thinking. "Minding my own goddamn business, and a car comes out of nowhere mashes into me. Over on Canton, behind City Hall. Know where I mean?"

"No."

"Right. They ask, I tell 'em I'm hazy on the where and what time. I come to. I drive myself to the ER."

"If who asks?"

"Doctors, police, the goddamn man from State Farm, whoever." He guides those big eyes over my way. "Nothing to do with you. You understand what I'm saying?"

I do. He's telling me that he'll take the heat, what he can, but what it feels like is he's pushing me away. Pushing when I don't want to be pushed. I want to pull. Grab hold of this big man and bury my face in his ratty coat. I want to tell Otto that taking a life is easier than I thought. It's the living after that hurts. I want to tell him the life I took is eating away at me and it feels some like he's living inside of me, and I can sense the bastard latching onto the part of me that makes it hard to breathe. It's hard to swallow and I let loose a little choking cough.

"Stop it," Otto says. "Whatever you got rolling around in that head of yours, just stop it." His voice is stronger now, telling me I get to choose what to remember, choose the things and the ideas I keep with me. Who I keep with me. "Shut it off. It's that simple. What you did's over and done. And right. And now it's time to shut it off. Like a spigot."

"You ever kill a man?"

"If I did, I wouldn't tell you."

Minutes later, I pull the Pontiac into the parking lot, the entrance to Baylor emergency across the street. Otto is looking at me, his head against the window cocked at a painful angle. He's wrong about one thing: it's not over. Over has a whole different feel to it. When it's over, you put it behind you, you give it away or throw it away and don't feel anything about it. It's over and you can breathe, only I can't breathe and I can barely swallow and I can't put what happened to Billie behind me.

With big, fat baby tears in my eyes, I stare back at Otto, waiting for him to tell me again that I did right. I'm ready for one of his hardnosed lectures about meaning and responsibility and value. I'm ready for this old guy, a guy's been through some shit of his own, to spell it out for me. Tell me about the value of a life. How Roe's wasn't worth shit. And mine is. Tell me again that I did right.

Otto says, "This here's a new beginning, you want to look at it that way."

"And if I don't?"

"Get going. Go on, before someone sees you." He waves me away and that's the end of my pep talk.

I don't move. Sit there stubbornly holding my ground and at the same time hoping he'll say something else. Something a little more insightful than "this here's a new goddamn beginning." But he doesn't. He opens the door, gets out, and makes his way slowly across the street. When he slips inside the glass doors of the emergency room, I crawl out of the car, take two steps and throw up on the pavement. After, I begin the long walk home.

In the morning, I roll over; pull the pillow over my head and try to drown out the noise. It's two more rings before I realize it's the phone next to my bed.

It's Pilar. She says, "I want to thank you for the sculpture," the one of her hubby, I suppose she means. No hello, no good morning, just straight to the thank yous. It's not a bad way to begin the day.

"You've seen it. What do you think?" I ask.

"Well, it's not ugly."

"I appreciate the flattery, but next time, don't feel you have to call."

Pilar says, "Why I called, Robert, that's my husband, he spent most of yesterday out there standing around. We both did. Not close, mind you, across the street with the others. Did you know the man who owns the building hired a security guard? He stands out in front of the place looking mean. He is mean, with a foul mouth on him."

"He's there to protect it?"

She says, "Are you kidding me? He's there to keep people like Robert and me from scaring away clients. It's a law office, Michael Barr, and the man's an ass. Get too close and he threatens to sue."

"Pilar, I was sleeping when you called."

On the other end of the line, I can hear the rumble of cars. I can picture it—a long queue of looky-loos, cars and trucks and tractor-trailers crawling north on Ervay and slowing at Wood. Peeking at the carved wooden column on the corner, at the sculpture of Pilar's hubby, and wondering what all the to-do is about. The volume on Pilar's cell is set way too high, so high that between the rumble of road noises I can hear Robert in the background: "Go on, ask." A pause. "Then give me the phone."

Pilar says, "How long does it take?"

"Does what take?"

"Till Robert gets better."

"I never promised he'd get better."

"I'm not talking about you. I'm talking about Robert. How long?"

There is a lull in the conversation. I glance at the canvas bag at the foot of my bed, hold the phone away from my ear, and reach over and unzip the bag. Pull out my baby ax and unsnap the leather sheath. There's no blood on the blade because I wiped it clean before I put it into the bag. No stains, no tell-tales whatsoever, but I'll have to get rid of it. I know that. It's something I don't want to do.

Pilar says, "Do you get channel 58?"

"I don't have a TV."

"Pastor Sammy's on, or will be later. Airing one of his crusades. The one here in Dallas. You should watch."

"Why?"

"Channel 58. One-thirty this afternoon."

I lay my baby ax on the workbench on top of a large sheet of brown paper. I run a pencil around the edge of the blade, down along the handle and up the other side. The tracing is a fraction larger than the real thing, but it doesn't matter because bigger might just be better. I've gotten stronger since I had this one made. I make some changes in the tracing by pressing harder on the pencil. The large blade gets even larger and the arc of the cutting edge flatter. The little blade, I make perfectly flat. I add a couple of inches to the handle.

I tape the drawing to the wall and stand back, imagine myself swinging the baby ax that isn't a baby anymore. It's time for a new name, and I've got one in mind.

It's 1:15 and I get another call. If I had to guess I'd say Pilar. I even know what she's gonna say: "The healing, what's taking so long?"

I pick up and hear a man's voice. "Miranda Tate?"

"What are you selling?"

The voice says, "Miss Tate, is that you?"

"Who is this?"

"You don't recognize me?"

The conversation ping-pongs until I figure out the clown on the other end is Pastor Sammy.

"I know who it is," I say.

"I want to invite you to watch a very exciting television special this afternoon."

"Yeah, one-thirty channel 58. Anything else?"

In the pause, I stare at the drawing of the ax.

Sammy says, "It's important that you stop what you're doing."

"Important to who?" I say, but Pastor Sammy is already gone.

The maintenance-workshop-general-fix-it room is on the ground floor. It's small and cramped, metal shelves filled with junk along one wall, a work bench piled with tidy stacks of tools along the opposite wall. There's a worn leather club chair and a twelve-inch TV in the corner. Otto's in the chair with his feet up. He looks tired and stubborn, his arms folded across his chest.

"You look all right," I say.

"You telling me or asking me?"

"What'd they say at the hospital?"

Otto says, "Nice lady down there said I'd live longer, I start taking the bus. She smelled good too. Had on scrubs with the words kiss me and honey and sweetheart printed on it."

"So?"

"So I say to her, I was to ask you out sometime, you okay we take the bus?"

I ask, "You hit on your doctor?"

"No. This was the lady took down all my information, helped me fill in all the paperwork."

On the small TV screen, I recognize Pastor Sammy. He has his hands in the air, his mouth flapping away but nothing coming out because Otto has the sound off.

"Well, you and the ER lady got something planned?"

Otto turns his head slowly, painfully, and looks me over. "You don't look good at all."

Pastor Sammy, on the other hand, looks spectacular, dressed in all white with gold piping, standing center stage at American Airlines Center. The place is packed: fifteen thousand hopefuls looking for sanction, for direction or—better—a shortcut to greater happiness and good health. Looking to come broken and leave whole.

A man comes on stage carrying a tall, thin, wooden sculpture. It's all of two inches on the tiny set, but I recognize it right away. Otto does too. The camera zooms in, filling the screen with its narrow wooden face. Otto's face. I can see little black knots below the eyes and the hint of a scruffy goatee that I don't remember carving. This was a present from me to Otto. A present he refused. This was months ago, back when I couldn't give them away. Otto finally relents, gracefully accepts his piece of kindling, he calls it, and later tells me he pawned if for a badly mistreated 30-inch widescreen HDTV. But he's watching a 12-inch. What happened?

On screen, the man passes the sculpture to Sammy, who grips it tightly around the neck with one hand.

"That's me," Otto says to the TV screen. He reaches up and rubs his own neck.

I say, "It's a piece of wood."

"With my face on it."

I slide over and turn up the sound.

Pastor Sammy peers into the camera and shouts. "Let me tell you something, brother. You watch it. Let me say something else, and I don't really care if you like this or not..."

"Is this man talking to me?" Otto says.

"...I'm warning you to stop what you are doing. I'm warning every magazine and newspaper and television news show; every man, every individual, who broadcasts and gossips and worship icons like these," He holds out the wooden Otto and glares at the crowd, castigating the masses, "You are in danger. And you'd better repent."

Sammy makes a show of putting both hands around Otto's wooden neck and squeezing, twisting the neck so hard that Sammy's face reddens. His mouth opens about to say something, but the words don't show up. He clenches his teeth, blinks away rage. It's part of the show; I know that, we all know it, but he's good at it, and I can feel my own throat tighten. I hold my breath, like I do watching an action flick whenever a car launches over a bridge railing and into the water below, the people inside holding their breath for about twenty goddamn minutes until Harrison Ford quits screwing around and pulls everyone up for air. I'm wondering now if I can hold my breath until Sammy lets go of Otto's neck.

I make it seven, eight seconds and then give up, suck in a big gulp of air.

Sammy prowls the stage, his head down, and then stops, rears up in front of a perfectly positioned camera, gets his voice back. It's harsh and raspy.

"I curse this, this creature and all hellish creatures like it growing in our city. I curse every man and every woman who worships such wickedness. I smite the person, and you know who you are, who carved this depraved figure. I smite thee with madness, and blindness, and a burning heart. And I smite any man or woman who dares to speak a word against this ministry. All these curses shall come upon thee, and pursue thee, and overtake thee, until thou follow the voice of the Lord."

"You still think he's talking to you?" I say.

"That man just put a curse on me."

"Not you. Me."

Sammy tosses the sculpture to one of his helpers.

"But any man, any woman, willing to turn away from these vulgar, primitive figures, and in turn raise his tongue in blessing toward this servant of the Lord, I bless thee. I bless thee with good treasure, and the work of thine hand. I bless the fruit of thy body." He raises his hands in the air. "I bless thee with healing."

Otto and I stare at the small TV screen, the crowd screaming and cheering like it's a goddamn basketball game.

"There's power here tonight, people," Sammy says. "Lift your hands and receive it." All hands shoot up. Sammy shouts over the roar, "I'm here to tell you, you will be healed tonight."

The camera zooms in on an old woman with a round, uncomprehending face. She's cheering too, if you can call it that, her hands in the air, mouth open and drool leaking over her thin lips. All around her the crowd is up on its feet. The round-faced woman is seated, unable to stand—and you know it, because if she could, she would, rocking back and forth the way she is, getting up her courage and a little momentum and then leaning forward pressing on the arms of the chair like she's about to stand, about to really do it this time, praying that angels will yank her to her feet. Only it doesn't happen. And the man next to her is just happy to see her try. He's bouncing on the balls of his feet, his arms way up in the air, looking at the stage and then down at the woman. He's animated in a clownish way, caught up in the circus, expectant. You can see it in his face, his mouth half open, showing off a set of perfectly shaped false teeth, so convinced that something good's gonna happen he's ready to take a bite out of it.

All this coming across in the three seconds the camera freezes on the couple, then we cut to Pastor Sammy, lumbering back and forth across the stage like a nervous, oversized rat, gazing squint-eyed at the squirming crowd, at the impassive ushers, at the catchers lurking at the edge of the stage. He shouts at them, all of them, angry and loud.

"Under this anointing, everything I say will come to pass. Listen to me. Tragedies will come upon the world, storms will strike, and floods and financial disasters will smother the land like a plague. And only those who have been giving to God's work will be spared. Give and you shall receive. Whatever you give, it will be used to measure what is given back to you. Increase your faith. Increase your seed in God's work and you—you way in the back there and you right here in front of me—, you will be spared."

The crowd eats it up. The applause is loud and genuine and frantic, the kind of spontaneous racket you hear at a horror show after you've had the shit scared out of you and just after you remember that this is why you came.

Sammy's voice is almost casual now, coaxing and supportive, asking the ushers to pass the envelopes, telling the crowd to make checks payable to Sammy Gann Ministries. Be sure to write legibly, print all credit card information on the envelope and don't forget to sign there where it says. Sammy tells the congregation, "Put your seed into the envelope, put your hands on that seed, and pray, and know that your prayers will come true. In the name of Jesus. If you are ready to give, say 'I am.'"

The camera cuts to a man in work clothes, the left side of his face slack, an envelope in his trembling right hand. Cut to a young Asian woman. Nothing wrong on the outside, but there's a whole world of pain behind those eyes. More singing, more cheers, more close-ups—a little black girl with withered legs, a white-haired guy in a tailored suit, a fat mom in a tight-fitting jumpsuit. All of them cramming cash and checks into little white envelopes, scribbling out credit-card information and then praying that all that money brings one whopper of a return. All of them mouthing the words, "I am."

It all comes off like an elaborate comedy routine that despite all the hard work, the clever dialogue, the light show and sounds, falls flat. It's just not funny.

Otto and I look away from the TV at the same time. I gaze at the neat rows of junk he's got lined up on the shelves. Paint cans and door knobs and rubber thingies. Shiny pieces of metal that likely replace parts of the building I know nothing about. I got replacement parts on the brain, and I imagine Otto a skilled surgeon, leaning over some large machine deep inside the building, dispassionately cutting out the parts that no longer work and replacing them with newer, shinier parts.

I'm looking at the shelves, at the parts.

Otto is looking at me.

"I can't watch this shit," I say, and I leave.

I'm standing out in front of my building under the awning, the Adam Hats sign putting out a soft glow, washing the red brick and stone trim of the building in a haze of light. It's not terribly cold. It's not raining yet, and it's not quiet. In fact, it's loud as hell, the distorted bawl of a guitar coming at me from across the street. Deep Ellum Live. It's a club for kiddies now, but it was the shit in its day. I saw Ziggy Marley there once, and David Byrne way after the Talking Heads but before all the gray hair. The front doors are on Canton, down to the right. It's almost eleven and kids are still shoving their way in. On a Sunday night, for chrissakes.

Otto eases out the door behind me, his wheezing giving him away. I turn and see he's got that lazy-eyed look about him.

"Don't you ever go home?" I say.

"I fell asleep."

I'm angry. Angry at the heavy-metal-psychedelic-bluesy-shit polluting the air. Angry at clouds for blocking out the moon. Angry at Roe. More than anything, I'm angry at Pastor Sammy Gann. For misleading people. For laying out the wrong choices: max out the old credit card and get a miracle or give nothing, get nothing. Most people see right through it because there are other choices. But Sammy's people, whole stadiums full of them, want something so bad their brains shut down. And when that happens it's easy to let other people—entertainers and politicians and parents and carnival barkers—do all the thinking.

"I don't know how people can be so stupid," I say.

Otto, picking up on it right away, says, "it's so stupid to want a miracle?"

"Want all you like," I tell him. "Stupid is giving your money to a man like Sammy."

Otto looks at me hard, like I just called him stupid, and turns away, bobbing his head and listening to the music. He's talking in a low voice, to himself at first and then to me, though he doesn't look at me.

"What if, say, the good pastor wasn't in the picture? How much would I give then?"

It's either a rhetorical question or he says it to goad me, trying to push me over some unseen edge, see what I'll do or say. Only Otto, lazy-eyed as he is, doesn't look in the goading mood. He looks more like he's got something on his mind. Like he's been waiting for me. He has this thing he does: tilts his head forward and looks up at me with those brown eyes hovering under the top lids, a sliver of white showing below the brown. He does it to get my attention. It looks good on him, and he's doing it now.

I hear some people shouting across the street and I zip around to see what's what. As I do, something inside pinches me, telling me to slow it down. My hand involuntarily moves to my chest.

Otto says, "How much would you give to do away with that pain? Cause some people would give all they got for a miracle like that. Good, hardworking people. People that save all their life for a rainy day." He pauses, looks up at the clouds and I'm thinking, *for chrissakes this is just the kinda shit you have to suffer through in a bad movie, and now I'm watching my good friend the-maintenance-man-protector-of-stubborn-white-girls pull the same shit.* "Hoping," Otto says, "that day never comes and they get to spend all that money on grandkids and kids of grandkids. Some people are willing to trade cars and houses and whole bank accounts for a miracle like that."

"People are stupid," I say.

"My daughter used to say, 'People are people,' but I think she meant the same thing."

"A daughter?" I ask.

"You didn't know, did you?"

I'm now angry with Otto, and I add him to my list. Angry for having a life I know nothing about. Angry at myself for not knowing, for making no effort to know. There's a pause in the conversation, a thousand-year silence that I'm suppose to break. Tell me about her, I'm supposed to say. What's her name? Why in the hell haven't you mentioned her before? Oh, and why bring her up now? But I don't say any of these things. I stand there and wait.

Otto says, "You and my daughter had some in common. She'd get so mad at people, she'd... well... She hated doctors." This is where I'm supposed to say that I hate doctors too, only I don't hate doctors, don't even hate that asshole Novak. Otto saying, "Made sense, really, if you knew what she'd been through." He says, "This one time, about your age, she needed a doctor. I tell her it's time for an exception. I talk to her just like I talk to you. Don't push, try to see it the way she sees it. It'd been some twenty years since she'd been to a doctor, but this here's special, I tell her. The streak has got to be broken. There's nothing a doctor can do, she tells me. There's nothing anyone can do, but to make me happy she'll go. On one condition. Know what that condition was? I bet you can guess, you give it a try."

"Tell me," I say.

"Don't want to give it a try?"

"Tell me."

"The one condition, she says is that I take her to one of Pastor Sammy's crusades."

"Oh, Jesus. What did the doctor say?"

Otto says, "Started as colon cancer, he said. Real nice about it, too. Lots of things he coulda done, we come to him sooner. By the time we asked for help, it had eaten up most everything inside."

"So, did you take her to see Pastor Sammy?"

Otto leans back against the building, folds his big arms across his chest and tilts his head at me.

"If you were to get inside my head, ask yourself what would I do, my baby girl is disappearing. I got no other hope, not one chance of beating this thing, outside of a miracle. You're me, not you pretending to be me. Just me. You know the man's a con, most everyone in the free world knows it, and you know in your heart that your daughter knows it. And she's asking me, you, to do something you do not want to do, and she knows it. Now you tell me, what do you do?"

It starts to rain. I turn and look up at the sky. I say, "I gotta go." I reach down and grab hold of my black canvas bag.

Otto looks down at the bag and breaths heavily through his nose, unwraps his arms. "Last night, I ask you to stop all this nighttime nonsense, and you hand me a picture. You still got it with you?"

"What picture?" I know the one he means, the girl in pink with the legs that don't work right.

"I ask if you found a spot for her and you tell me nuh-uh."

I pull the photo from my jacket. Hand it to him. He holds the picture up to the soft glow of the sign. "Cute."

"Yeah, you said. Her name's Emmy."

Where he'd put her, Otto tells me, where he'd put her is right in front of the man. Right there where he has to look at her every time he opens his door. The man? I ask and he gives me the look. He'd put her, Emmy—he says the name like I might have forgotten who we're talking about—no. not put, he'd *carve* that little girl's face right on Sammy's goddamn front door.

I walk up Crowdus to Elm and go left. A truck pulls up to the sidewalk next to me, an old Nissan clunker. Mary Ellen's clunker. She's got the corner loft on four directly above me. We haven't seen each other in weeks. Last time I passed her in the lobby, she grinned at me, a grin that reminded me of Handy, of how much I miss him, and I didn't say a word to her. Since, we have grown less chummy, if that's possible. She's originally from Florida, which might explain the sunny disposition, and her hideous paintings, lots of hokey sunsets in blues and dopey pastels.

Mary Ellen leans over, giving up a wide smile, and rolls down the passenger window. I'm surprised to see what might be actual pleasure on her face.

"You're coming, aren't you? Don't tell me you're not coming." She jams the Nissan into park. "You're not walking are you? It's miles. And it's going to rain."

I lean closer so I can see her face, say, "It is raining, Mary Ellen."

She says, "You got on the wrong shoes for rain. You need something with a thick sole."

She can't see my shoes, can't even see my knees. I look down at my Doc Martens and the extra fat soles. I say, "I've been warned."

"Don't worry about it," she says. "Get in, I'll drive you."

"To where?"

"You're funny. Get in, already."

Half the building I live in, and probably half of all the other lofts in Deep Ellum, are occupied by artists—painters and sculptors and photographers and printmakers. And lots of wannabes—graphic layout specialists, color theorists, Web designers, and computer animation geeks. None makes art and any one of them makes more money than the rest of us combined. And there's the don't-wannabes, the contrarians in black with scruffy beards and army boots. The ones that look so much like an artist ought to look, I count them too.

Mary Ellen's in all black. I'm in all black. And when we get to Froggy Bottoms, an upscale dive in West End, the gaggle of people bunched around tables in the corner, they're in all black. These are my people—artists and wannabes and don't-wannabes. People I haven't seen in months, some I know only by face, some not at all, and yet I feel a warmth spread though me. It's a warmth I miss only in hindsight. Seeing these people here and now, I pine for the hours we haven't spent together, the months since Novak diagnosed my little problem, the weeks since Handy left, the days I've holed up in my studio, venturing out only at night.

I try shaking the feeling I've had since cutting Roe twenty-six hours ago. Or longer, since seeing Billie lying dead on the floor. Maybe it goes back as far as Handy's disappearance—that my old self, the one that didn't care too deeply or too long about anything but soft wood and sharp tools, has slipped away from me for a while and now wants back inside before I do something really stupid.

Maybe this is what I need: this artist's night out, this gathering of misfits probably drawn together to discuss a cause in need of volunteer painters and sculptors and photographers.

The bar is dead—one youngish beer-pusher, chin down, scrubbing the bar top, a waitress, a bunch of clowns in black schmoozing in the corner. That's us.

Mary Ellen and I thread between tables. I'm moving slow and she gets up behind me, bumps me with her hips, says, "You know the crew." We get to the tables and she starts throwing out names. "Bruck, Tracey, Aline, Dwight, Shawna. Ronnie lives in the Murray building on Commerce. Jared's in the Continental on Elm."

Him I know, sort of. He works with old clothes and bicycle parts, wraps the parts—sometimes whole bicycles— with tightly knotted cloth and then paints the cloth. Hangs the whole shebang on the wall like a giant, cloth-covered Christmas ornament. I like them.

Jared makes a space for me at the table, says, "What's in the bag?"

"Dirty diapers," I say.

"Really?"

"Wanna smell?"

Three tables have been shoved together, those trendy tall tables without any stools. The ones where you stand around on sore feet and aching backs and try to take a load off by leaning on the table with your elbows until you tip over someone's beer. In the center of our table, a plastic take-out box is piled high with fried mushrooms. It's one of those white hinged Styrofoam jobs divided into three parts, the mushrooms spilling into all of the parts. I'm tempted to reach over and pop one of the mushrooms into my mouth.

Mary Ellen moves to the head of the tables. There's a column next to the table, and she places an elbow way up high on a column, places her other hand on her hip, and cocks the hip. It looks goofy, but it gets our attention. "Okay, why we're here," she says, and I watch her voice light up the group. Mary Ellen definitely has some kind of voice, squeaky and overenthusiastic at the same time, a cheerleader's voice, and I brighten at the sound of it.

She says, "Our goal is to ID this guy. Not to catch him. We just want to know who he is. Get a good look at him." Murmurs all around. "We each take a couple of blocks, roam, you know; look around. If you see him, get up close enough to make a positive ID and then walk away. That's it."

One of the nice things about being with your own people, at least to my way of thinking, is that you no longer have to spell everything out. You intuit, you fill in the gaps with whatever fits, or when you're completely lost, like now, you fake it.

"These any good?" I ask eyeing the mushrooms.

"I see questions," Mary Ellen says. "Okay, we get the name, face, whatever, and I give it to Pastor Sammy Gann. He gives us the reward."

I stiffen at Sammy's name, involuntarily reach for my bag and get ready to run. The compassionate, art-loving, good Pastor Sammy has managed to herd my fellow troublemakers—a group who are about as amenable to herding as humming birds—into doing his dirty work for him. He wants to catch me red-handed, offer up independent witness of my crimes. Prosecute, probably. And he's using my own people to make his case.

"How'd you hear about the reward?" I ask.

"Who cares how?" Jared wants to know about the money. "The question is, how much?"

"Ten thousand," Mary Ellen says. "Could be more, but the ten thou is a lock."

Jared put his elbows on the table, says, "We split, what, nine ways? That's eleven hundred each. It ain't much." This coming from a guy who dresses old bicycles in Goodwill clothing.

"Yeah, right," Mary Ellen says. "Some of you I talked to already liked the idea. For those I forgot to mention, I say we split whatever we get."

"What I mean," Jared says, his voice taking on a distinctive whine, "it's not much money. After the split, I mean."

An ugly guy across the table from me, it's either Dwight or Bruck—I don't know which, but I go for Bruck—says, "Is she in?" and points at me. The guy's shaggy, has a sketchbook in front of him on the table, a pencil in hand, gazing raptly at me. Ready for inspiration, the moment it strikes.

"Okay. These are all good questions," Mary Ellen says, her voice taking on greater gravity.

"Is she in?" Bruck says again in that gin-and-smoke voice of his.

"She's in," Mary Ellen says.

Bruck says, "How many times we gotta split this fucking pot? No newcomers, I say."

That seals it. I want in, even if it means roaming the streets looking for myself.

Mary Ellen drags her arm off the column, straightens her hips, moves over and shoves her way up to the table next to me, directly across from Bruck. Her supportive tenor's all but fizzled out.

"Pardon me for saying, dickbreath, I brought you in and I'm bringing her in. You don't like it, then do your own thing."

In the silence, I stare at the mushrooms, at the hinged lid of the container gaping back at me like a big, full mouth. I make eye contact with Bruck, glance at the mushrooms and lip-sync the words, "I'm starved. You mind?" Mr. Killjoy looks over at me with a distasteful grimace that might be ready to slide into sarcasm, only he doesn't know if I'm making fun of him.

"He's got a point, though," Jared whines.

"So you're out," Mary Ellen says. "Beautiful, that's seven ways. Who's good with math?"

Aline looks at Tracy and Tracy shrugs.

"Jesus, Mary Ellen," Jared says.

"This dude, what if I know him?" Shawna says.

"Excuse me?"

"I mean, what if he's one of us?"

Mary Ellen, her fussy sweater hugging her tiny waist, moves back to the head of the tables, asks how many artists Shawna knows, by sight, outside of this room? Shawna doesn't answer.

"He's not one of us," Mary Ellen tells her. "The guy's not even an artist. Come on. You seen his stuff? It's like he's working with a jackhammer. And he doesn't even use color."

"Gray," Bruck says.

"Gray?" Mary Ellen says. "Since when is gray a color?"

"It's the new blue," Aline says.

Mary Ellen rolls her eyes. "Bleary-eyed colorless sticks. That's what I see. An affront to rational taste, if you ask me."

"There's that," Shawna says, "but sanguine, too. The one on the other side of the Convention Center, on Austin, this Amazon-tall woman with the heels, that woman has got some kinda confidence." Absently, Shawna reaches for her beer, downs what little is left, and sees through the bottom of her glass everyone staring back at her. "I'm not saying it's good, it's just, there's something there."

I see it in my mind, my people, my peers strolling the streets like a gaggle of tut-tutting rubberneckers, staring at the side of the warehouse on Austin, at Billie's thick hair pulled back, a scarf around her neck, her arms pressed to her sides, trying to figure out what it is about this woman that looks so familiar.

"Billie," I say without knowing why. "They call her Billie."

"It is good," Bruck says to Shawna. And in a tone that strikes me as very unBruck-like, he says, "The figures, the poses, it's all done in a way that is intensely humane."

Shawna reaches for her glass, lifts it absently, remembers that it's empty and puts it down. Her face is bland, but her lips are moving. Barely, like she's talking to herself. Or rehearsing.

"The sculpture, graffiti, whatever you want to call it," she says, "it's in the middle of nowhere. The ones I've seen, anyway. You got to know where it is. Might even stumble on it and still not know what you're looking at. And yet, it's got a life separate from itself. Know what I mean?" I nod, out of politeness. The movement draws her look, and she latches onto me, not looking at me so much as through me. "I mean, we're sitting here talking about it, right. Some of us maybe haven't even seen it, and yet here we are. Talking about this sculpture, like that, giving it life."

Mary Ellen shakes her head impatiently, her tone mocking, "Yes, yes, I can read it now: 'The work pushes hare-brained spiritualism to a fresh level...'"

"The faces," Bruck says. "I like the faces. They remind me of people I know."

"Who?" Mary Ellen says.

"I don't know who, but I can tell you what."

"Okay."

Bruck says, "The artist. It's a woman."

Mary Ellen fixes him with one of her more severe squints, says nothing but wants more, like the rest of us, like me, all of us listening to an urban legend in the making, a legend we all know is horseshit but leaning forward all the same, waiting.

"It's sensuous, contemplative in parts, at least to me," Bruck says. "Calm may be putting it too strongly, but it's definitely saner than anything a man would do." He pauses, takes a long gulp of beer. "I don't want to catch this woman. If it were up to me, I'd join her." Bruck looks at me, says, "Looks like you're in." He turns and walks away.

I'm still staring at his ass when I lean over and whisper to Jared, "What's his stuff like?" He tells me, picture

Chuck Close and Julian Schnabel. Ahh, I say, and can't picture it at all.

"Okay," Mary Ellen says, "we're all artists, right, so we know we can trust each other, but just for fun, raise your right hand and repeat after me." Hands go up, Mary Ellen's, mine. Jared doesn't move, and then his hand lifts off the table maybe six whole inches. Mary Ellen's voice, a rousing squeaky cheer, "We find the guy, we split the pot."

We all repeat the words.

One of the girls, Tracey maybe, orders a screwdriver. Aline orders a light beer. I ask if anyone minds if I have a mushroom.

I reach for the pay phone, dial the number, and wait.

Pilar's sleepy voice says, "What, hello."

I say, "It's me. I need a favor."

"Miranda? Are you okay?"

"I'm downtown. I need a ride."

"It's late."

"How's Robert?" I say and she doesn't answer right away.

The phones at Froggy Bottoms are in a secluded, little alcove next to the men's bathroom with noise-amplifying ceramic tile covering everything. I hear zippers sliding down and oh-boy-that-feels-good sighs and tinkling water. Not once do I hear one of these pigs wash their hands.

"What's the address?" Pilar says.

The road to the Global Healing Center is familiar, the entrance gate an ornate wrought-iron thing with vertical bars wide enough to jog through. Pilar drives past the gate, follows the bend to the T in the road, and takes her time in a loopy U-turn. She scowls at me, her mouth clamped stubbornly shut, hoping I'll change my mind. She owes me. She knows it, but that doesn't keep her from wishing she wasn't here. Coming back to the gate from the opposite direction, she stops the car. Tells me again not to do what she knows I'm gonna do.

I lean forward, unzip my bag and reach inside for the hinged plastic container. Pop it open and offer Pilar a fried mushroom. She's pissed at me, but decides, yeah, one a.m., cold greasy fried mushrooms, why not?

We sit for a few quiet minutes and eat cold mushrooms together. I hand her the photo of Emmy. "So this is the one," she says.

"That's the one," I tell her.

I can see lights on in the tower, other lights coming from the dome, and below that several small square windows glowing yellow. Beyond the gate, the drive sweeps around to the left leading directly under the covered entrance to the building, a colonnade of fat wooden columns on the left, glass doors to the lobby on the right. I can't see any of this from the car, of course, but I remember it.

The column on the end, closest to the street, hardwood with lots of knots and a couple of deep crevices big enough to slip a finger into—that's Emmy's column.

"You're going to get caught," Pilar says

"You have no idea."

For whatever reason, my memories of Mother and me together are frozen in time. I'm twelve, she's older. I see snapshots of a gangly little girl, of a teacher giving her time and tolerance and answers. Answers only Mother could give. Answers about rebellion and conformity, about bravery, cowardice, sex, self-love, and death. And men. Mother had a trunkful of answers about men.

Loving a man was hard, she told me. Hurting him was easier. Find what he most valued and then tear it to shreds. Burn it or run over it or hide it. If his most valued thing is a secret, then expose it.

The trick, though, was that men won't easily give up their most valued thing. They squirrel it away, refuse to look at it, to touch it, to mention it, even. To learn what the thing is, you have to get close; become a friend, a confidant, a partner. I don't know what Pastor Sammy most values, but when I do, I plan to tear it to shreds.

I slip between the bars and wriggle my bag until it squeezes through. I move fast, hurrying across the parking lot. The Global Healing Center is dotted with surveillance cameras: the corners of the buildings, the tower, every other light pole in the parking lot, several of the taller trees. And the building entrances, of course. The portico next to the lobby has four small cameras tucked way up high in the corners. Nobody watching, according to Pilar, just hours of playback should anything happen worthy of watching after the fact.

One of the cameras is perched directly above Emmy's column. I march over to a lanky tree and yank out the tall stake holding the poor thing upright. The stake is just long enough to reach the camera. It takes several jabs to get the lens pointing down at me—not straight down, but angled to get a good look at me, a good look at the show. The other cameras I get pointed at Emmy—one looking her square in the face, the other two sort of three-quarter views, left and right.

There's plenty of light under the portico, so I don't bother with my flashlight. I drag over one of the dirty-collared trash cans and use it as a scaffold. I pull out the photo, grab my grease pencil, and make a few tentative marks on the column. Climb down and take a look. More marks, more looks. When it's done, the sketch of Emmy is tall, eight feet or better, her head turned slightly away, her hip cocked, and her long legs as impressive and reliable as prairie aspen.

I reach into my bag for my baby ax, but it's not there.

I know it's not there, but I let my hand sweep around the inside of the bag anyway. In the five years I'd been using the ax, it's always been there. Always nearby, always waiting, just in case. I'd gotten lazy the last couple of years—and stronger and better and more focused—but lazier, too. I'd grown used to it, roughing out a new piece, taking out large chunks of wood in a single whack. It was a part of the process. A part of me, fit into my hand like a foot fits into your ankle. What I hadn't realized until now was how much the ax, the tool itself, was a part of the outcome. Without knowing, I'd changed the way I work, the look, the form, the depth of a piece. Everything getting bigger, way bigger, and taller, with more angles, more severe, more hard-edged. But Emmy would be different. Different tools meant a different outcome, a way softer take on the little girl.

I reach into the bag for my No. 9 gouge and mallet and I go to work.

Monday morning, I show up at the machine shop around eleven, unannounced, ease through the big barn-style doors, and see Crawford across the shop, standing in front of his lathe. The green one the size of an SUV with the cream-colored doors. His gaze holds on me, angry that I didn't call ahead. Angry that I can't follow a few simple rules, like don't bother him at work, like call ahead, like stay out of the goddamn shop. Crawford is one of the best metal men I know, a beefy dock-worker look to him, and an old-school chauvinist, the type that believes women should be shielded from all the ugliness in the world. Like machine shops and square-jawed laborers who work in machine shops. And here I am, marching across the shop floor, with a handful of other button-pushers standing in front of giant, brightly colored metal boxes, punching numbers on consoles and giving me furtive glances.

Crawford looks back at his gauges, twists a knob, looks at the gauges again. He opens a small locker next to the lathe and hands me a paper sack with the ax inside.

"This one's a piece of work," Crawford says.

I take hold of the sack, slip the ax free. I say, "It's too goddamn heavy."

"That's what I told you when you showed me the sketch."

"I wanted size, not heft."

Crawford says, "You like thinking you can do better? You can't. This here is a jewel. High-carbon steel, balanced the way you said, but better. Quench-hardened. Tempered to a strength you won't find on this planet. Look at that handle. Hand-finished African purple heart, that's what that is."

"I can hardly lift it." In fact, it hurts to lift. I involuntarily reach for my chest with my free hand, up high near the collar bone, and rub. The arm and shoulder and chest feel bruised. A bruise that starts on the inside, working its way out.

He grabs the ax with his meaty hand. "You're not strong enough."

"It's got nothing to do with strength. It's about balance, rhythm…"

Crawford, about to say something shitty, changes his mind, watches me massage my chest, studies my eyes. "You don't look well."

Mother would have said, "Miranda, you look like shit. You don't take care of yourself, you don't make good on what God gave you, you don't respect yourself, then who exactly do you think is gonna do it?" It was another of Mother's life lessons. She'd say, "Honey, you got one job in this life, and that's to convince yourself that you're worth it. You're worth the time and the pain and all the aggravation that it takes to make a person worthy of respect."

Respect yourself, and people respect you. I get it. I got it the first thousand times I heard it. More than once, she put it another way: You disrespect a man, you make it hard for that man to respect you. This one never meant much until now. It's what I was doing to Crawford. Disrespecting his work. Disrespecting him.

I stop rubbing my chest and grab the ax out of his hand. Swing it a couple of times.

"Mother," I say.

Crawford knew Mother, and he knew she was one tough goddamned woman. I meet his glare, nod at the ax, telling him without telling him that he did good.

I say, "That's what I'm gonna call it. Mother."

I seat myself in a booth next to the window. Lunch at the AllGood Cafe, and I'm looking forward to it. I set the ax in its brown paper wrapping on the seat next to me. I'm tired, sore, tired. I'm still thinking of Mother, wishing the two of us were here, right now, having lunch together and then thinking better of it. It wasn't her snappy replies that got to me, it was the nonverbal cues—her eyes, the slant of her head. Sometimes all it took was a sigh, and I'd feel as though I'd been poked with a railroad spike.

If she were here, I'd tell her, "I'm tired. My arm hurts, my chest. Hell, I hurt all over." She'd tell me "So, do something about it." "Like what?" And she'd look across the table at me, tilt her head, maybe yawn. Her way of telling me I already know the answer to that one.

The *Morning News* feels light. I thumb the Metro section, scan the page and find what I'm looking for: *Man Found Fatally Stabbed.* A Dallas man stabbed and killed early Sunday. The body found at the Harwood Center, inside the Federal Street tunnel that runs through the building. Police aren't giving up the name, but describe him as in his 40s. The victim was robbed, everything taken, found completely naked. The vic's truck is missing. No witnesses.

If I didn't know better I'd read it as a car-jacking gone bad. A few homeless dudes now roaming the streets in Roe's upscale duds,

I order, eat, drink, look out the window, fondle the ax.

I ask the waitress for another glass of OJ and head for the pay phone. I call Pilar at the office. She picks up on the first ring.

"Is Sammy in?" I ask.

"Miranda?"

"Is he in?"

Pilar says, "If I ever began a conversation that way, my mother would twist my ear till I screamed."

I take a long breath. "Good morning, Pilar. Sleep well? I'm interested, really."

"He's in," she says, then adds that he might be out front. That they had a little incident last night.

"Is that so?" I ask.

"Uh huh." And Pastor Sammy's not sure what to make of it. Needs a little time to pray on it, maybe consult the good book. It was either vandals, a sin—which, the mood he's in, is punishable by death—or it was a miracle. Sammy hasn't decided on the spin.

"Spin," I say, stalling. "Tell him not to make up his mind until I get there."

I flip to another page of the *Morning News*. Scan the headlines, nothing. I ask the waitress for yesterday's paper. Or older, the last few days if she has it. She snaps her fingers as if she remembers something and scoots away. Returns with a pile of newsprint, some with egg on it. It takes a few minutes before I see the headline: *Graffiti Sculptor Cuts Deep* by Jeffery Henson.

The phone number for the news room is at the bottom of page 2A, right next to the box apologizing for yesterday's screw-ups. I dial, get transferred four times, and a man says, "Yeah."

I say, "Is this Mr. Henson?"

"Who is this?"

"I'm the person doing the carvings."

Henson says, "You got the wrong number."

"On the sides of buildings. Wood Street, Austin, Evergreen, Browder."

"Browder?"

"Yeah, Browder. You ever get out of the office?"

"You're the graffiti sculptor?"

"That's the best you could come up with?"

"It's what we call him, her, you, if you're telling me the truth. You'd know that if you'd read any of my stories. So you say there are four of them."

I can almost hear him scribbling down notes. I say, "Nine. Well, ten if you count the one last night at the Global Healing Center. And before you ask, her name is Emmy."

Henson says, "Just whose name are we talking about?"

"I called because I thought you might like to see it. Give you an excuse to get out of the office."

"An interview, you mean."

I say, "Come out to the Healing Center, you'll figure it out."

"Look, you want me to fight rush-hour traffic, you need to give me something newsworthy."

I can hear Henson tapping his pencil on his coffee cup. Okay, I tell him, not entirely sure how to go at this.

"Pastor Sammy Gann and I are partners." The tapping stops. Henson, playing it cool, not jumping in with the questions, showing some poise.

One last thing, I tell him. I need a ride.

My mind is on Pastor Sammy. What I'll say to him when I get to the Center. How I'll say it. Come on strong, go right at him, angry-like, or be cool, make him ask the questions, me giving up only one or two words at a time, if that. I'm thinking about the one or two words when I hear myself say, "Billie Hannah."

"That again," Otto says, cheery disinterest in his voice. He's in the hallway outside my door, his back to me, on his knees, all hunched over the plastic cover of an electrical outlet on the floor. An outlet I don't recall ever being used. Wires spring out of the hole in the wall. Parts of the building are ninety years old, and there's lots to be found in these walls. Most of it bad.

He glances at me sideways, at my black bag, says, "I see you got your tools with you. Got any wire cutters in there?"

I say, "You open up Pandora's Box and you forget your cutters?"

"I misjudged," he says. "That ever happen to you? You start something hoping for a little fix, and the more you work at making it right, you know that a little fix just won't do."

"Maybe you should have left it alone," I say.

Otto says, "That what you do? See something broken, you leave it alone?"

"I gotta be someplace." I march past him to the end of the hall, hear some asshole outside laying on his horn and glance back at Otto. He hears it, shakes his head, says, "Where you off too in such a hurry?"

I say, "It's not important."

"You were smart," Otto says. "You'd give the man what he wants."

Lately, this is the way we communicate—me not giving away anything and Otto stepping over my flimsy hurdles and reading my mind—and, it's starting to grate on me. I say, "I don't know what he wants."

"You do."

I tell him, being a real smartass about it, "He wants a big fat sculpture of himself, the conceited pig."

"That," Otto says, "And what else?"

I look up, like the answer's floating overhead, and tell him that he wants me to stop the graffiti art.

Otto turns all the way sideways and looks up at me.

"That too, but a man like Sammy aims a bit higher. He wants what you got, and he don't have it. Admit it or not, what you do makes people better. Maybe better than they been in years."

The asshole outside starts in on the horn again. This time more insistent: three long howls followed by a couple of short yelps.

"Friend of yours?" Otto says.

"Give me a break."

Otto rubs his hands on his pants. Dark gunk streaks his khakis. He eyeballs me, cocks his head the way he does.

"Sammy looks at you, he sees himself. Only you got the juice right now and he don't. Can you give him that? Can you give him the power to heal? Cause that's what he's after."

"I wouldn't if I could."

"No, but Sammy doesn't have to know that. He's a con man, so he sees you as a con. Why not let him see what he wants? Use it if you can."

The asshole laying on the horn is Jeffery Henson, sitting up high in a large, square-edged SUV, the driver's window down, squinting at me as I come bounding out the door. I bet anything this is the way the man goes through life—impatient to get on with it, always in a hurry to kick over the next stone. It's the bedrock of slash-and-burn journalism; keep moving. He has gray hair and a scowl with lots of fine wrinkles, and he needs a shave. He's out of the car, taking me by the arm, directing me into the driver's seat, saying, "You drive, if you don't mind. I'd like to ask you a few questions on the way. Take some notes."

I resist the tug on my arm, don't move, don't speak until he looks directly at me. I say, "At feeding time, old rancher-types drive into their fields and lay on the horn. It gets the cows a-coming."

Henson says, "Yeah, well, we don't have all day."

"It's rude, is what I'm telling you."

"What is?"

"You, treating me like a cow."

"Oh, for chrissakes," Henson says. "I'm sorry for honking. Will that do it for you? Now let's go."

He grabs my bag and puts it in the back. I hoist myself up into the front seat. Lots of leather and plastic made to look like real wood. A young man's in the back with a camera aimed at my face. I hear the click and whir of the speed-winder.

The SUV's running, so I move the seat forward, buckle in, wait for Henson to strap in and punch it. The cameraman, still spying me through the lens, bangs his head on the side window and curses. Henson glares at me. I take Canton three blocks west, then zig up Central and zag onto

Commerce. I make each turn with a little extra zip. We approach the Magnolia Hotel and I slow to get a good look at the place. It's one of my favorite buildings—the massive stone columns, the arched entryway, all those 1920s details. It's a shame there's no wood.

Henson glances at the hotel, reads my thoughts, asks me why on the sides of buildings? I don't answer and he says okay, why at night? I tell him it's dark at night. We must be getting to it, because he slips a small notebook from his pocket, makes some squiggly lines on the bottom of the page, priming his pen. He asks how much I get paid. He makes a little dollar sign on the top of the page. I tell him for the graffiti? One handful at a time. Henson pauses just a beat, like I'd caught him off guard. I take one hand off the wheel, mime reaching into a collection bucket, pulling out a big wad of bills and jamming the bills into my pocket. The young dude in back likes what he sees through the lens, giggles. Chuckles? Young men don't giggle much. *Click, click, whirrrr.*

At Akard, we stop for a red light.

"The way newspapers work," Henson says, "you say it and I write it down. This thing you're doing with your hands, I can't print that."

"Have you seen them?" I ask.

"They're ugly," the dude says. "It's why people like them."

"So why on the sides of buildings?" Henson asks.

"Ask your man here. He seems to know what's going on."

The dude says, "So people can see them that don't go to galleries. Art for the masses, that kinda thing. The ones I've seen are more in-your-face then what you get in a regular gallery. They got that mad-as-hell look about them."

Henson says, "That's enough, Chad."

The light changes and we're moving again, coming up to the onramp for I-35. "Chad," I say, "you see them as angry?"

"More like hurt," he says. "Like people who want to get even."

Henson says, "What's the connection between you and Pastor Sammy Gann?"

"I'm not sure how to answer that."

"On the phone, you said you were partners."

"I'm not ready to talk about it."

"For chrissakes," Henson says. "All I have so far is me asking questions and Chad here giving the answers." He seemed about to say something else, but then looked way, staring straight ahead at the dark, at the traffic lights.

"What do you know about Pastor Sammy?" I say.

Henson finally on solid ground, a topic he knows something about, relaxes, tells me Pastor Sammy Gann is first and foremost a money machine bringing in over $200 million a year. The money's donated for missions and crisis relief and feeding programs in Dhaka and Calcutta and West Hollywood. But the missions never get built, the programs never funded. People give because the man promises miracles, guarantees them if your donation is large enough. Henson stops talking and looks sideways out the window following the taillights.

"Is that where you come in? Are you the new miracle worker? Rumor is your art, if it is art and if it is you, can heal."

I say, "Do you believe that?"

"It's not important what I believe. I'm just here to write it down."

"They do," Chad says. "I've got footage. People stand around, some afraid to get too close. Others trample people to get up front and touch it. Why all the aggravation if there's nothing to it?"

"Is that the way you see it, Miss Tate?" Henson's sounding professional now, almost distant, knowing this might be the single usable sound bite in this whole lousy interview.

"Uh huh."

Henson says, "You're admitting that the graffiti sculptures can heal?"

As he says it, I see the entrance to the Healing Center, slow the SUV to a crawl, and turn into the parking lot. I feel suddenly like a tour guide, perky, my voice projecting.

I say, "And directly ahead of us, we have the Healing Tower."

"Miss Tate," Henson says. "Are you saying that your art can heal?"

I say, "The dome, see the tip of it there? Below that dome is the Healing Hall of Faith. You or Chad here have any prayers you'd like put on the fast track, that's the place to do it."

"If you don't want to answer my question, just say so."

"What was the question again?"

"For the record: Are you telling me that the sculptures heal?"

I pull the SUV into a parking slot and look back over my shoulder. directly into the camera. *Click, click, whirrrr.* I say, "Why don't you take that up with Mr. Money Machine."

The three of us cross the parking lot, aiming for the portico, and I can feel it coming on me—that wave of sadness, the one I feel each time I get close to Sammy, an awareness that sickness and tragedy gravitate to this place, this man.

Forty or so people crowd around the column closest to the road, near the carving of Emmy. It's twice the size of the little girl, cut deep into the column. The last time I'd seen her—the wooden Emmy—she was all contrasts, nothing but lights and darks, with a dazed look to her, the halogen lamps freezing her, off balance, staring up into the light. Now, in the daylight she appears poised, smoother, rounder. Light comes at her from odd angles, bouncing off the walls and the landscape and the people standing nearby.

Henson and Chad slink into the crowd.

A guy inches up next to me. It's Emmy's father wearing a pressed white dress shirt, white tee underneath, and the collar wrinkled where a tie might have been.

"It's you," he says. Yeah. It's me. He asks if this is my work.

"It's what I do," I say.

Dad says, "Pastor Sammy's assistant called me this morning. She invited me to come and take a look."

It's a statement, but behind it is a question, and he's asking me to help him make sense of what he sees. Why a sculpture of his little girl? Why here? And what, exactly, is a father's role in all this? I don't see Emmy or Mom anywhere, but I know they're here. I can feel it: Mom also dressing up for the occasion, wearing something churchy; Emmy in her pink dress, not the one from Saturday, another one.

Dad stares at the sculpture, at the mass of bodies crowding around, at Chad now strong-arming his way to the front of the mob, his camera held high overhead, clicking away. This event, whatever it is, becoming bigger than Dad expected. Bigger than he can understand. It's a public happening, not really about his little girl any longer, if it ever was.

"I'm sorry," Dad says. "I don't know your name."

"Miranda."

Dad says, "Miranda, what do you think about me? A man who comes to a place like this for help. A man who drops everything to go see a sculpture of his baby."

"I think you're a good father."

Dad stares at me guiltily, then swivels back to look at the wooden Emmy.

"What is it about something revolting that makes you want to touch it?"

"You want to touch it?" I ask.

"Do you want me to?"

What I really want, suddenly, urgently, is to pee. What is it about this place that makes me rush for the bathroom?

On my way to the restrooms, I'm surprised to see Pipsqueak standing near one of the lobby doors keeping an eye on things, a flesh-colored bandage across his upper lip, the lips swollen, parted, and the teeth clamped tightly shut. The Squeak is standing rigidly at attention with just his head swiveling side to side, looking for something or someone.

There's a lot I don't like about this place, a lot I don't know, a lot that scares me. Pipsqueak's unpredictability is one of the things that scare me. And when I get scared, I get angry. And when I get angry, I do things I shouldn't. The bag in my hand, I place gently on the ground, reach down and ease the zipper open a few inches—just enough to slip my hand inside and remove the mallet. I stuff the handle into the waistband of my jeans, around back.

Pipsqueak finally sees me moving right at him. Sucks in his stomach, acting tough.

I say, "How's the mouth?"

"Bitch," he says, but it comes out as "vish," or something close.

His lips are badly swollen, the mouth wired shut, and a mass of braces on his teeth, all of which make it hard to insult anyone with any real sting to it. I laugh when he says it, one of those involuntary little hiccups of a laugh, because the word, the way he says it, sounds genuinely funny. Pipsqueak thinks I'm laughing at him, naturally, and his face goes red. He puckers those big lips and makes a soft yakking sound like an angry baboon. He wants to grab me by the throat and squeeze, and I dare him to do it, standing as tall as I can, as tall as The Squeak in fact, and glare back at him.

He says, "You did this to me," or it could have been, "You, come with me." In that mumbly-jumbly voice of his, it could been anything, maybe extending an invitation for a smooch out back behind the Cotton Bowl, a date to go boxing. Whatever it was, the confidence in his voice makes me want to hit him with something heavy or kick him in the balls, do it first, with attitude, tell myself not to be afraid of this guy.

An old couple brushes past and totters through the doors into the lobby. I watch them go, and when I look back at Pipsqueak, see a tiny rivulet of drool coming out of the corner of his mouth. He doesn't know it's there, can't feel it. I imagine the guy walking around all day slobbering on himself, nobody telling this asshole how stupid he looks. I reach up, point at the spittle, about to say something caustic when he grabs my arm, his stubby fingers clamped above the wrist. He jerks me close to him, barking at me in baboon-speak, spraying me with spit. The guy is strong, and he's nuts, making a scene here on the front steps of the Center, but he can't help himself. I stare pseudo-casually away, which infuriates him, and he wrenches my arm backward, throwing me off balance.

It's time, and I reach behind me with my free hand, take hold of the mallet and bring it around in front of me. In Pipsqueak's face. I say, "Remember this?"

He flinches, immediately narrows his eyelids, and begins smacking his lips. The height of friendliness in baboon society.

The lobby bathrooms are done up in a sort of manger theme. There's a wide ledge on the far wall decorated with miniature bales of hay where moms get to change dirty diapers and babies get to woogle around in the itchy grass like baby Jesus. The lighting is yellowish and dim. The rest of the room is a celebration of dusty neutrals—ochre and umber and sienna.

I say, "I really have to pee." This to the four side-by-side toilet stalls and to the pairs of feet shuffling beneath the doors. All the stalls are full. The fronts are painted to look like two-thousand-year-old barn doors. Churchy types behind the doors, I imagine, ladies who take their time getting comfortable before getting down to business, take in the surroundings—the look-alike Dead Sea Scroll tissue dispensers, the coat hooks molded into trumpeting angels, the hand-painted toilet seats.

I rap on the closest door, say, "I don't mean to be rude, but I'm having a sort of medical emergency here."

"Patience, dear," a voice says, the tone mumbly, like someone eating potato chips with their mouth closed.

"And to patience, godliness," a buoyant voice behind door number four adds.

"And to godliness, brotherly kindness," says Number One, "and to brotherly kindness—"

"I'm not kidding around," I say. "You don't hurry up and I'll squat right here. Give the place a real nice sheepy smell."

"You wouldn't," says Number One.

It's easy to be mad when your bladder is about to rupture. It's not the women I'm mad at. Clearly their business is more important than mine—boning up on Peter and Luke, tending to nature's humdrum needs, bingeing on Pringles. I'm still thinking vividly about what I'll do to Pastor Sammy when I see him—a clear mental picture of my hands around his neck, shaking him violently, his face going red, the ugly rug slipping to one side of his head.

I'm staring at the stall door when I set my bag on the floor, unzip my pants—as loudly as possible—let out a big breath and say, "You finish up in there, watch your step. There's a puddle out here and you don't want to leave the Nativity with whiz on your shoes."

Behind door number two, I hear rustling, the cheerful sound of a toilet flush, and giggling. The stall opens and Emmy, wearing a pink striped shirt hanging out of her jeans, the jeans still unbuttoned much like mine, pulls hard on the door and falls forward, tummy first, onto the polished terrazzo floor. She's not hurt, not even surprised at the misstep, and has a sort of whoopsy-daisy look on her face as she peers up at me. Mom, standing behind her, reaches out to help her little girl and then stops herself.

I take a step closer, not so much to help Emmy, already spraddled on the floor, as to step over her little body in my rush for the toilet.

"Don't touch her," Mom says. "She wants to do it herself."

"You mind if I squeeze in there?" I say as I push past her into the stall and shut the door.

It takes me all of ten seconds to do what I have to do, and I enjoy every moment of it. Zipping up, I hear Emmy say, "Watch this," and Mom saying, "Emmy, please," her tone worried and encouraging at the same time. I ease out of the stall and scoot over to wash up at the cattle-trough sink.

Mom watches me in the mirror, both of us taking inventory at the same time. Me in scruffy jeans, a vintage black tee with "AC/DC Live" printed on the back, unwashed red hair, one or two new freckles I hadn't noticed before high on my cheeks. Mom's in a cozy slouch sweater and gray skirt.

She says, "It's you."

"Your husband said the same thing."

She says, "I don't know what to say."

"I have that effect on people." I dry my hands, reach into my pocket, and pull out the photo of Emmy. "Here."

Emmy, up on her feet now, has made her way to the large, fresco-like painting on the opposite wall—a sort of medieval Nativity scene with an ox and an ass nuzzling the Christ Child. The horsey, Emmy calls it, is high on the wall just out of reach, so she climbs onto the fat, rustic baseboard and launches herself upward grabbing for the horsey's nose. She gets close, too, and then lands in a heap on the floor.

She's still untangling herself when she sees the photo in my hand, cranes her head around, and waits to see what's next. The sudden quiet in the room is prayerful and restrained. The church ladies in the stalls stop their shuffling. Mom stops fussing with her sweater. She looks at the snapshot, but doesn't take it. Her eyes dart from the photo to the nativity scene on the wall, with the ox and ass and baby Jesus, to Emmy, trying to draw a connection between the painting and her little girl and me. Or at least, that's how I see it. A woman who only hours ago was teeming with hope that her little girl would some day be running and jumping and grabbing for things just out of reach. A woman used to a solid foundation where cause precedes effect. She can see the effect, all right—Emmy is doing just what any healthy four-year-old ought to be doing. But what she can't get her mind around, not exactly, is the cause.

"Emmy…" Mom says to me. "You know about MD?"

I shake my head.

"Muscular dystrophy."

"Jerry's kids," I say, still holding out the photo.

"Well, yeah, that's sort of the happy version. The unofficial MD holiday. All the other days, it's not so much fun." We both turn to look at Emmy. "Started out she had trouble walking. Waddled around the house and we thought it was cute, something she'd seen in a cartoon. It wasn't. She's four now, almost five, and she developed it when she was three, we think. She fell a lot and couldn't pick herself up. It got so she couldn't sit upright without help. We took her to a doctor who diagnosed MD, no doubt about it. It could be worse because it comes in several flavors. That's what he called them, flavors, like Emily's up and caught herself a bad case of Rocky Road. It turns out she's got your basic vanilla. With vanilla, we get twenty, twenty-five years with her. All the while watching her waste away."

Mom stops, collects herself. "We went to other doctors, counselors, support groups, the whole thing. Know the first thing they tell you? It's inherited. I did it, or my husband; it's his fault, one of us. I didn't know. The thing is—and they tell you it just doesn't happen—I always believed she'd grow out of it."

Emmy is now playing hop-scotch on the unlined floor, bouncing unsteadily on one leg and then the other, stepping back, spinning circles and singing a song with nonsensical lyrics.

Mom says, "There's no cure. But look at her."

"I am looking at her. She looks happy."

"She does, doesn't she."

I hear the rattle of wrought-iron latches. A woman inches out of stall number three. She glances at me, at Mom, at Emmy, says, "I'll be right back," and scoots out the bathroom door.

Just as quickly, doors one and four open up and the women step out. Number Four, a sweet, putty-faced matron in a fitless dress, hoofs it to the sink and begins scrubbing her hands. Number One, with the mumbly voice, stands there, slightly bulge-eyed, her hands clasped in front of her like a schoolmarm, watching me.

Before anyone says a word, Number Three is back. Following her are a string of looky-loos, noisy, energetic women tired of staring at the wooden Emmy, now almost frantic with the expectation of seeing the flesh-and-blood Emmy.

The line of people streaming into the bathroom is steady and unending. It's not three minutes before the manger is standing-room only. Some of the women steal glances at me, some cozy up to Mom—knowing, but asking anyway, if the little girl is the one carved on the column outside—but most content to watch Emmy playing ballerina.

Emmy looks like she's forgotten the world: dancing, hopping, kicking one leg and then the other high in the air, occasionally falling to the floor in a playful sprawl. And then just as fluidly picking herself up and beginning a clumsy, twirly, arm-swingy rhumba.

Emmy's a girl who knows how to fall. She'd had years of practice at it, knows all the nuances of the butt flop, the knee scuffing stumble, the face-first tumble. What she's learning now is the joy of picking herself up.

Number Three pushes her way through the crowd to me. She has a large nametag pinned to her blouse in the shape of a bird. The name, Annabeth, embroidered in blue across the bird's body. She touches my arm, says, "A guy, he's outside waiting. For you, I think."

I say, "Pipsqueak. Short guy, big arms, never shuts his mouth unless you wire it shut?"

"That's him. Boone," she says. "Some people around here call him Little Boone, but he doesn't like it. He can be mean."

I grab Mom, tell her I could use her help. A man outside this door…That's all I get out when Mom says, "What about him?" I tell her that I'm unwelcome here.

"I don't understand," she says.

"I'm not sure I do, either."

Mom says, "Does any of this have to do with Emmy?" Mom makes a connection that I hadn't. Yeah, it has to do with Emmy, and me, and Pastor Sammy and the Global Healing Center, but I don't say any of this.

Mom says, "He wants to hurt her?" I tell her no, he wants to hurt me. She doesn't ask his name, what he looks like, or why exactly he's after me. Just spreads her arms, waving at the women around her, many pushing and shoving close to hear what's being said.

"I have an idea," she says.

"You don't know this guy," Annabeth says. "What if this idea, whatever it is, doesn't work?"

I unzip my bag and pull out the mallet. I say, "I can always hit him in the mouth with this."

The women all around me are inspired with new purpose, though what that purpose is, exactly, isn't clear. Some see Emmy's dancing as a sign—good things can and do happen. Some are staring at me, and what they see I can only guess: a sculptor, a woodworker from the far shores of Deep Ellum, an attention-grabbing fake. But most of the women are huddled tightly around Mom, who is diagramming her scheme on the palm of her hand.

This group of women is about to put themselves in harm's way. Because of me. I'm anxious to get going, to get out of this goddamn crowded manger, its air foggy with Diva and Fifth Avenue and White Diamonds—unwelcoming old-lady odors. A woman next to me looks pickled in the stuff.

She hasn't opened her mouth, but I know the voice is high and squeaky. I know because the woman is the image of Ethel Mertz, the curly hair and round face, the wide open mouth. For chrissakes, I'm in a 1950's sitcom—the episode where Lucy talks her women's club into staging an operetta, only she's too scared to go on stage. When it comes time for her big solo, Lucy hides behind all the other women. It was both funny and sad—Lucy Ricardo smitten to jibbers with her one chance at stardom, but when it was right in front of her, her first impulse was to turn and run.

I pick up my bag and set it on the counter next to the sink. I look at myself in the mirror, brush red hair out of my face, remind myself that I'm not Lucy.

I drop the mallet into the bag and casually take hold of a small wooden handle, like the handle of my baby ax without the blade. This one's fiddleback maple with a wavy, rippled grain, about fourteen inches long and light as a penny compared to the mallet. I slip it into my back pocket.

I zip the bag, wash my hands, move over to the towel dispenser and sneak quietly out the door.

I don't see Pipsqueak until I'm halfway to the lobby. And I didn't believe I could get within a thousand feet of the guy without getting a whiff of him—oxidized sweat and testosterone and steroids—yet there he is, hiding behind one of the stone columns. Most of his body's hidden, all but the wide shoulders and one pumped-up bicep, the short sleeve scrunched high into the armpit showing off the muscle.

Walking up to him, I say, "That thing about big muscles and teeny weenie peckers, is that true?"

Pipsqueak doesn't answer. He pokes his head out from behind the column, looks past me down the hall and then behind him back into the lobby. No one in sight. Then asking, "Wa 'ook so long in 'air?" Pipsqueak's lips move like an old sock puppet, his smackers going extra wide to compensate for the jaw. His speech is measured and some of the words aren't fully formed, but I know what he means.

I say, "A lady in the stall next to me was telling a joke. About this pecan head, a real 'tard called Little Boone. The guy keeps getting into trouble, and he can't see that he's doing it to himself. It's funny," I say, "if you're not retarded."

Pipsqueak doesn't move, but I can see the blood pumping in his arms, his wrists, the back of one hand. The large veins popping out from the skin. All that hate and anger squirreling throughout his body.

I say, "Want me to tell you the punchline?"

He reaches out for my chin and I slap his hand away.

He says, "Everyfing's a zhoke oo you, is 'at it? Wha' you did oo me, oo fink iss is funny? I godda ea' through a straw. Iss hard to breath. I go innoo a coughing fit, I could suffocae mysel."

I say, "Does it hurt to laugh?"

"How 'ould I know."

I say, "I Love Lucy, you ever watch that show? There's this one, Ethel says, 'What do you mean you didn't have a baby?' and Lucy says, 'I didn't. I didn't have a baby. It was a piece of cheese.'"

He touches the bandage on his upper lip, giving himself time to think about it, says, "You gotta fing for babies, is 'at it?" he says. "'at little girl, she means somethin' to you. What you did out front, you think that can protect her? You think if I wanted I couldn't tie them legs of hers into knots. A cinch knot, like my daddy showed me, so tight nobody'd get her undone. I'm through with her, I'm startin' in on you." He brings both hands out in front of him, clamps the hands together and squeezes. The muscles in his neck go wide and flat, his lips press tightly together, and his jaw strains against the fine wires holding it in place.

Amazing how quick I start to understand him. It's hard to tell if this is supposed to be intimidating or entertaining. The poor schmuck drooling now, the slobber inching its way down to his chin.

I say, "I never told you how the joke ends."

"Shut up." Pipsqueak says it as we both hear a door open. Mom sticks her head out of the restroom and then gets shoved from behind into the corridor. The other women are desperate to see what's going on. One by one, my rescuers pile out until we've got the whole clan in the corridor. Watching.

"What do you want?" I say to Pipsqueak.

He looks at me, lowers his voice, says, "You got no idea what's going on here."

"How about you fill me in?"

"What you did to that little girl. Sammy don't like it. You think you the only one can do that? You ain't that special, and you ain't the first. You ain't even the second."

I say, "The second what?"

Now in a voice meant to be heard, he says, "I godda search your vag there." I know what he means. I put the bag on the floor, unzip, and pull the opening wide. Pipsqueak sees the mallet and smiles, like he's got nothing to worry about. He says, "Sean says to keep you out of the building. Off the property would be better."

"Sean," I say, "the guard with the buzz cut?"

"What he says goes."

I say, "I'm not going anywhere until I talk to Pastor Sammy."

Pipsqueak says, "I was kinda hoping you'd resist."

He reaches forward with his stubby arm and I slap at it, but this time it doesn't move. He's all muscled up now. The hand and forearm and bicep fused into a club. He grabs a big wad of my tee shirt in front. His eyes lock on mine and he performs this little show in slow motion, daring me to do something about it. His grip causes my tee to bunch tight over my breasts. I'm not wearing a bra, and my left breast is swollen into a ponderous half-moon as supple as a hubcap. Pipsqueak likes what he sees—the nipple showing through faded cotton.

"So what now," I say. "We just stand here and you stare at my tits?"

Pipsqueak looks down at my tits, not sure what he's seeing—the right one on the smallish side, the left an extra large. It's all the distraction I need. I snake my right hand around back, grab hold of the handle and whip it out, hitting Pipsqueak on the elbow, hard. He bends the elbow, but keeps a hold of my shirt. I pivot into him and grab the stick with both hands. Before he can react, I stick-punch him in the belly, low where it hurts.

He stumbles and hunches over. I whack him on the side of the head with the handle. I wind up, ready to give him one last shot when a pair of smallish legs come into view. Emmy moves in close to me, so close that I can't step into the swing without knocking her over.

Pipsqueak takes deep breaths through his nose. He reaches for the wall and pulls himself upright, checking his jaw now, feeling his head, says, "You don't know what you just done."

The women get close, unsure what to do at first, then wrap themselves around me like a musty blanket and shuffle me away from Pipsqueak and into the lobby.

P ilar sits at her desk, hunched over with half a sandwich in her hand trying not to get any crumbs on her black suit. I've seen her wear it before, maybe the one nice suit she owns, and the color looks good against her maple skin. The sandwich is sourdough with orange cheese and something pasty slathered on the cheese. Whatever it is, it's dripping onto a newspaper spread on the top of her desk.

"I'm not the first," I say, repeating Pipsqueak's words. "I'm not even the second. What does that mean?"

She's eyeing the sandwich, looking at the sliced edge, admiring the geometry of it, maybe. She hasn't taken a single bite. "Good morning to you, too," she says, not looking at me, and I notice how strangely her hands are shaking, a loose tremor that reminds me of old women drinking tea.

"What's going on, Pilar?"

"I'm surprised it took you so long."

"I'm not the first—"

She says, "What do you think it means?" There is a venom in her voice that I hadn't heard before. She looks up and I see dark circles under her eyes.

"Why don't you tell me."

Pilar says, "I just figured something out. What you do, what Pastor Sammy does, it's a business with you people. The entertainment business. Put on a good show, make the church-goers happy, hypnotize them into doing all sorts of stupid things, I don't know."

"What's wrong, Pilar?"

She sets the half sandwich on the newspaper and swivels her chair around to face me.

"Why should anything be wrong? Revenues are up for the quarter, thanks to you. And this stunt of yours has backfired. Sammy's not angry, he's elated. It's a miracle and where better for a miracle than here? Like having a heart attack in a hospital. It's all very convenient."

"It's Robert, isn't it?"

"So now you want to talk about Robert. Why, so you can tell me that a relapse is his fault? He didn't believe enough, or suffer enough. Or give enough. I've heard it before, but I've never heard it from you. Until now."

"What happened?"

"You lied to me, that's what happened. You said he would get better."

"I didn't."

"No you didn't," she says, her voice coming out in a whisper. "And I believed in you even more because of it."

I tell her I don't know the future any more than she does. It's what makes us who we are. It explains the foolish things we do.

I'm talking to Pilar, but about myself. About the foolish things I do, now thinking that the last several weeks have been one long fool's errand. Saving Billie from her husband, Roe, Pipsqueak, Pastor Sammy Gann. And now Pilar turning her back to me, seeing the world in a whole new way she doesn't like. Her practical nature hardening. I'm about to say that not knowing the future is the basis for hope. And denial. We hope the bad things will just up and go away if we hope it enough. Things like loneliness and pain and cancer. And we deny things can get any worse if we do nothing but hope. Only things can always get worse.

"Not knowing," I say, "is what makes us human."

"You sound more like Pastor Sammy every day."

She means it as an insult, and I take it as one.

I say, "You want to talk about it?"

Pilar says no and that ends it. She briefly looks at me, and it's a look that I've avoided for some thirty years. A look of blame. It's why I've been silent for so long, why I work at night. I'm the kind who goes to great lengths to avoid blame. What I said earlier, the part about not knowing the future, isn't entirely true. I sometimes pick up the phone and know who's on the other end. I can smell a warm wind and know rain isn't far off. I do a carving of someone, and I know that someone gets better. I know it before it happens. Pilar's wrong to worry about Robert. I know it.

"I'm not the first," I say. "What does that mean?"

"You're not the first healer Sammy's talked into joining him."

"You think I'm here to join this circus?"

"Aren't you?" she says. "You made sure it's all on camera. You get a ride with that newsman. Who arranged that, your publicist?"

"Where's Sammy?" I say.

"He's not here."

The door to Sammy's office is open. "I can see that. Where is he?"

A voice off to my right says, "I can show you the way." Officer Sean Harris is standing in the doorway to Pilar's office. Mr. No-Nonsense. Looks you right in the eye and says whatever's on his mind. Pipsqueak stands behind him, and he lets loose a dry whisper of a chuckle. The bandage on his lip is peeling away at one corner. He has one of those long-handled flashlights in his hand. Here I see into the future again, and I know that Pipsqueak is bad news. If I don't stay clear of him he'll hurt me, or worse. Or I'll hurt him, or worse.

"Sean," I say, "it's nice to see a friendly face." It stops him, me remembering his name.

Mr. No-nonsense says, "Please follow me."

Officer Harris leads us along a curved corridor, through a door and into a narrower corridor. He's in front, not talking to me, not making eye contact. Pipsqueak is behind me, occasionally giving me a little poke in the back with the flashlight. I feel like a ten-year-old, and the little brother I never had is trying to get me in trouble. Trying to get me to tattle, or better, to take a swipe at him. I do and Officer Harris will turn just in time to see me, the aggressor, assaulting his buddy in blue, and I look like the asshole. They both pile on and I end up with more bruises I don't need.

I stop long enough to put some distance between Officer Harris and me. I turn and Pipsqueak instinctively lowers the flashlight to protect his stomach. I can smell his breath—peanut butter and old sausage.

I say, "You keep pushing me, and I'll push back."

"Amen, sister. I get my arms around you, and you can push up against me all you want."

"It's always a pleasure, Little Boone."

I catch up to Officer Harris. We come to a door. He knocks, doesn't wait for a response, and uses a key card to unlock. The room is wide and shallow, and the back wall is stuffed to the ceiling with rack-mounted computers, flat screen monitors in all sizes, satellite receivers, DVD players, surveillance gear, and something that looks like an old-fashioned radar unit. The front wall is divided in two. The bottom half is a built-in console with eight thousand knobs. The top half is all glass.

Sammy waves us inside, and we stand in the middle of the room, looking out through the glass into a sound stage as big as a hangar. It's dark, but I recognize the set of "A Fine Day," Sammy's television show. The stage is a replica of the Oval Office, with the heavy presidential desk and tall windows overlooking the rose garden. The roses are painted on the wall, of course, but they look real enough from here. Sammy's done away with the white walls and put up a forest of dark wood paneling and ornate moldings—black walnut and Indian ebony and some knotty-grained cedar, it looks like, all of it stained a glossy, crude-oil black and brown.

To the right of President Sammy's desk is a ponderous painting. It's brightly lit—the only thing in the room that is. It's of an old guy with a white beard and an orange robe and a blue scarf and who looks a lot like God, except I know better. It's Ezekiel talking to a boy on his right. The boy's hair is long and girlish, but it's the face that gets me; the boy's face is Pastor Sammy Gann's.

There's no telling what Ezekiel is saying to little Sammy. Maybe recounting how he got booted out of Israel for harassing the Jews. Maybe warning Sammy about sin and punishment. Maybe suggesting that Pastor Sammy consider adding a winding river ride to the Center. Something for those dry Texas summers; a splashy tour through the Hanging Gardens of Babylon, perhaps.

Ezekiel was a big deal twenty-six hundred years ago, the first prophet of Israel, but none of that matters because to Sammy's devoted followers he's a stand-in for God. The painting's location next to the desk—positioned so that it's constantly on-camera—the boy's altered features, and the spotlights all speak louder than words: Pastor Sammy and God talk all the time.

Sammy sips from a twenty-ounce bottle of Mountain Dew and gazes reverently through the glass.

He says, "It was the Lord who told me to start this fellowship. ' Go ye into the world, and preach the gospel to every creature.' And that's what I've done. Our show is translated and broadcast to millions around the world." He takes another sip of the Dew. "It's my prayer that the Holy Spirit will raise up a new generation of ministers. People willing to take the message of healing around the globe."

It goes on like that, Sammy telling me what a bang-up job he's done, reminding himself who he is, how much he's had to give up, how much he's suffered, and how his suffering is changing the world. If I have any doubts, just look at all that exotic dark wood. Look at that gaudy painting, for chrissakes. If that's not testimony to Sammy's suffering, then what is?

I think about interrupting, asking if he's got one of those little fridges hidden away somewhere with another Mountain Dew inside.

When he stops talking and looks at me, I say, "You murdered a friend of mine."

And for the briefest moment, Pastor Sammy doesn't know what to say.

"Ｎone of us is free of sin. Not me. Not you," Sammy says, saying it like he knows something. For a moment, I think he's talking about Roe. About me and my baby ax. About killing a man. "You're on the wrong path, Miss Tate. Only trust in Christ will save you. What an incredible exchange: your worst for God's best."

I look at him, at Pipsqueak behind him scratching at his privates, at Officer Harris standing guard at the door. Sammy taps a finger on the glass. We both look out at the soundstage, at the mass of wires and light fixtures hanging overhead, at ladders and dollies and the scaffolding holding up the walls. I'm tempted to tell him how phony it all feels, when Sammy says, "I reach millions of viewers every day. Those with need, go right into their living rooms and bedrooms. Into hospitals and retirement homes and—"

"I get the point," I say.

"I go where people need me."

"You go wherever there's a television set."

"You honestly think I had something to do with Billie's death?"

I say, "Roe killed Billie. I know because he told me." I lie, but so what.

Sammy says, "Then why accuse me?"

"Because he takes his orders from you. What I want to know is, why?"

"That's why you came?"

"Not really."

Sammy is waiting for me to say more. What do I tell him? That I'd like to grab him by the throat and not let go—right there above the starched white collar where the skin is pink and fleshy. That I want to find out what he most values, so I can stomp it into the ground. I don't know what to say, and I'm half a mind to turn around and beat it back to my loft in Deep Ellum, haul a six-foot chunk of telephone pole upstairs and do what I do best.

I can't do that, of course, because a childish wanting has taken over, a wanting that says friendship and loyalty and justice and punishment are worthy pursuits. Pursuits only a child believes in. Life can be unfair. Even a kid knows that. And when life strikes me as particularly unfair, as it does now, a part of me wants to line up all the bad guys in the world and cut out their hearts. I end up frowning and shaking my head like a little girl who just can't find the words. All of which seems to please the daylights out of Pastor Sammy.

He stares at the painting of Ezekiel, motions me closer to the glass, reaches out and gently places his hand on my shoulder in a pose identical to Ezekiel and little Sammy. It's effortless and practiced. Confident.

"You still don't understand what's happening, do you?"

I say, "I know that a friend of mine is dead."

Sammy tells me God has placed hands on his heart. I don't know what that means, and it's possible he's referring to Ezekiel with his hand on Sammy's shoulder. He wants to know what God can do for me. What he can do for my family. Wants me to tell him about the struggles I'm facing, right now. It's kinda cute the way he says "right now," in a low-key way, like he's really talking to me. Like I'm not supposed to know he's given this little sermon a thousand times to tens of thousands of people. He wants to know—

and here I'm not sure if "he" means God or Sammy—of a burden so beyond my faith that only a miracle can lift it. A burden so heavy that lifting it is proof of God's intervention. Sammy knows with absolute certainty that God loves to intervene in the lives of His people, especially during times like these. "Challenging times," he calls them.

"Call unto me," he says "and I will answer thee, and show thee great and mighty things, which thou knowest not."

I say, "Is there something you're trying to say to me?"

He takes small sips from his Mountain Dew and pats down the fringes of his toupee. The orange cap of the Dew—the exact same orange as Ezekiel's toga, I swear it—is resting on the sill of the window next to an ashtray. The cap's upside down and I can see inside: "Free Mountain Dew." I slip the cap into my pocket.

Sammy says, "What you don't understand is that God wants more for you, and for me, than we want for ourselves."

"Is that so?"

"He wants to take away your sins."

"That's it?" I say.

Sammy picks up a half-smoked cigar from the ashtray and puts it to his lips. He lights it and the room quickly fills with smoke. For a moment, his face is lit by the flame. It's a soft, doughy face. He looks up at Harris, sets the cigar in the ashtray. Sammy, with his wrinkled gray suit, the wilting hair, the phony smile, says, "He wants you to come work for me."

I pause before speaking, making sure this isn't some kind of joke, and then I tell him to go to hell.

"Look," Sammy says, "I'm about to march out front there and tell that crowd the sculpture of that little girl—"

"Her name's Emmy."

"That Emmy is God's work. That this is a place for God's work."

I say, "You want to take credit for the healing."

Sammy says, "I'm willing, if you'll let me, to take a burden like this from your shoulders. A burden you do not want, are not prepared for."

"Why you?"

"Miracles are my stock in trade, Miss Tate. Who better?"

Sammy is escorting me out of the building, Harris and Pipsqueak hanging back like a couple of prison guards in case I decide to make a break for it ,when Harris's walkie-talkie squawks. A man's voice says, "Harris, you there? You gotta come see this."

Harris speaks into his talkie, "What do you got?"

"Better you come see for yourself."

There is a short conversation about what to do with me—nobody willing to let me loose in the Center all by my lonesome, and nobody willing to miss whatever there is to see—so we all trudge back in the direction we just came, right on past the television studio until we come to a door with bold lettering, "Security Operations Center." Below it in a smaller more inviting font, "Authorized Personnel Only." Harris runs a key-card through the reader and ushers us inside.

The room is high-ceilinged and brightly lit with four enormous, flat-screen monitors arranged in a semi-circle around us. Each monitor is the size of a garage door and divided into a grid of sorts. I count twenty-two TV-sized images around the perimeter and one big-ass picture in the middle. On center screen is an aerial view of the Global Healing Center. It's not a photograph, because I can see ants parking their cars and zigzagging their way to the main entrance. I see a whole lot of ants surrounding the portico, crawling on top of each other, it looks like from here.

"Is this a live feed?" I ask.

Someone behind me laughs. Probably Pipsqueak.

Harris nods.

Sammy and Harris are watching me, and I can tell they get a kick out of this: my first look behind the curtain of Sammy's house of worship. The technology is overwhelming; it's goddamn Mission Control for televangelists, is what it is. I get it now: the room is a showpiece, a stop on the tour for VIPs and special donors.

Four high-tech workstations sit in the middle of the room. Each station is nothing but a pricey slab of granite on four legs, nothing but a keyboard and a headset on top. No phones, no messy papers or printers or junk of any sort. The giant monitors are positioned ten feet in front of each workstation. Standing back as we are, I can view all four monitors at once.

Harris moves up close to a technician standing sheepishly next to his workstation. No greeting, no handshake, nothing. Harris glances at the three empty seats and says, "Where's Johnson, Clark, Barrett?"

The tech sees Pastor Sammy, hesitates, says, "Bathroom. Clark's getting a Coke, Barrett's kid is sick." He points to his giant monitor. "Take a look."

Sammy moves close where he can get a better view, and his expression says he knows exactly what he's looking at. Everyone knows what they're looking at but me. Even Pipsqueak is glaring upward at the monitor and shaking his head like he's none too happy.

Sammy mumbles to Harris, who mumbles to the technician. The tech sits, flops a headset over his ears, punches some buttons. The center image blinks to a wide-angle view of the main entrance. He types something and the view widens. The scene is a sea of heads. It's hard to tell the size of the crowd, because the camera can't get them all. I'd guess two, three hundred—five times what it was twenty minutes ago. The place has a dank and chilly atmosphere. It's started to rain, and the people at the fringe of the crowd aren't covered by the roof. There's a lot of pushing and shoving. I can't hear it, but people are shouting.

Sammy nods anxiously at one of the smaller screens.

The tech reads his mind, taps the keyboard. The center image changes. It's now a close-up of the wooden Emmy. The color is off, but the definition is unbelievable. I can see a fine crack in her lower lip where I let the chisel get away from me.

I glance at more images. A side view of the crowd: people gathered tightly around the sculpture, jostling for position, a woman sobbing, a man in a wheelchair waving people out of the way so he can get up close. The center screen flips to the man in the wheelchair. The chair is one of those ultralight jobs with the wheels canted inward and the name Dutch embroidered in large letters on the back of the chair. In front of him, a woman with her back to us is huddled close to the wooden Emmy.

"What's that woman doing?" Sammy says. "Zoom in. There." The image changes, and the people in the crowd are now life-sized. It's disorienting, as if we were standing in the crowd directly behind her, looking over her shoulder. She's young and thin and hunched forward, holding onto Emmy's ankle or shin. Bodies push against her, and I involuntarily lean to my right to push back. She lowers her head and tightens her grip on the sculpture.

"What's she got in her hand?" Sammy says. He reaches forward, shoving at the air, trying to move the woman aside. "What's that woman doing? Someone tell me what she's doing." We all stare at the giant screen, at the woman's narrow back and strong arms and determined stance.

Dutch grips both wheels of his chair and pushes, but there's nowhere to go with all the feet and legs and hips in the way. He tries swimming through the crowd, clutching at arms and loose clothing and whatever he can grab in front of him and tugging forward in an awkward breaststroke. He's nearly within reach of Emmy when he grabs hold of the woman's belt and jerks. She doesn't give, but turns her head, and it's the first time I see her face. It reveals no sympathy, no bitterness. None of the bottomless loss pouring out from those around her. Her hand moves down to her side, and we all see it at once.

The tech says, "Oh, that's not good."

"Pen knife," Pipsqueak says. "Nothing to worry about."

"It's a knife," Sammy says. "And why are you standing here?"

I glare at Pipsqueak ready to stick out my tongue if he'll just look this way.

"What's she gonna do with a pen knife?" Pipsqueak says.

"Shut up, Boone," Harris says.

"Yeah, shut up, Boone," I say. I can't help myself.

Pipsqueak says to Harris, "You want I walk Miss Tate out of the building?"

"Not another word," Harris says. He turns away from us and barks commands into his walkie-talkie.

The woman turns back to Emmy, and it's Sammy who first understands what's happening.

"No," he says, stretching out the word. "She can't do that."

The woman has used the knife to pry a small piece of wood from the sculpture. A splinter, really. I watch her put the splinter in her pocket. The people around her stare, temporarily motionless, and then a man barrels forward, grabs hold of Emmy's foot and yanks. It doesn't budge.

A woman barges on screen, this one old and wide-bodied and gray-haired. She's carrying something heavy over her head. The crowd widens, giving her room. She's got a brick in her hand, makes a bee-line for the sculpture, and gives the brick an overhead, two-handed thrust. It careens off Emmy's knee and hits a man in the foot. The man goes down and the gray-haired woman scoops up the brick, ready to give it another toss, I guess, when Dutch reaches up from his chair and grabs her wrist. He works the brick out of her hand, plops it on his lap, wheels himself through a gap in the crowd, sets the brake, raises the brick over his head and lunges forward whipping the brick out in front of him. Something snaps, and a piece of Emmy falls to the ground.

"It's a foot," I say. "He got a foot."

Sammy cranes his head around to look at me. "That's all you have to say?"

I say, "Good for him."

"This is your fault," Sammy says.

The technician cups his hand to his earpiece, listening, taps a key on the keyboard, and the center screen changes He says, "It gets worse."

Sammy looks up at the monitor.

"Oh, my God."

I turn and look at the center screen. What I see is a traffic jam. Yawn. Hardly the kind of thing that warrants an "Oh, my God."

I'm looking down on the parking lot, only the view is wider, a lot wider. I see every inch of pavement and all of it jammed with cars. The stalls, the aisles, even the plant beds that rim the lot are blanketed with F150s and Dodge Rams and a few beat-up foreign jobs. I see the gate at the south end of the lot, a giant spiderweb of cars and trucks and SUVs converging on the Center. And beyond the gate, the road is backed up in both directions. A couple of cop cars are angled onto the shoulder, trying to pass but stuck, lights flashing away. There's even a fire truck up near Loop 12 waiting patiently in line.

The tech points to one of the smaller screens. The screen, I realize now, that everyone but me is staring at. The small screen blinks, the large screen blinks and the two images swap places.

The center screen is now a close-up of a man's back, the man wearing an ugly sweater striped blue and gold. The man's hanging eight feet off the ground, his arms clutching the wooden Emmy around the neck. One leg is wrapped around her arm at about the elbow. His other leg is searching for a foothold, kicking her in the hip, hoping, I suppose to soften her up. The view widens. The mob is crushing in on him, the guy up high enough to walk on people's heads if he wanted to. Lots of hands reaching up, most of the hands pushing him higher. "Attaboy. You can do it," they seem to say.

One pair of hands is grabbing at a pant leg.

But that's not the weird part. The weird part is all the blood. oh-my-God amounts of blood. On the big screen it's dark and purplish, much of it spread across Emmy's shirt, her shoulders and neck. From this angle it's hard to say exactly where it's all coming from.

Mr. Blue-and-Gold is getting tired, jittery, losing his grip, anyone can see that. My bet is, less than five minutes before he blacks out and belly-flops into the crowd. He keeps one arm around Emmy's neck and jams the other hand deep into a split in the wood behind her ear.

A woman with a short spiky do and a matching blue-and-gold sweater reaches for the guy's leg, finally gets a handful of ankle, and puts all her weight into it. She's dangling from the ankle when she spins around, looks up, sees the camera and stares directly at us. "Do something," she says. Her lips don't move, but for chrissakes, do they really have to?

The woman with spiky hair is crying, big fat baby tears that leave black streaks on her cheeks. Her head's bent back, talking to the guy now, her hubby probably, the dumb spaz, pleading with him to come on down. Telling him to get his skinny butt back to Earth. The guy cranes his head around and peers down at her, looks into her face, and he's young, way younger than I thought. His forehead's streaked with red, and he's telling her he's not letting go because letting go means giving up and, well, he's not giving up, not yet, maybe not ever, so enough with the ankle.

Next to Mrs. Blue-and-Gold, a busty, button-nosed woman is trying to claw her way up onto Emmy's hip. If she can just get a leg up, if she can just get a little goddamn help here... An old man huddled close to the woman grips a tire iron in both hands, jamming it into the base of the sculpture and prying away large splintery chunks of wood. The woman puts her foot squarely on the man's back, finally making some progress, when the old logger twists and elbows her in the calf. She lands on top of him.

A man has a brick in both hands banging it against the fold in Emmy's pink dress and basically wrecking the shit out of her Sunday best.

Harris says, "Pastor Sammy," but Sammy's in his own world, mumbling to himself about signs and sacrifices and sprinkling blood on the altar in front of the Tabernacle.

"How do you want to handle this?" Harris says.

The tech zooms in where blood is dripping from Mr. Blue and Gold's shoe onto Emmy's knee, and a stooped, not-entirely-healthy elderly lady is rubbing her hands in the blood and smearing the mess on her cheeks and neck and bare arms.

Sammy rouses himself. "Where is it all coming from?"

"This man falls and he's going to hurt himself," Harris says.

"He's already hurt," I say.

The tech listens to his headset, yanks it off, and hands it to Harris. Harris listens, looks to Sammy, finally says, "Get them inside the building if you can. Away from the girl... Yeah, away from the sculpture, the girl, what else would I mean?" Harris hands the headset back to the tech, says, "Get everyone out front, ASAP."

The tech slips on the headset, punches some buttons. "All-officer check-in, pronto." He cups his hand to his earpiece. "Clark, stop what you're doing and get out front... Well, go out the back and circle the building."

Sammy says, "I want to hear. Put it on speaker."

Harris glances at me.

Sammy shouts at him. "Put it on the speaker."

The tech taps at the keyboard and the room is alive with voices and background noise. Heavy breathing, boots on pavement, running. "Clark here. Daniel, you still there?"

The tech says, "This is Officer Turner. I've got Pastor Sammy and Officer Harris here in the SOC. You're on speaker."

More heavy breathing. Clark says, "Okay, right. Turner, we got problems. I got a woman down between the west doors and lot B. She was trying to get into the building. Says she was shoved to the ground. People stepped on her. She was down there for a while until a couple of Samaritans dragged her out here. She's got broken bones. Cuts on her legs and stomach. This lady's not getting up."

Officer Turner says, "I'll call an ambulance."

Clark says, "Scratch that. The lots clogged. Cars, people everywhere." The connection stutters. "Wait, I got an old guy sitting on the curb. Some blood on his face and hands. Southeast corner lot A. I could use some help."

The video image wobbles. On screen, a man squats on the curb, both hands covering his face. Blood on his hands. A woman crouches next to him.

"Hey buddy," Clark says, "someone want to tell me what's going on?"

"Give me a sec." Turner glances at Harris.

Harris's face tightens, says, "Boone, get out there."

"Not Boone," Sammy says. "Send someone else."

Harris considers this for a long moment. "Rovell, Get him out there ASAP."

"Okay, Clark," Turner says, "What else?"

"Hey buddy, I mention it's raining?" No one speaks. "Son of a bitch," Clark says. "I see Peterson trying to break up a fight. He needs back-up. Now."

"Delay that," a fuzzy voice says. "This is Peterson. I got it. Four males, mid twenties. These assholes are fighting over a chunk of wood looks like from a fence post."

"Weapons?" Turner asks.

"It's mostly wrestling. Three-on-one. Then the guy on bottom gives up the post and it's three-on-one with another guy."

Turner says, "What else?"

Peterson says, "What else what?"

"Is the area secure? You know the drill, draw me a picture."

"Shit no," Peterson says, "it's not secure. Too many people,. way more than we can handle. You remember when Tech shut out A&M a few weeks ago? Tech wins and the fans rush the field and tear down their own goalpost? That's what we got here. All these assholes are looking for a goalpost."

Sammy glares at me. "You still don't understand what's happening, do you?"

Pipsqueak is a man who likes to be where the action is, so when Sammy tells him to wait here and make sure that she, meaning me, stays out of trouble, Pipsqueak is not happy about it. I can feel him watching me even with his eyes on the giant monitor. Watching and waiting and wanting to ask me something. Wanting to tell me something, is more like it. Like what he's going to do to me if he ever catches me alone some night down on Elm or Clover or Canton. The fat-lipped, dogbreath peckerwood hates me so much that it oozes out of him.

I walk to the door, look back, and make eye contact with Pipsqueak, daring him to stop me, but it doesn't make any difference because he wants me to make a run for it. Or slip out the door, unseen, or just plain leave so he can get out front and tell Sammy I've escaped. I walk out. On my way, I swing by Pilar's office and pick up my black bag. And Sammy's wrong. I do know what's going on. At least I think I do.

From where I stand, at the outer fringe of the crowd, it's loud. The kind of pining, chain saw, shout-in-the-ear loud that causes hearing loss. And most of it, though not all of it, is pointed in the direction of the wooden Emmy.

Even from this distance, Emmy looks aged and bloodied. The ravages of worship have been hard on her. Her arms look pock-marked and chewed up—attacked by angry horseflies maybe, or locusts or big fat killer bees hiking up from South America. Grimy hands have stained parts of her skirt a dark shiny brown. The column was as thick as an oil drum only an hour ago, but now it's been whittled to half that. From about waist down, she's been picked at with tire irons and car keys and ball point pens. Her legs and feet are entirely gone.

A cross the parking lot, I see a long line of tall black figures trooping between the parked cars, their fat heads held high looking for something or someone to criticize. These are my people—Bruck and Dwight and Tracey and Shawna. Some others, I forget their names. And Mary Ellen, of course. Her page-boy do clammy and pasted to her head, her hips swinging wide, wagging along ahead of the colony. Bruck sees me first, but it's Mary Ellen who changes direction and points the procession my way. When she reaches me, she's ready to bite.

I put a surprised but altogether friendly smile on my face. "Long time," I say.

"It was day before yesterday."

"It was yesterday, Mary Ellen. Last night."

"You tricked us. Made us think you were helping us catch this guy."

I say nothing.

"So," she says, "anyone claim the reward?"

Bruck is standing by himself in the rain, gazing up at the Healing Tower. The downspouts are plugged, and dirty brown water is spilling out of the gutter onto the stone façade. Bruck has icky little drops of water hanging from the end of his nose.

"So, where is it?" he says.

The entrance to the Center is one big mass of humanity, three or four hundred people crammed under the portico and the rest of us standing out here in the rain. I'd aim us inside, out of the rain, if I thought we had a chance of squeezing through the crowd, but we don't, and besides, I think security locked the doors. I point over the heads, in the corner, way over there. Bruck raises his chin, takes a serious gander at Emmy, says, "Who's it supposed to be?"

"A kid I know."

Bruck says, "Tall kid. What's she, about eight feet?"

"I'm not real good with perspective."

I say it as a joke, but it's true. When I was young, I never noticed. Then, when I got to UT, several of the figure-drawing teachers ganged up on me and pointed out that everything I put to paper was getting smaller and smaller. Even when I was trying to draw the thing life-sized, a hand or a foot say, or Bruck's runny nose, I couldn't. The teachers wanted to know exactly how I expected to get anywhere if I couldn't draw a nose on paper the size of a real nose? Good question. The following semester I transferred to the sculpture department, and things got worse—everything got bigger.

Bruck says, "She's beaten up pretty bad. That doesn't bother you any? All these antagonistic shits tearing up your work?"

"Not really," I say

"What's with the red?"

"It's blood."

"Blood of the Covenant, that sort of thing? It's spooky, but nice touch."

I say, "Not my idea, but thanks."

Bruck says, "I like what you did with the hands."

"You can't see the hands," I say.

No one can. The jagged folds of Emmy's skirt have been rubbed smooth, and her hands are tucked shyly beneath the folds.

"Yeah," he says, "but I know they're there. I see the
rest of the girl and I know what the hands look like. Small,
with long fingers. And strong. The kid's not stupid. She
shows those hands, and they're gone." Bruck turns to me,
about to say more, and then glances past me and sees Mary
Ellen coming our way. He says, "I think that little girl's hiding
something, or guarding something. Something she doesn't
want these clowns in front of her to get their grubby paws
on."

Mary Ellen marches up and punches me in the
shoulder. "What I want to know is who handles your
advertising? Jesus, great turnout."

Before Sammy left the SOC, he barked at Harris to
get him something to stand on: a platform about so tall.
Move the people away from the sculpture and put it there,
maybe off to one side so he and Emmy are framed in the
same shot. Call Communications and get a film crew out
front, now. Sammy told him he wanted it all on tape, disc,
whatever. Harris said, "Want what on tape?" and Sammy said,
"All of it."

It takes a few minutes to set up the stage—a plywood
box maybe two feet tall with just enough room for a slow
dance. Time enough to get Mr. Blue-and-Gold down and
strapped onto a stretcher. Mrs. Blue-and-Gold is calmer now
that hubby's been restrained. His face and stomach are
soaked with blood, splinters of wood poke through his shirt
and pants. People in the crowd pick at the splinters. Someone
tears away a piece of his shirt.

As he's carted off, eight burly security guards
surround the sculpture and ask all the believers to take a step
back. Or else. The guards cordon off the area with a bright
yellow ribbon, holding the ribbon out in front of them in
fisted hands. When someone gets too close, they bare their
teeth.

A paunchy guy helps Pastor Sammy up onto the box and hands him a microphone. Sammy's still in the same wrinkled gray suit, the wilting hair, the phony smile. He takes the mike and raises his slim, almost feminine hands. A gold wedding band's on his left, so wide it covers the bottom of his ring finger knuckle to knuckle like a chunk of lead pipe.

He speaks into the mike, his voice a whisper, "Can I tell you a secret?" The crowd rustles. "I say, can I tell you a little secret? Something I've never told before." The crowd settles and Sammy's voice deepens.

"One day, a little girl appeared to me. I was deep in prayer, you see, and the little girl appeared twice one day and the next day. She was tall, over six feet. Her dress down to here and it showed her knees. To me, she looked like an angel. She asked me to pray for her. I asked the Father, 'I come to you now, in the name of Jesus, asking you to help this child. Heal her soul and her body. Fill her afresh with the Holy Spirit, that she may experience your power. Dear God, let this child walk after the spirit, let her endure no more pain, let her be strong in this battle. In Jesus' mighty name I pray, Amen."

Sammy nods and music begins, a low chorus rumbling from speakers in the portico ceiling, deep male voices coming from the left and altos and sopranos on the right. He reaches down and takes someone's outstretched hand. It's a small hand, and he yanks the hand and the arm and the body up onto the stage. It's a clumsy process, unrehearsed, and the girl's dress flips up, showing her white panties. She turns around and stands there looking out at the crowd. The girl is Emmy.

"That the kid?" Bruck says.

"Uh huh," I say.

"Sammy said she was six feet tall."

"They're always bigger in visions."

"What's wrong with her?"

"Nothing," I say. "She's a good kid. Likes to dance in the bathroom. You should see her rhumba."

Bruck says, "Is that part of the show, the rhumba?"

"If Sammy shuts his mouth long enough, it might be."

I spot Pilar with a large umbrella fending off the rain and wave her our way. Mary Ellen has wondered off, and Bruck is standing beside me, water still dripping from his nose. I introduce Bruck as a good friend, though I don't know why. He puts his arms around Pilar and me and squeezes us under the umbrella. His hand on my shoulder is large, the fingers beefy, the nails flecked with paint and the whole package smelling of paint thinner. A smell I can't get enough of.

We're snuggled up so close Pilar whispers into my ear, "I'm sorry for blaming you."

I say, "If you need to, you can push some guilt my way any time."

"I'm worried," she says and turns away, uncomfortable. "What these people did to that statue, they did to my Robert. I think you knew it would happen, wanted it to happen."

I say, "I didn't know."

Pilar takes my hand. Her fingers are cold against my palm. "It's how you stay so calm. You see it coming."

"Not like this, I didn't."

Pilar says, "An old man's looking for you. A black man in kind of a blue shirt. A little bald spot on top. Do you know him?"

Otto is standing on top of a tipped-over trashcan, one of those heavy concrete jobs big enough to hold two or three Ottos, when I find him. .He's up there to see over all the heads in front of him, he says, to see what this Pastor Sammy character looks like in person, to see what there is to see, though he doesn't mention the sculpture. And now that he's here, he's getting a kick out of Sammy.

"Put a little mustache under that nose, and he's a Nazi. If I was to salute him," Otto says, "you think he'd salute back? German or no, he's way better than on TV. The set I watch him on, the thirteen-inch in my shop, this is way better."

"You coming down anytime soon?" I say.

"I do and I'll lose my place." Otto says, "A few days ago, this guy had his hands around my neck."

"It was a piece of wood," I say.

"With my face on it."

"But it wasn't you."

"If it was, he'd of choked the life out of me."

Sammy's yammering on about God and glory and concealment. God the trickster, he says, likes to hide his words, or maybe it's that he likes to hide the meaning of his words. It's hard to know where Sammy's going with this. God conceals the deep truths, he goes on, truths that can't be mined by scratching the surface. Sammy reaches behind him with the microphone and rubs the tip of the mike against the wooden Emmy: *Scratch, scratch.* The deep truths, he tells us, are a precious ore, gold to be pulled from the earth and purified. He's here today to share with us one of these deep truths.

Otto puts his hand on my shoulder and eases himself off the trashcan. Squeezes my arm, says, "I think we're finally getting to it."

The afternoon sky has morphed into a sloppy purple-gray. Bulky rain clouds are suspended overhead, a couple of the clouds shaped like buckets, big cartoon-looking buckets, the kind hanging from a string above your front door waiting for you to walk outside and get drenched. It has that kind of feel to it. Like a cartoon: the crush of too many people, the crummy November rain that won't give it a break, and Sammy with his voice box working overtime.

"Ye that fear God, listen to me," Sammy says.

We all listen.

He tells us that he's walked in the spirit world. He's seen things we will never see, sights we will never understand. And he tells us to stop this.

"This…" but he can't find the words. His face goes red, his feminine hands go up in the air, and I see dampness in the pit of his arms. "This, this," he says pointing up at the wooden Emmy's missing legs. "Stop this. Right now," he shouts at us. "I command you to stop it."

He points to a man directly in front of him.

"You there. Stop tearing down God's work. What you have in your hands there, those small pieces of scrap, are God's gift to this child, to this Center." This thieving, he tells all of us, is the enemy of righteousness, a perversion of the way to the Lord.

His little harangue reminds me of a pep rally gone bad. The mood was festive just a few minutes ago, but now we've been scolded for scribbling on the bathroom stalls.

What Sammy does is whine—the way grandmothers plead with grandkids saying, "Really, I mean it, seriously, cut it out," but never for a minute intending to show the little shits what's what. Sammy doesn't say, "Or else," but that's what he means, threatening us with a plague of leprosy. He doesn't tell us this plague will make our eyebrows fall out and our ears swell into huckleberry potatoes. Doesn't say our fingers and toes will shrink into lifeless peanuts. He lets us think these things for ourselves.

What he says is, "Do as I command, or this plague will rise as a bright spot under the skin and turn to scab."

What he says is, "The next person to touch that sculpture will grow fat as a stall-fed calf," doing a pretty good Texas accent the way he says it. Sammy's throwing us a low blow with that one, knowing what really hurts isn't God's disappointment in us sinners or an unlikely bout of leprosy, but getting fat.

It all comes off so corny you want to tell him to put a lid on it. But what makes it so dead-skunk-on-the-road stinky is that under that pasty-faced exterior, the guy knows what he's doing. A guy who buys thousand dollar suits that don't fit. On purpose. A guy humble on the outside and mean on the in. Mean enough to peddle hope to the highest bidder. Self-obsessed enough to kill and think no one will notice.

Here's a man who raked in over two hundred million last year. A man with a private jet and a couple of mansions. An expense account that would humble small banks. A ba-zillionaire, and he looks more like a guy sells shower curtain rings on the road. A guy with a pitch. At the same time, a guy not afraid to show us his warts—the frumpy suits and the sweat stains and the dopey toupee. And his childish anger that comes off so genuine you want to give the wimpy little squealer a big wet hug. Here's a guy you can feel for. Or could, if he wasn't, deep down, a callous, bloodsucking, parasite—a man who gets people to cash in IRAs so he can gas up the old Gulfstream, and single moms to hand over food stamps, and kids to pitch in a little lunch money when they can.

Here's a grown man with more influence than the goddamn governor of Texas. Any governor. All of them combined, maybe, and with all that influence he's standing here bullying us to stop picking at his precious sculpture.

I'm not sure why it's taken me so long, but now I know what Sammy most values. It's not his devoted followers, their adoration, their health or safety. It's not his television show. It's not money. It's not even the most obvious of wants for a modern, jet-setting messiah—to be able to heal.

It's simpler than that.

It's the Global Healing Center. This building. It's more than brick and stone and exotic wood to Sammy. Pinch the corner of the Healing Cathedral and Sammy flinches. Break a window and he bleeds. Take a brick to Emmy's wooden knee and he limps. The building is one big voodoo doll of the man.

I've heard stories that Haitian slaves used to disguise their voodoo *lwa*, their Gods, as Roman Catholic saints. The boss man sees a dumb African with a doll of St. Apollonia— the patron saint of dental disease—and he thinks here we got a convert. Only it's not St. Apollonia, it's the voodoo Mother Goddess. Be nice to the Mother Goddess and she looks after you, makes it so's the mastahs don't break any bones when they beat you. Ignore her and you might catch a nasty case of leprosy or get fat.

In North Texas, we do it a little different. We disguise our gods as amusement parks and television studios and global healing centers.

Sammy booms over the loudspeaker, "Don't hate this young artist for rewarding me evil for good. Don't hate her for what she's created. It's not her fault. It's mine."

I've missed something, I'm sure of it. A transition from, "...stop picking at my column" to "she's the evil one." I look around and Otto is still here, but "here" is a different place. He and I are into the crowd, out of the rain and under the roof now. Closer to Sammy and Emmy. My head hurts and the muscles in my arms ache. My fists are clenched around the strap of my black bag. The skin on the back of my hands is see-through pale.

The music gets louder and Sammy says, "I asked her for a token, for a decoration for the entrance to this fine Center. I asked this young artist to do the Lord's work in the only way she knows how. If you want to blame someone, blame me. If you want to point to someone, point to me." The voice gets louder. "If it's responsibility you seek, seek me."

Henson, pushing his way to the platform, shouts up at Sammy. "Are you saying that *you* healed that little girl?" Chad stands behind him, the camera clicking away.

Sammy rests his hand on Emmy's shoulder. "This child here asked me to pray for her."

"In a dream, is that right?" Henson shouts. "A six foot tall child asked you to pray for her, in a dream."

Sammy says, "What happens between her and the Lord is between her and the Lord."

"Is that a yes or a no?" Henson asks .

Bruck and Mary Ellen, with her sour face and round cheeks, sniff me out. Behind her are Tracey and Shawna and the kid with the goatee, I can never remember his name, all of them dressed in black. Next to the goatee, I see Pilar coming at me, and behind her a handful of the surly blue-hairs from the bathroom. And way over, near a guy with a movie camera on his shoulder, are Emmy's mom and dad. Mom and Dad are looking at me, doing that thing with the eyes: "let's talk, let's get together and hold hands and stand too close and try to find just one goddamn thing we have in common." One thing other than Emmy, or poor health, or the hope that tomorrow we'll all wake and everything bad that's happened in our lives will be suddenly, permanently, forgotten.

It's a cult—a nihilistic, soggy-ass, knotty-pine-worshipping cult. And I'm its cold-to-the-bone ringleader, for chrissakes.

Otto puts his arm around me, and I'm wondering why in hell everyone I get next to is glomming onto me. He says, "You're shaking." He glances down at my wet tee shirt. "Be still, now."

I hear my teeth clacking against each other. My head and neck are into little micro-spasms that come and go, and I get the feeling the only thing holding me together is Otto's big arms around me in a kind of bear hug from behind. Sort of boosting me up, it feels like. He's got parts of his crappy corduroy jacket—the one he's still wearing—wrapped around my sides and a little in front. If he could, the old fart'd zip me up inside and the two of us would merge into one person for a little while.

I hear Sammy's voice, weary and hypnotic. "We ask your blessing, Lord, and hide ourselves in the shadow of your healing wing."

It's what Otto's doing, hiding me under his wing.

Mary Ellen says, "Give me your hands." I don't move, so she reaches down and takes the bag from me and gently pulls on my left hand. To Shawna she says, "I don't think it's supposed to be this white," meaning my hand, I think.

I'm not paying attention. In fact, brief snippets of attention keep slipping away from me. I catch the beginning of a sentence and then I hear the end of a sentence, only it's not the same sentence. There are words or phrases or whole paragraphs missing.

Bruck pulls off his sweater, says, "Here," and pushes it at me. I'd take it but Otto's arms are wrapped around my shoulders, Mary Ellen's got my left hand and Shawna the right. Shawna's cuddling my palm to her cheek, divining my temperature, if that's possible.

"Go away," I say. "Will you people back off?" but it's not their fault I'm getting smothered and squeezed. I know that. It's the people behind them, and those behind them, on and on. The rain is coming down harder and the crowd is pressing in, all shoving to get under cover. All of us getting closer to Sammy, closer to Emmy, the real one and her legless look-alike. All of us in one giant fishbowl of our own making.

We're still pressed tight up against each other, Otto and me, Otto tugging on the jacket, trying to stretch it out to cover both of us. It's not working, and it's about zero degrees here under his wing. He brushes damp hair out of my face with one of his big mitts, whispers, "Tell me what you're thinking, Miranda."

"It's this building," I say. "This Center."

"It is, huh?"

"It's what it stands for."

Otto says, "Girl, you just be quiet, now."

"To him," I say, looking up at Sammy. "What it means to him. He'll do anything to protect it."

"Whatever you got in mind, don't do it."

"That's what I been doing."

He says, "Just keep it up, you'll be all right. We got to get you outta here. Get you to a doctor."

"I can't do that," I say.

Otto takes in a deep breath and I can feel his belly pressing against my back. He lets the air out slowly.

"Life is about choices, Miranda. You can make choices, can't you?"

I got an old black man with his arms around me, talking into the back of my head and he wants to know can I make choices.

I say, "There's something I gotta do."

"You do and you'll hurt a lot of people," he says.

"You're wrong," I say. "We do it right and no one gets hurt."

"No one?"

I shake my head.

Otto leans over, his face next to mine. "Not even Sammy?"

"When you were little," I say, "did you ever play with voodoo, maybe stick a few pins into a doll? You know, just pretend."

"You want to put on the sweater," Otto says, "I'll help you."

"This doll," I say, "you look at it and think of a guy you know. It's nothing like him, but that's who you see, right there in front of you. This asshole, a guy who did something bad, something rotten, maybe to you or someone you know. And this shit-sack, he has a way of hypnotizing people into thinking he's angelic. Only you can see right into his head and you know he's guilty and needs to be punished, and at the same time you know it'll never happen."

Otto says, "You can do that, get into people's heads and take a look around?"

"And this guy, one day he walks up to you. He's meaner than ever and more cocky, 'cause no one can touch him. He hands you the doll, dares you to try and hurt him. He's right there in front of you, screaming in your face. 'Do it,' he says. 'Go on,' he says. 'I dare you.' What do you do?"

Otto stands tall and I can feel his chin brushing the top of my head. He takes another long breath, says, "I don't take kindly to anyone shouts in my face. Never have."

I feel an unexpected wave of affection. The way Otto breathes before he speaks, the arms around me, supporting me and protecting me at the same time, the way he saves his words and uses only what he has to.

Bruck is listening, making a face, trying to take it all in. He says, "Sammy, right? We're talking about Pastor Sammy. He's the asshole with the doll, am I right?" Then says, "I'm in."

"**T**here she is," Sammy says into the microphone. "In the back there. Hiding. That woman, under the man's jacket."

I'm grinding on a molar, thinking, and I give Otto a wriggle, a signal to get his grubby paws off me.

"My child," Sammy says, talking to me like we've never met. "'Hide not from me,' the Lord said. I may hide from you, a child with no faith, but thou shalt hide not from me. Come up here and join me."

Otto whispers, "Here we go."

A woman with a rain-soaked face and yellow skin nods at me. Gives me a helpless grin. *Go on*, she seems to say. *He won't hurt you.*

"Come," Sammy says.

Otto clutches me with those long arms of his, but when I manage to squirm around and look up at him, he unwraps himself and sets me free. He says, "Do not disappoint me, girl," speaking to me like a daughter—the way I imagine he spoke to his daughter.

Moving against the crowd, I feel stronger. It's the resistance I need, the push-back. There's a clingy cobwebby feel to it—some people moving out of the way, but most making me rub up against them to squeeze by. Others, I have to give them a shove or aim for the shins, swinging the heavy black bag out in front of me, all of them wanting the same thing: good, old-fashioned human contact.

When I reach the stage, I set my black bag next to Emmy's small, white canvas shoes and step up onto the makeshift platform. Up close, she's smaller than I remembered. And younger; four, not five. Frail in a way I'd somehow forgotten. Elf-like. She wraps an elfish arm around my skinny leg and hugs my thigh.

I turn and face my audience. All eyes are on me, and for the briefest moment, I see what Pastor Sammy sees: a zillion heartbroken faces looking up at me, waiting for someone to convince them that life isn't all that ruined, that there's still hope.

I bend and unzip the bag, take hold of Mother, stand tall, and raise the ax over my head. It's a sight—a preacher and a girl and a woman with an ax. I reach over and take the microphone from Sammy, say into the mike, "This ax, I had it made to fit my hand." I turn and glance at the wooden Emmy. "I didn't have it with me, when I made this one. But I've got it now." My speech is slow and halting. "With this," I say, "sculptures like Emmy here, I can do the rough in a few hours."

Emmy lets go of the leg and when she does, I move quickly and take two short whacks at the base of the column leaving a small wedge-shaped piece of wood sitting in its groove. The wedge I toss into the crowd and it starts a fist fight.

Sammy is glaring at me, furious that I nicked his precious sculpture.

"I can mend her," I say, and before Sammy interrupts, "I can do it now, with you here. Watching."

Sammy yanks the mike out of my hand, shouts, "You will not."

I lean over and whisper in his ear and that stops him. He turns to the audience, says, "Lift your hands, people. Father, today we believe. In Jesus's mighty name, we come to you. Believing today for miracles. Believing for signs and wonders. That the bondage of sickness will be broken. That we will be healed. In the name of Jesus, I pray."

The maintenance crew rolls out an aluminum scaffold, locks the wheels, and jimmies a couple of planks between the diagonal bracing. The planks are splattered with paint and rest about six feet off the ground. I hoist my bag up and climb the narrow rungs. This close to the sculpture, I smell pine and pencil shavings and pancake syrup. I'm hungry. From my pocket, I pull out a photo. It's a news photo, but clear enough and a good likeness. I stare at the photo for several minutes, then I shove it back into my pocket and grab hold of Mother.

The first swing hurts. The second and third aren't so bad. After that, I don't remember the pain.

I begin with the legs, shaping them into a single unit covered in pressed wool slacks, the creases as hard-edged as sheet metal. The skirt goes away and in its place I carve the bottom of a suit jacket. When I move up to the arms, I whack off the elbows in two quick swings. There's a scuffle for one of the bony knobs.

Emmy was carved into the face of the massive column—shallow, only a foot or so deep. This time I go at it from all sides whittling this knotty chunk of pine into a tall human toothpick. I scope out Sammy to see what he thinks so far. He's leaning against the wall next to the entrance, three beefy bodyguards next to him giving him breathing room, his arms folded across his chest, smiling. He knows what's coming, the giddy shit. It's his disciples that don't have a clue.

I t's dark and raining when I finish. I've got a headache from the halogen lamps—a billion watts of intense light, the glare making the sculpture's features look hard-edged and mean. I put my tools inside, zip the bag, and climb down. The place is thick with bodies, and a couple of bozos roll the scaffolding over someone's foot. Next to me, the guards are refereeing a skirmish for the last unclaimed wood chip.

In the confusion, I try to slip quietly through the crowd, but it doesn't happen. A woman puts her arm around me, says "hold it" and "you don't mind, do you?" and "take the picture already, Harold." A girl wants me to sign her sweatshirt. A man in a plaid flannel work shirt asks to see my ax, and another guy in a trendy lambskin blazer, this one older than the first, says why don't we get a cup of coffee sometime? He'd like to talk about my career, if I don't mind.

I grin for the camera, make a big check mark on the girls sweatshirt, tell the guy no, he can't see my ass. To the dipstick in the jacket, I say I'm due back at the convent—I'm late, in fact, so get the hell out of my way. It gives me the half second I need to grab my bag with both hands, grip the thing to my chest, and bulldoze my way into the parking lot.

I'm making my escape. I've had enough with needy people, enough with Emmy and Mary Ellen and Bruck and Otto. And enough with Pastor Sammy.

I'm zagging between cars when I slip into a dark fissure between a couple of SUVs. It's then that I see Pipsqueak in front of me, blocking my way. I don't know if he's waiting for me or if he's just lurking between parked cars looking for trouble. He's sporting an official-looking ball cap with a little bird logo on it, the cap throwing a shadow across his face. All I can see is his mouth, the lips kind of bluish and the jaw clamped shut.

He says, "I see what you did. We all see what you did," speaking slow, making an extra effort to form the words.

I say, "This isn't the time. I'm tired, sore. I'm hungry. I'm hormonal, if that means anything to you."

He says, "You cut up the girl and underneath was him. I think he was there all along. I think you planned it. Or you and Sammy planned it together, a way to make a bigger show of it. Get these idiots thinking they seen a miracle, and I'll be damned if Sammy isn't inside there all along."

I set the black canvas bag on the ground and look up into the night, past the tall poles and the yellow lights, and I can't see a thing—nothing up there but darkness.

I say, "What do I have to do to you to get you out of my way?"

"While you were up there swagging? your ass, I heard some people whispering. There's an element that don't like what you're doing. Some of them don't like you."

"You're still mad about the mouth. Is that it?" I stare at the band-aid peeling away from his top lip. "It hurt, didn't it. And that little poke in the tummy. How'd that feel?"

He says, "You take it too far sometimes."

"Get out of my way."

He's irritated, ready to get ugly about it, but cautious, too. A guy as strong as a Buick, and he's wondering if I've got a mallet or a stick or both hiding in my back pocket. Then he shakes his head and smiles like he remembers why he's here, glances over the hood of the SUV to the portico, at Sammy up on the platform ready to make a speech.

"He's taking credit for it. You know that, right? He'll be preaching on it for weeks. How the Lord gave him the idea. How he prayed on it and made it happen."

"It's what he does," I say.

Pipsqueak says, "What these people did to the girl, and some of the ones in town, I wouldn't be surprised it didn't happen again."

I squat, reach inside and take hold of Mother and show Pipsqueak what I've got in my hand. The ax is heavy, pulling on my arm like a bowling ball. My hand's shaking, the muscles in my forearm freezing into a nice long cramp. In the show, up there working on Sammy's toupee, I bruised something in my shoulder; I'm sure of it. If Pipsqueak makes me swing this thing, it's gonna hurt. I move closer and look at the hat and then at the eyes I can't see. "You got anything else you want to say to me?"

Pipsqueak looks up, works the muscles in his jaw, his lips slightly apart like he's talking to himself. Like he's deciding what to do.

"This new one," he says, "what's to stop 'em from picking it to pieces?"

The AllGood Cafe is busy for a Wednesday morning. We luck out and get the same booth as last Sunday, next to the window, under the big red sign with yellow letters. Otto leans his shoulder against the glass and picks up a flyer from the table. It's a list of local bands playing the AllGood in November and December, and I'm sure he couldn't care less. He's hiding behind the flimsy paper, his eyes glued to the page like he just can't decide which band to see. He's brooding over something. What, he won't say, and I'm not asking.

Otto says, "This Friday, you got an all-female rock band who've never played together, don't know how to play, no rehearsal, nothing. Get this, it's being filmed, the pilot for a reality-show."

"I'm having buttermilk pancakes with pecans," I say.

He sucks in a big breath of air through his nose. "Fishing for Comets, Biscuit Runners, Asylum Street Spankers. What kind of names are these?"

"I changed my mind," I say. "I'm going Mexican."

"What's Mexican about it?"

"Eggs and black beans, salsa, tortillas."

Otto says, "So now you serve black beans with an egg and it's Mexican?"

"Do you want to talk about it?"

The waitress comes with two cups, pours coffee, and takes our orders without writing anything down. I sip the coffee and gaze out the window. Otto doesn't touch his and looks the other way into the crowded café, at the walls, at the framed photos and old posters and giant, painted avocados and cherries. I catch him staring at a poster that reads: "Don't Follow Leaders."

He places the flyer on the table and says, "What's to stop 'em from picking it to pieces?"

It's the way we talk—leave out the transitions, the context, and go straight to the heart of the thing—and I'm starting to like it. Sometimes it takes me a moment to get my bearings, and I count to six or seven, thinking before I speak. This time I count to three, but I know where we are.

"That's what Pipsqueak asked me," I say.

"I know who you mean. So, what'd you tell him?"

"I didn't."

"It's a secret, huh?"

I say, "There's nothing to stop them. That's the point, Sammy'll try, the greedy pig. I see him spending whole days thinking up ways to protect his little miracle. Months, if it lasts that long. He'll post guards, put up fences, threaten people with curses. He'll put it behind bulletproof glass, but it won't make any difference, because people want a piece of it and nothing he can do will stop them."

Otto says, "And you're okay with that?"

"Why wouldn't I be?"

"This man smokes a friend of yours. He tries to steal whatever you got. And you give the man what he asks for, is that it?"

"That's what's bothering you? He got what he wanted? You think I gave in."

He says, "Let me get this straight. This is your way of torturing the man."

"Watching his precious sculpture get picked to pieces, yeah, I guess it is."

That's not good enough for Otto. In his part of town, justice is more tangible, about shove and shove–back. Something's going on inside that head, something I know nothing about, and I have to remind myself how little I really know about him—he fixes things, he had a daughter, that's it.

"If I was younger," he says, "I'd of scorched the place, burnt it to the ground."

"That's not me," I say.

Otto says, "No, it is not." He says, "I been meaning to tell you, Handy called this morning."

Two hours at the Jonsson Library and I find out I have two choices: give up one of my breasts or die. It's the odds that piss me off. Twenty-two hundred to one a woman under thirty gets tagged with breast cancer, and I'm the one. To cheer me up, I pore over a cute little comparison table: National Cancer Deaths. It's got a handful of nifty headings: cervical, ovarian, skin, colorectal (a sort of double-whammy of bad news), lung, breast. The table is neatly sorted by state. I find deaths, breast, Texas, 2,891. Wyoming, 49, a state I never much admired until now.

I'm zagging through the Baylor Medical Center parking lot, my head down, rehearsing, when I see Dr. Novak cross the street in front of the ER. He stops at a black Mercedes and takes in the mess on his hood and windshield. It's bird-shit season in North Texas, and the goddamn grackles are painting the town with little white dollops of poo. Novak's parked under a hundred-year-old oak. He looks up into the tree—a handful of guilty grackles staring back at him—and then at his car, at the milky white goo covering his windshield.

I feel sorry for the guy. Still, I can't help saying, "You got shit on."

There's no one else in the parking lot. It's mid afternoon, all the emergencies holding off for nightfall. He unlocks his door with a beep, says, "It's nice to see you Ms..."

"Tate."

"Miranda," he says in a tired voice, and waits for me to say whatever it is I came to say.

So I say it. "I'm ready to live." I wait for a smirk or a shrug or one of the trite little comebacks they teach you in med school.

"That's a start," he says.

It's the middle of the morning when I pick up the phone and dial the number Otto's given me. It's an ancient phone with a long cord that reaches to the window. I shuffle over, stand there looking down on a couple of kids in knit caps. It's cold out, and the taller one is wiping snot from his nose with his shirtsleeve. The other one is telling a story, waving his hands and sort of kicking at imaginary bad guys. It's the kind of story that holds your interest because of all the gyrations. A story you just gotta see.

The tall kid's listening, not giving anything away. He reminds me of me—hard to read, patient, not a lot of wasted energy. The other kid could be Handy, wired, loose jointed, trying to get his arms around everything at once.

The phone rings six times. Seven, eight, nine. Then a man says, "What?"

I don't say anything at first, and I swear I can hear him impatiently bobbing his head, snapping his fingers trying to move things along.

I say, "You remember Zimbabwe? All the walking, the days we spent hiking through the scrub, as wet as it was, like marching over soggy mattresses. How the baboons would sit in the path and bark at us, the mean little shits making us go out of our way to walk around."

Handy says, "They were hungry, is all."

"Or the damage an elephant could do to a fever tree just by scraping the mud off its back. And the giant baobabs no one could hurt."

He says, "I remember clouds as big as cities."

"And the goddamn red clay that stuck to everything. Do you remember how tiring it was, all that walking?"

"You forgot the purple sunsets."

"That's the thing with us, Handy. I remember the blisters and the angry animals and damaged trees and the sticky mud. You remember the color of the sky."

He says, "Otto tells me you've got a lot on your mind."

I twist the telephone cord around my finger, fooling with it. "Why we were there. Why I was there. Do you remember?"

He says, "If you mean the time in the village, we were looking for Sekai."

"And later?" I say.

"Looking for the men who took her. What's this about, Miranda?"

"The last several weeks," I say, "that's what it's been like for me. Hiking down paths I've never been on, no idea where they lead. Only this time, anything gets in my way, I grab a club and start swinging, and I keep swinging until there's nothing left. I go out at night, mostly, and the buildings hover over me like giant baobab trees. I hadn't thought of it until now, but that's how I see it. I'm trekking through a forest looking for someone."

"What are you telling me?"

I'm watching the kid below me on the street. He might be dancing now, or imitating someone dancing, his mouth wide open shouting or singing his tale, spur of the moment, in the only way that makes sense to him.

"It's a story," I say, "About slaying a beast."

"How does it end?" Handy asks.

"I'm not sure."

There is a long pause and I can hear breathing on the other end of the line.

Handy says, "You know what I think? I think this beast you're looking for is you. You're the most fearless woman I know. People, situations, they don't frighten you. But this thing in the forest scares you. It scares the shit out of you. I'm glad you're willing to talk about it, but I don't want to hear any more about baobab trees and baboons. Tell me about the cancer, Miranda. Tell me how you're going to fight it and keep fighting it until there's nothing left."

I'm still at the window looking down on the kids in knit caps. The tall one is sitting on the sidewalk with his back against the brick wall of the building across the street. His head is pointed up at his buddy, some teeth showing, the other kid into a new story, this one slower with a few Tai Chi moves to it.

I tell Handy that I met with Dr. Novak earlier today. Saying it like we had a real heart-to-heart, like we discussed things at length, me sitting on the edge of the exam table, and Novak scribbling notes in a thick manila folder. I tell him I'm having the surgery next Thursday. Handy says he's proud of me, and my throat goes tight.

I swallow hard and say, "Why I called, I wondered if you'd given any thought to coming home?"

T wo weeks after the surgery Detective Stanislaw comes to my door. I open up and stand there in a ratty bathrobe, nothing on underneath but twenty pounds of gauze and tape. I carry a pillow in front of me, pressing it against my stomach. It's to numb the pain, the nurse said. A couple of days, she said, but it's been weeks, and I can't give up the damn pillow. Detective Stanislaw gives me a frown but doesn't mention the pillow. Says he's got a few questions is all, real nice about it, won't take but two, three minutes is all.

It's from the detective that I learn what time the fire started.

He wants to know where I was around two a.m. I tell him Dr. Novak over at Baylor just cut off one of my tits. I haven't left the loft in fifteen days. Haven't bathed in five, haven't brushed my teeth in three. I don't tell him that I'm suffering a little post-surgery gloom, but I think he gets the picture.

I say, "If you're asking me where in the loft I was at exactly two a.m., my guess is over there." I point to the bed, but he doesn't catch it because he's eyeing a work bench on the other side of the room with a dozen long-handled chisels lying on top, the ax pushed to one side. I try to see the room the way he sees it—an artist's loft with high ceilings and brick walls and a big fat view of the freeway. A bunch of worn tools and what looks like fresh wood chips on the floor. A woodsy smell to the place—pine and green cedar and pin oak and whatever kind of trees they turn into telephone poles. It looks like a pretty good life to Detective Stanislaw. That's my guess.

He asks, I answer. The whole thing takes about twenty minutes. On his way out, I throw him a sultry look— me with my greasy red hair, a blue and white striped pillow clutched to my stomach. It's a look I'd seen in an old black and white movie, the tough, good-looking cop and the maybe-guilty leading lady, and I ask what happens if he catches the guy?

"For arson," he says, "what happens is twenty years. If people were in the building, add on another ten. Less if whoever did it did it for the insurance. This case, I don't think it's about the insurance. What do you think?"

I tell him I think it wasn't me, so I don't have to worry about it. I'm sure he believes me, cops being such a trusting group and all.

Where it started, I get from Pilar—outside and moved in, zoomed through the walls and ceilings until the lobby was toast. The Healing Tower is extra crispy. Parts of the offices and conference rooms just sort of melted. She's not sure about the Healing Cathedral. She heard a rumor it's still standing but everything inside is all black with soot. The fire sprinklers slowed things down some, and anything not burned or smoke-damaged is soaked or covered in a thin layer of chemicals, or both.

How it started, I get from the reporter, Jeffery Henson: unleaded gasoline. Traces of fuel, he calls it, found on the base of the sculpture. He's sorry, he says. He knows how I must feel. Henson's clever, and I wonder if he's being sarcastic. We say our goodbyes and that's that.

I hear a key in the lock and stare at the door expecting Handy to come bounding in, all get-up-and-go and good will, but it's not Handy. It's Otto.

I say, "I told you, you don't have to look in on me."

Otto says, "I'm here to check your switches. Make sure they all working, up to code, that sort of thing." He reaches over and flips the light switch closest to the door. His movements are slow and precise. The lights go on and he glances at me.

"Is there something wrong with your bathtub?"

"Not that I know of."

He says, "Some reason you're not using it?"

"Maybe we can do this another time." I say it without thinking, without meaning it, really. It's the way Mother and I talked. Pretending not to understand each other, or feigning indifference when we did, and I can think of few things I enjoyed more.

I want to tell Otto I'm glad he stopped by. Really. I want to tell him lots of things, but I don't. I drop the pillow to the floor and move up next to him. So close that he involuntarily inches backward, and I reach out and put both arms around him. I squeeze his large body against mine, his stomach pushing into my belly and chest, and for a few moments, I don't feel any pain at all.

www.ingramcontent.com/pod-product-compliance
Lightning Source LLC
Chambersburg PA
CBHW032034240626
47154CB00003B/910